ROCKSTAR echoes

ROCKSTAR
echoes

zach taylor

For the generation still chasing

greatness, meaning, and legacy.

PROLOGUE

Arrowhead Stadium, Kansas City, MO

CLARA COWLEY

stood side stage. She didn't need to take notes. After thirty years documenting the rise and fall of rock's greats, Clara could feel a moment before it happened.

She'd been on this story almost from the beginning. One day, she hoped, she'd repay Aberdeen's publicist, Aiesha Holt, for the free meal that first got her here or maybe Markus Kenney, one of the band members, and their manager, Paul White, for that weekday panel that set it all in motion. Well, for her part at least. The air was heavy with equal parts humidity and expectation. Something else? Wonderment. The space between chords went sharp. People held their breath without knowing why.

Now—they would know, after months of suspense.

Social media was buzzing, thanks to Aiesha and the last few weeks of the man, the replacement, the enigma of Kline, who was about to take the stage. Even as legends paid homage to Lloyd Brannon, the energy was saving itself for what came next.

Next to Clara, a younger woman bounced on her boots like she might take off. Clara turned. Red hair. Leather jacket. Cheap eyeliner. Energy vibrating just beneath the surface.

RAYNE HARLOW.

No deal. No fame. No safety net. And no idea Clara knew exactly who she was.

Clara had seen her live once. Watched recorded sets and shaky videos from LA's legendary shithole dive bars. The kind of rooms every artist had to pay their dues in, though most never made it out. Maybe even viewed some of her OnlyFans content. For research purposes, of course.

That was enough. The girl had something—furious, unrestrained, and real. The same thing the man they came to see had in spades. Rayne thought she knew why she was here.

But did she?

Rayne folded her arms across her chest, eyes locked on the stage. She needed to check scores. See what her take was, following the day's college football games. The phone stayed in her pocket as thousands of phones recorded what was on stage. Some to catch history. Some to catch music brought to life. Some to catch another Kline Thomas viral moment.

"I am so fucking nervous, man," she whispered.

Clara didn't respond.

The man about to step onstage wasn't just a risk. He was an unknown entity.

KLINE THOMAS.

The final act on a bill of legends.

Clara wondered how many saw his name and thought: *Who?*

And for good reason.

She'd heard the questions.

How the hell did this happen?

Straight from the backwoods of Alabama—rock's sludge pit—to center stage like he was born with it.

Clara couldn't reconcile it either. In a month, he'd gone from beer joint cover band to the biggest spotlight in rock. No stumble. No stutter. Just arrived ready.

Ready to perform and write.

Ready to be a rock star.

There was more to that story. There had to be. What had it taken for Freddie? How long did it take for Morrison? There had been an evolution for Layne and Chris. Kline was packaged, drop in ready. Wasn't that what Aberdeen had wanted? Was he what they expected? There was no way. But, that was before last night.

Her eyes cut to Rayne, a mirror of the man she came to see. One was on the stage. One was in the wings. Clara wondered if either of them understood that. No, not yet. Eventually, but not today. She wondered if things would ever change for the young woman. She played like Nancy Wilson, sang with the wounded soul of Courtney Love, and wrote songs that were a frying pan to the face like L7.

Rayne called herself a friend, but Clara had doubts. Kline didn't have many of those. Not real ones other than the one he brought with him from Alabama.

EDDIE CORNELL.

Husband. New father. Affable. Instantly lovable. Kline's loyal best friend.

The rest? Shoved into this with him. Along for the ride.

Clara included.

She'd watched him over the last month—torn apart and shoved forward, chasing a ghost. A ghost with a shared past, tied to him like a millstone around his neck, he'd never known existed.

Now? He knew.

And Rayne? She didn't know why she was here either, not really. Not from the perspective of what happened last night in that hotel. Maybe Kline didn't know why he was here, either, because of what he'd learned. Maybe that was why he called her. Maybe he just had no one else to call.

Still, Clara played dumb. She always did. It served her well. Her eyes went back to Kline.

They just keep underestimating you.

Good. Let them. When the world was ready?

Show them who you are.

She could tell the younger woman beside her thought the same thing. Not just to the man who'd called, but also to herself.

"Who are you here to see?" Clara asked casually, playing ignorant. She'd been in the same room with Rayne. Had watched from the shadows. It was a test. Rayne's eyes turned to her, looked the much older woman up and down, but she slid her mask on. She knew exactly who Clara Cowley was. Knew Clara had seen her play. Knew she'd been in the same room. Knew she was being tested. Cherie Antoinette gave nothing away and smiled.

Just playing the game like everyone else.

"Aberdeen. With the new guy. Kline." Rayne shouted the name like it had just come to her. "Got a text this morning. No way I was saying no. Side stage? With this bill? You kidding me?"

Rayne grinned in her half-truth, but her eyes didn't follow. "Wish it wasn't so last minute, but—" She cut herself off. Clara imagined there had been something in Kline's voice when he called. Desperation. Like he had no one else. Rayne had come running, but likely not for altruism. Clara suspected what her endgame was.

Maybe not. Perhaps Rayne had chalked it up to nerves as she lined up someone to watch her young daughter that Clara knew she had. Knowing the woman, Clara imagined she even rustled White for babysitter money, cab fees, and a hotel room. Always hustling.

Clara watched her eyes. Women who smiled like that are used to being onstage—not beside it. Rayne had a mission. But Clara wasn't sure Rayne believed in it.

On her other side was Paul White. Dialed in. But worried for good reasons, after what had reportedly transpired last night and this morning. Clara had the revelation that he had been so focused on Kline versus Aberdeen that he didn't know the snake he might have let it. It wasn't her place to say anything. Besides, she was rooting for Rayne.

The crowd roared as the tribute set ended. Classic Aberdeen. Safe. Reverent. The crowd ate it up.

Clara watched Rayne watch them. Not with awe.

With hunger.

Then Kline walked by them. Head high, smile tight, body tense.

Rayne lit up, barely hiding it. He hugged her quick, said something Clara didn't catch.

But Clara saw his eyes. So did Rayne.

He wasn't ready.

The man she saw rehearsing and performing in the Eveningview mansion, day after day and night after night always had a plan. From setlist to the direction he wanted to take the band to the lyrics he shared. This one looked like he was drowning. She couldn't blame him.

Clara had heard rumors. A song. A secret. One of those collapse-under-its-own-weight moments.

She didn't know how he was even standing. From what she'd heard, he almost hadn't.

The first song hit like fire. Kline lit up the stage like he'd been born there. Confidence. Charisma. A voice like gravel and heartbreak. His song—and a hit.

The crowd turned. Cheered. Believed.

He directed them, and they sang it back like it was charting.

It wasn't.

It had barely dropped. But from the call and response? It would be, very soon. She'd heard it, of course. From infancy to the master. But to hear it played in front of thousands? To see him perform? She had goosebumps. Clara had been waiting for this rebirth.

To her side, Rayne danced like she meant it. Clara had seen her when she didn't think anyone was watching. There were other motives, sure—but she couldn't help herself.

She believed in him. Maybe loved him.

Even if she hated what led them here—Clara understood. She wanted to hate what he stood for, most off all and it went back to what Clara had just pontificated upon. Dropped in. Success. Stage.

But Kline hated himself enough for all of them. And that didn't just quench the fire— it made him a martyr worthy of admiration. Something he wouldn't let himself have.

She was his antithesis. His Janus—two faces split by time and guilt. Just as he was Lloyd Brannon's echo. Not just metaphorically.

Clara could hear it—Lloyd's dead voice, echoing through.

Kline owned his song, but that wasn't the test.

The second song was. The one that wasn't his. Lloyd Brannon's final track. His best. The one that would pull at every exposed nerve. Before, Kline didn't know what it meant.

Now, he did.

He stepped to the mic. Lights shifted. The band played.

MIKE KILMORE,

first and only Aberdeen guitarist.

Musical maverick.

Best friend of the departed Lloyd Brannon.

Appeared to Kline's side.

Whispered something. Pointed to the screen.

Kline turned.

Froze.

Whatever was on that screen, Clara didn't need to see it. She saw his body tense. Fury bloom.

He missed the beat. Missed again.

Kilmore smirked. Didn't even try to play.

This had been the plan.

Kline balled his fists. Kilmore flinched.

Clara willed it not to happen. *Rock needs this.*

The fans were still cheering. Waiting.

Then—Kline flipped him off. Both hands. No hesitation.

"Oh God, no," Rayne whispered, barely audible.

He walked offstage.

Past Clara—no surprise. Past Rayne—which was.

But where he stopped? That was the biggest surprise of all.

He stood an inch from Paul White's face.

"You fuckin' knew it. All along. All of it. It just never stops, does it, you piece of shit."

He was shaking—so furious, so raw—he couldn't find anything else to say.

White didn't respond. Didn't flinch. Just bowed his head in shame.

Kline Thomas stormed off.

Kilmore shrugged, turned to Eddie Cornell, and calmly took the mic, as if it were always his plan. Because it was.

Rayne opened her mouth. Closed it. Took off running after Kline. Clara didn't move. Whatever just happened—this wasn't an ending. It was the beginning of something darker. Bolder. Greater.

Excerpt from "The Voice Was Never Theirs"
BY CLARA COWLEY

Forgive me that this first entry is long.

I promise I will do my best to shorten them, going forward. But I must set the stage before we get to the action. Is that fair? There are things you must understand, up front, or you might lose interest. I mean, that's really on you. It's my book. I do want you to read it. You need to read it. If you don't, only you miss out.

Call me a boomer. Or Gen Xer. Whatever. There's a line I want to open with from the perfect movie, The Princess Bride:

"Life is pain, highness. Anyone who says differently is selling something."

Do you hear it now? Was it a throwaway line from your childhood? If it was, put this book down. I mean that as a compliment. I'm happy for you. You made it. This is a cautionary tale to tell your kids or grandkids as you celebrate at your beach house on 30A down at Florida's Emerald Coast, a place Kline once told me about. Good for you.

But.

You aren't where we are. You aren't where the people in this story were.

If it isn't a throwaway, you lived through the period of the least economic growth in

memory. You were told, as the blimp told
Tony Montana, "The world is yours."

But it wasn't. Get in the breadline.

I'm starving. We are all starving. Remember
Billy Crystal's bit about the Man in Black
being "mostly dead"? Our generation is mostly
poor and fully cynical. What did we get? A
series of unfortunate events. No great war.
No great music. No great economy. What did
we make? Fine—I'm already halfway down that
rabbit hole. Back on track. We can do one
thing.As Jen Farrow sang Rayne Harlow's words
in "I Make Me?":"I think I should find this
alarming." Fitting, because all the people
in this story were starving, just as Rayne
wrote. Just starving in different ways.Yet
here we are, trying to live the thesis of
Incubus's title track "Make Yourself."
We make ourselves. That's all we can do.

Ultimately, the fate of the figures in the
story of Aberdeen and the Painted Queens—of
Kline Thomas and Rayne Harlow—came down to a
single event. People like clean beginnings,
easy answers. It would be tempting to point
to the death of Lloyd Brannon. Or that night
at the hotel bar in Atlanta. A story for
another day, which I will not be covering
in this book. But I will.

But doing that would cheapen it—for Kline,
for Rayne, for the Queens. None of them were

side notes. None of them were accidents. Without every single one of them, this story doesn't get written at all. And since this story is really about Rayne and the Queens, it is important to point out how all of this matters.

Lloyd's death was a smoldering coal. The fire was already there.

So, what was the moment? What was the day that pushed it all forward, that cracked the old guard open and let the ghosts in?

It wasn't a grimy bar floor.It wasn't a stadium full of fans.It wasn't even about the art.It was about the other side. The dark side. The part no one wants to talk about.

It didn't happen in a dive bar or on a stage. It happened under fluorescent lights, with contracts instead of chords.And it was about the only thing that ever really mattered here—money. It began with Paul White doing what he did best. But that doesn't sell you, the reader. You want blood, not pen strokes. I get it.

So, let's get something straight from the very beginning: all the tears, sweat, blood, and death in this story started inside those very pristine offices I just mentioned. The kind where artists never realize the "deal" isn't a deal at all. It's indentured servitude to the label, dressed up as "making it."

Even on that day, a group of brilliant women went begging, not knowing what was really happening. Even as they concocted a plan, the machine was already in motion.

If you can't hang with me, put the book down and walk away. I'll wait.

Okay, you want blood? Let me give it to you. Absolute bloodletting.

There are memes, plenty that poke fun at Kline Thomas. I won't get into them. My favorite: "When I meet my wife's other man."

There's a picture of Aberdeen with a couple in front of them. A VIP meet-and-greet. Getting one of these doesn't cost much—a few hundred dollars to get a picture with your favorite band. It's sterile. You come in. You talk to the band for a minute. Maybe tell them what they meant to you. In this case, the woman did just that.

The man? He asked what the hardest song to perform was for Lloyd Brannon. How he built his setlist. What a particular song meant to him. He asked about tonal shifts. Why Lloyd changed from this key to that and why. Was it emotional? Did it have meaning? Why did Mike Kilmore shift from this progression to another at that particular moment? What was the meaning of Kenney's sample in that transition from this verse to that?

He got no answers. He didn't expect any.

Maybe that's what he needed for the future.

In Atlanta, a couple met Aberdeen and asked these questions, which I later refreshed the band's memory about. So, I showed them a cheap black-and-white picture. None of them remembered it. Why would they? Sure enough, there it was. Sure enough, it was exactly like that old Jamey Johnson song—some things don't translate unless you're standing there, seeing it in color. Lead guitarist Mike Kilmore said, "Well. Huh," while scratching his mane of salt-and-pepper curls.

Ben Cantrell and Jose Madera said, and I quote, "No fucking way."

And Markus Kenney didn't say anything at first. He shook his gorgeous Afro, glasses sliding, and said, "Well, that tracks."

Kline and Chrys Thomas. With Aberdeen in the background. Fans with the band they worshipped. At least one of them. The other had existential questions about himself, his life, and what he was meant for. The answers he got that night—or the diversions—hm.

Did any of them know what would happen later that night? Did any of them know how their lives would change?

I don't mean just from Aberdeen's perspective, or Kline's and Chrys's. But it holds true. Kline was there. He was right there. The entire time.

One night, Kline Thomas would sing their music in his own way, go viral, and get noticed by Aberdeen, as well as everyone else.

Across the country, a woman—broke, unknown, burning out—played a dive bar no one filmed. She didn't know it, but that night, everything began.

And thank the rock gods, I saw it. I don't know how. Call me Claravoyant. Call me Cassandra. Call me what you want. I call me lucky. I was there through it all. My greatest regret? Being paid. Being fucking paid. I wasn't paying attention.

Were you? I don't think so. And that's not an indictment of me. It's an indictment of you.

Honestly, it isn't fair to either of us. I was hired to curate a story I had no idea would matter this much. Trust me. Keep your money. Embrace and enjoy.

I spent an entire life—no shit—waiting for a story that would define my career. I missed grunge by a few years. I went pro during nu-metal. What a goddamn disappointment.

And after? Nothing. Twenty years of cultural wasteland. So, when the moment came, when she took the stage, I was sitting at a bar, waiting to die.

She played "Fuck Your Dick, Man." She smashed a cheap guitar. And I watched her smash the fourth wall, even if she couldn't

walk through it yet. You read about Joan of Arc
burning at the stake. My breath lit her clothes
on fire. That's not bragging. That's an
indictment of me. Just as Atlanta was a torch
on a witch's pyre at Kline's feet. We didn't
know what we saw. But we saw it.

   This story is about Kline, sure. We follow
him through all of it, and he deserves
that. Every ounce of recognition. He
was a transcendental artist. Performer.
Transformer. Writer. Architect. Artist. He
wanted you to hear him, to hear a generation
that felt lost, deceived, misunderstood. He
wanted you to hear it in the sound that made
you understand. He couldn't do that with
Aberdeen's mix of jazz, funk, and quasi-metal.
On the other side? Rayne couldn't convey her
thoughts into lyrics and put it to the very
sound Kline needed. One had the lyrics.
One had the sonic ability.

   But if you think this story is about Kline,
put the book down and walk away. It's not.
And he wouldn't want you to think it is. He set
the path. He wrote the words. He walked away.
But not before handing the Crown of Swords to
Rayne fucking Harlow. As you read this, you'll
ask: would she have made it without him? Where
would she be without him? Isn't this book
about him? Is there a book without him? No.
Destitute. No. No.

And yet, without her? Where would he be?
Also no. Destitute. No. No.

Kline was an echo of Lloyd Brannon. Later,
in this story? He would become a mirror of
Lloyd Brannon. Until he shattered it. Rayne?
Same story. Again, later.

Rayne carried a different message.
One Kline knew he couldn't give. Shouldn't
give. Tried to give.

He asked the question.

Rayne gave the answer.

Are rock stars born, or are they built? Do
they fall from the sky, or claw their way up
through the gates of Hades just to stand on
Olympus? And when they get there, when they
finally tower above us all, who the hell are
they then?

Kline ran a gauntlet that defied the hero's
quest. He had ten of the twelve steps, neat as
chalk marks. Did he meet his mentor? Yes. But
not the way you think.

He met his mentor. Met his god. Met his Zeus.
Asked the questions. The mentor didn't answer.
The hero didn't let that bother him. Then Zeus
stole his woman.

Only then did his call to adventure begin.
Yes, he refused the call. Yes, he crossed the
threshold. He faced tests. Found allies. Made
enemies. He entered the innermost cave. Faced
his ordeal. Seized the sword.

But did he have a road back? Did he find resurrection? Did he deliver the elixir? No.

And Rayne? Rayne heard the hero's call. In her own way, she answered.

Two of them made the journey with an apparition leading them. Neither knew what, or who, led.

Hold up, let me light a cigarette and smack this bottle top on a wooden picnic table to explain, for those who don't understand. Paper and tobacco, for those who don't know what I mean.

This is me, old woman, beer in hand and a smoking cherry, looking at you. Get ready.

Where Kline gave out, she rose. Frodo carried the ring, but Sam was the one who climbed the mountain. Three went in. Two came out. One wasn't Gollum. The ghost.

This isn't three Israelites and an angel in a furnace. Three went in, four were there, three came out. This was three went in, two came out. Just like Tolkien said. Can you understand? That was the burden on Kline's back.

When those two came down the mountain, let me borrow a line from Joan Osborne:

"What if God was one of us?"

Full stop. Think.

Who was God? The ones who made the climb and believed? The ones who walked out of the

furnace, or Mount Doom? Of those who did, who
was God and who was the apostle? Does
it matter?

I'll never know. And if I don't, neither
will you.

Because what came out was music.

Music.

MUSIC.

I have to say this: I love Kline Thomas.
Who he was. What he sang. But this book is not
about him. This story isn't about him. It won't
seem that way at first.

This story is about Rayne Harlow. That will
make it harder for you to follow.

A challenge, then. Are you brave enough?
Do you feel enough?

It's okay to walk away. I wish I had.
But here I am. And I'm better for it.

calculating

01

Pacific Coast Records, Los Angeles, CA

Ten weeks earlier

PAUL WHITE

checked in with reception. Gloria gave him the polite smile she always did—but no "he'll see you now." No rush. No urgency.

Bad sign.

He declined the offer of water, coffee, or tea and made his way to the waiting area. Plush chairs. Platinum records. Hollow victories.

Across from him, four women in their twenties or thirties. Artists, clearly. A punkish redhead, platinum blonde vibrating in her seat, a stone-faced Asian woman, and a towering blonde with the build of a power forward.

"Pitching or signing?" White asked.

"Pitching," the tall one replied, arms folded.

"You a manager?" the Asian woman asked. "You don't look like talent."

"I represent Aberdeen."

Recognition clicked instantly. Of course it did.

"What's left to represent?" the tall blonde muttered, flat and cold.

White didn't answer. The question didn't deserve one.

Gloria appeared. "Mr. Holden will see you now."

Time to beg.

As he stood and followed Gloria down the hall, the women exchanged glances.

"Did he say Aberdeen?" the platinum blonde asked.

"Yeah," said the redhead. "Guess they're still trying to replace Lloyd," she guessed. Multiple sets of eyes rolled. What else would there be to meet with Pacific Coast Records about?

"Good luck with that," the platinum blonde muttered, grinning. The three other women knew what she meant. Two of them laughed. She referred to his charisma. His beauty. His willingness to take off his shirt for every show for twenty years. Oh, and his skill as a songwriter and artist, sure.

But the tall one didn't laugh. She was staring down the hall after White.

"If they ain't found him yet, they ain't gonna. Not in this town," she said quietly.

:

GREG HOLDEN

watched White enter, beady and dark eyes, shark like demeanor and predatory instincts. Lifer in the industry. Fattened by decades of backing the right artist at the right time, sat on his throne. His office was a monument to ego: floor-to-ceiling windows, a desk that could land aircraft, and the ever-present cloud of cigar smoke.

The cigar wasn't lit yet. That meant the mood was worse than usual.

White walked the gauntlet of the conference table and stopped short of the antique chair. He waited.

Holden didn't stand. Didn't smile. Just stared over the chewed-up cigar.

"Sit, White. Let's make this quick."

White sat and folded his hands.

"I came to ask for time."

Holden laughed like someone had just told a good joke at a funeral. "Time? Paul, you've had five years of time. One half-assed album of B-sides that you literally called Besides. Zero momentum. And now your golden goose is dead." White forced a stone face at the complete irreverence in referring to the death of an artist that had made PCR a lot of money. More importantly, the death of a good man he called a friend.

"They still have fans. Still have value."

White stayed still.

Holden leaned back, finally lighting the cigar. "Let me ask you this—what's the plan, Paul? You come in here, no singer, no record, and ask me to extend the deadline on what's already a contractual graveyard?"

"Four years of hiding behind Lloyd's back while he sold paintings and played psychedelic shaman for the socialites. Pontificated about women's reproductive rights on every podcast in greater L.A." Holden crossed his meaty arms and leaned back. The chair creaked under the weight.

White betrayed no emotion.

Holden hadn't dealt with this—not directly. White had.

He'd profited from Lloyd's side projects, sure. But the real returns weren't just financial. They were musical. Emotional. Holistic.

The music. The experience. That's what made it all worth it.

Until the Lloyd Brannon Foundation came along. Until she came along.

And wrecked any semblance of hope—*killed it with the stroke of a pen.*

Now? There was no fulfillment. Not in the work. Not in the legacy. Not in the man.

"I gave them space. I got nothing but piles of bills, an unfulfilled contract, and promoters for this tour circling me like vultures to show for it."

White's jaw tightened. He adjusted his glasses.

"The tour isn't really your concern. You sue them now; you get a hollow win. The catalog's worth pennies on the dollar, right now."

Holden studied him. "You don't even *have* a plan, do you?"

"I have options." White bluffed. White finally leaned forward, voice low. "So do you, Greg. You sue them and kill Aberdeen; you inherit the ashes. You give them three extra months, maybe you get a phoenix instead."

Holden didn't reply. Just stared. Holden looked at the women sitting outside his office, waiting for a chance he wasn't going to give them. An all-women band? Hard pass. Though, he did acknowledge that at least they were good looking. Still, not marketable. He gave Gloria a look that said, 'get them outta here.'

Then: "Three more months. No more. I'll even book Eveningview for you, because I am such a nice guy." That was surprising. Or a fuck-you. He couldn't be sure. But he'd take it. It was a move in the right direction. A carrot on a stick that would get the band in motion. Far better than those sessions during COVID that had gone nowhere. Just yelling and silence.

White nodded once.

Holden waved him off with the cigar like a king dismissing a jester, a final slight push of the shoulder. "Go on. Find your miracle. But next time, don't come back unless you've got a voice that can raise the dead. I don't care where you get it from. That album better be made, and someone must play these gigs they're on the books for." Ever the pompous ass, he made sure his voice carried so everyone around could see him being both the nice guy and the man in control.

Back at the front desk, White handed Gloria a small envelope. She tucked it into the drawer with practiced ease and shot her sweet smile at him. She was still quite the looker, despite the lines that had appeared on her face the last few years.

"How'd it go?" she asked.

"Same as always," he said. "Everything on fire. No water." White's eyes went to the four women. He hoped they had better luck than he.

He turned to leave, pausing at the sight of the four women still waiting. The tall one met his eyes. Unreadable.

"Good luck, ladies," he said and kept walking, but his gait said everything he wasn't.

Time to start looking.

They waited until White was out of sight.

The tall, muscled blonde narrowed her eyes. "So, they're desperate. That's useful."

No one said anything, but they were already calculating. There was leverage here. They'd find it. They needed a break.

Excerpt from "The Voice Was Never Theirs"
BY CLARA COWLEY

"Rayne Harlow wasn't late on rent. She was short. There's a difference.

Late is a delay. Short is a condition.

That's how this started.

Not with ambition. Which she had.

Not with a record deal. Which she didn't have.

Not with fame. Which she'd get, but not the way she envisioned when she left home at sixteen.

It started with a woman standing in a living room with an eviction notice, a daughter in the other room, and a voice in her throat that no one wanted to hear unless she screamed it while naked. In fact, no one cared if she screamed at all. Silence was easier.

I know Rayne Harlow gets framed as a schemer.
A manipulator. A woman who knew exactly how
to weaponize her looks, her story, her scars.
She, and the Painted Queens, are proud of that
ability. Unapologetic.

But I've always seen her differently.

I saw her when the lights were off and the
bills were due.

When she was just a mother with a dream and
a dream that cost more than she had left to
give. Desperately trying to break out of the
generational struggle that her family had
faced for decades. Rayne carried the fear that
despite doing everything she could do to avoid
being her mother, it sure looked like she was
headed down that path, just with a guitar in
her hand instead of a needle in her arm. But,
both dropped drawers when the bills were due.
It just looked differently. I promise you; it
felt the same.

That's where her legend began.

Not on a stage.

But in a one-bedroom apartment where the
rent was short? She had to do what she had
to do. Sex work. Not like her mother, but sex
work all the same. But before she did, she
wrote a song that I would one day hear and
would change how I looked at women in rock
and roll, forever."

de-lin-q-ent

02

Apartments on Fountain Ave.
& Vine St., Hollywood, CA

Rayne sat cross-legged on her bed, strumming, humming, and writing. Not her strength but still her job

"Mommsy? What does de-lin-q-ent mean?"

LANNA paused between each syllable, trying to sound it out. Rayne froze, rigid. Then, she laid the acoustic guitar down on the bed, slid her tan, bare legs over the comforter, and hit the carpeted floor in a rush. Rayne entered the small living room and found the child. She snatched it from her tiny six-year-old fingers.

"Where did you get this?" She tried not to act concerned.

"It was under the door when I opened it. What does that mean?" Rayne read it carefully.

"It just means late. It's nothing." It brought back many painful memories from childhood.

"Baby, I appreciate how curious you are, and I love how much you love to read. But you don't open and read things that aren't yours. Okay?" Rayne's mother would just have slapped her. And had, over far less. Rayne crunched the letter in her fist without realizing it.

"Listen, I have to run down to the office for a second. Just watch some TV or your tablet. I'll be back in a few minutes and make you a sandwich." The child looked up at her, curiously, as if she thought she was in trouble. Rayne bent down and hugged her.

"You did nothing wrong, baby. You just got to learn that not everything is for you." Rayne pushed her towards the well-worn couch before slipping on jean shorts over her muscled and tattooed thighs and heading out the door.

A few moments later, the landlord greeted her.

"Hi, Rayne. What can I do for you?" He already knew why she was here.

She held up the paper. "What is this?"

He pretended to read it, handed it back, arms crossed. "You know how this works. I'm sure you've seen it before." His smirk widened. "And I'm sure we can think of something. You know…"

She knew exactly where he was going. She'd heard this line too many times. *What would my mom do?* Rayne knew.

"Oh, fuck you, man."

He held out his palms, rocking back.

"You're all the same. Always thinking with your dicks first."

She wadded the paper, threw it at him. "Fuck your dick."

Rayne stormed out of the office and back to her apartment where Lanna sat on the couch watching her tablet. The TV played in the background. Rayne put an arm around her child's shoulders and pulled her close. A tear of frustration started to fall. Rayne looked away and sniffled, hoping Lanna wouldn't hear, but the child wore her pink earphones.

Her mother would have told her to find the street corner.

She had until close of business Monday to stop the eviction process. Rayne opened an app and looked at the subs. They weren't due for re-ups this month, and she couldn't see how she could get more followers in that short amount of time.

The notification for private messages showed dozens, hundreds perhaps, of unread messages. She knew what those were. Requests for personalized content.

She did the math.

Rayne looked down the top of her daughter's head and kissed it, pulled her in close. She stood, patted Lanna's leg.

"I have to do some things in my room, just for a while. Just keep your headphones on. Okay?" The child nodded as if she hadn't planned to do anything else.

"I heard you singing when I got home. Are you working on a new song? I like when you sing angry songs, Mommsy." Knife to the chest.

Rayne closed the door, undressed, and looked in the long mirror as she pushed tears away. She set the stage like she always did—except this time, it wasn't for art. It was for survival. Again. Just in a different way than the way she'd seen as a little girl. Survival left no room for dreams.

Excerpt from "The Voice Was Never Theirs"
BY CLARA COWLEY

"It's easy to blame Aberdeen's Mike Kilmore. But to vilify him the way he's been? That's a bad take. Lazy, even. And deeply misunderstood.

I'll be the first to admit—Mike Kilmore was never hard to dislike. He was a walking caricature of rock and roll: loud, indulgent, ego-driven, and allergic to subtlety. But a bad person? No. Not even close. And his story—his part in all this—isn't as simple as wanting to replace his best friend or trying to sabotage Kline Thomas before he could step into Lloyd's spotlight.

Do I absolve him of the hell he put Kline through? Absolutely not. I couldn't even if I wanted to.

But if you're looking for villains, maybe start with Paul White. Or Aiesha Holt.

There's plenty of blame to go around.

Because Mike's choices were never about a mic. They were about money. He just needed the band to think it was about the mic. Think about what that says about Mike Kilmore. He was ok failing as a frontman, long as he got what he wanted. What would his best friend, Lloyd Brannon, say about trading art for money?

Money is the root of all evil and has no place in art.

And when money gets involved, the lines blur fast."

folder

03

Kilmore Residence, Calabasas,CA

World-renowned guitarist Mike Kilmore sat at the dining table of his childhood home—the one his parents left him—trying not to clench his fists as his financial advisor flipped through a folder with surgical detachment.

"I ran the projections three times," the man said calmly. "There's no path forward unless something drastic changes. You're leveraged in every direction."

Kilmore stared at the condensation sliding down his glass of water.

"You're telling me I'm broke."

"I'm telling you," the man replied, adjusting his glasses, "you're nearly half a million in the red. And that's if the album goes platinum—because of the recoupment to the label."

Kilmore barked a bitter laugh. "We haven't gone platinum in over a decade."

"Exactly."

Silence settled. The air was heavy with old hardwood and pressure.

"The market tanked. You bet wrong. The alimonies did the rest."

The folder slid across the table. Spreadsheets. Color-coded tabs. Asset lists. Debt.

Kilmore didn't touch it. He wanted to scream at the man who once told him it was time to diversify. But what good would it do?

"If the record hits, and I stay in the band?" he asked quietly.

"You'll still be liable for prior losses. Tax debt doesn't go away. Neither does the alimony."

"And if the record bombs?"

The advisor took his time. "You walk away. Clean. Creditors eat the corpse. You declare. The label absorbs the loss."

Kilmore's jaw tightened.

Better to fail.

Kilmore's fingers twitched.

The advisor stood, gathering his things. "There are no good options. Only consequences. I'll follow up next week."

Kilmore stayed seated; eyes locked on the folder.

When the door clicked shut behind the man, he whispered to no one.

His eyes drifted to the wall — a picture of Lloyd, flanked by gold and platinum records, crooked where he'd hung them after moving back into his parents' house. The house he grew up in.

Lloyd would've told me to take the hit and fight my way out. Never sacrifice art.
But I'm not that strong.

Excerpt from "The Voice Was Never Theirs"
BY CLARA COWLEY

"I didn't expect much that night. An all-female punk band in a dive bar, another scream into the void for women in this industry.

But when Rayne Harlow took the mic, the air shifted. It wasn't performance—it was defiance. Her voice demanded to be heard.

They existed at that moment because the world gave them no other choice. Because silence, for women like them, was just another way to starve.

That night wasn't about the music.
It was about survival. About finally being too loud to ignore."

truth

04

Harvard and Stone, Hollywood, CA

The redhead with a guitar slung across her back nearly got knocked off her feet as the six-foot-tall drummer squeezed past her on the cramped stage. Clara Cowley, perched at the bar with her IPA, snorted and jotted a note in her battered notebook.

She didn't bother turning toward the guy beside her when he leaned in.

"You here for the Queens?"

Clara raised her glass. "What gave it away?"

The Edison bulbs overhead cast a warm glow that did nothing for her aging eyesight. She squinted through smudged glasses and cursed the dimness, her years, and the fact that she still did this—scouting punk clubs like it was 1994.

The guy beside her smirked. "You came to the right show. Those girls are incredible. If that's your thing."

Clara finally looked at him. Mid-thirties, maybe. His band tee—Chevelle and Breaking Benjamin—still looked freshly merch-tabled. Post-grunge DNA. The kind that traced lineage but never inherited the crown. Her flannel was older than he was. Her notebook rested on her thigh; his phone flickered blue every few seconds. She slouched into the stool—no apology, no posture. He stood straight, tapping his fingers in bad rhythm. She wondered why he liked those bands. She knew why she did, but she wasn't in a mood to be disappointed.

She tapped the pen against the page. "What makes them special? Besides playing half-naked."

He just grinned. "You'll see."

A pop of feedback rang out as plugs slid into instruments. The redhead stood between a platinum-blonde bassist built like a pretty tank, all curves and softness. A tiny guitarist with inky black hair, and a tattoo that ran all the way down her bare back. And then? A towering drummer behind them all. All wore lingerie bottoms, fishnets, and pasties—or was that electrical tape? Clara shivered at the thought of pulling that off. Some people like pain, she reckoned. The redhead's knee-high patent leather boots caught the light as she stepped forward.

The small guitarist pulled out a Gibson Flying V and plugged it into…

Is that a Mesa/Boogie? Clara squinted. Probably one of the new Gibson rebrands. No, that was a Mark IV. Interesting.

A snap as the cord was slid into the amp. The hum of the tubes warming up. The clank of glasses and mindless banter.

No intro. No sound check. Just a jagged thrash-metal riff from the tiny guitarist, straight from the mind of Hetfield or Buzz Osborne. All down picking excellence. The combo was both bright in the midrange but sludgy with a midrange bite. *Thum-thum-thum-thum! Chug! Chugga chug! Wail! Thum-thum-thum-thum! Nah, nah!*

Pause. Silence. Clara's mind wondered where she'd heard that sound. The Melvins? Queens of the Stone Age?

Tsk. Tsk. Tsk. Counted in. *SNAP!* Double strike on the snare.

Clara flinched as the room exploded in sound. Messy, off-time, but somehow precise. Then the sounds collided in a stop-start rhythm. The redhead blazed through a punk rhythm—no FX pedals, no finesse. Just fury. The band crashed in behind her. The guitarist ripped a filthy solo high up the neck, her fingers a blur. Bent strings and guitar neck. Shook out the last of the sound.

Clara winced; hands half-raised to her ears. Tour shirt man beside her just grinned wider.

The redhead swiped her shaved-side hair with a flourish, glittering braces flashing under the stage lights.

The bass pounded—steady, relentless, like a second heartbeat.

"This one's for all you lazy motherfuckers staring at a screen and paying us to get naked," she sneered, pointing into the crowd. "Yeah, you jerk-offs, jerking off. Thanks for the cash. It's called

'Come to My Kitty.'"

Clara rolled her eyes. *Of course it is.* Subtlety was dead. All that play and those lyrics? Ugh.

But that first line stuck with her. What exactly did she mean? It didn't take long to figure it out when she spied a QR code and scanned it with her phone.

On one hand, Clara was revolted. This kind of content creation felt like the worst kind of sellout—sexual exploitation as business model.

And yet... there was something clever about it. Clara scrolled through tagged photos, matching usernames to performers.

The roar pulled her eyes up from her screen. She took a sip and leaned toward Chevelle/Breaking Benjamin guy.

"I've covered Love. Manson. Morissette. I've met Jett. This? Not that special. It's ok." She set the phone down.

That's not fair, she thought. The further into the song they played, the tone became cleaner, the timing perfect. Clara looked up from her phone.

He was still grinning, knowing.

The redhead stepped onto a floor speaker, slung her guitar around her back—and leapt.

Clara sat up.

The singer caught the metal bar above the stage with the crook of her knee, swinging upside down, hair flaring like fire, and started playing again—flawless, fierce, inverted.

Clara's jaw dropped.

The redhead's back arched in a contorted bow, abs flexed, every tattooed muscle taut under the light. Then her green eyes locked on to Clara's.

A jolt shot through Clara's chest.

Still hanging upside down, the guitarist pointed straight at her—no mistaking it. A taunt. A challenge. A bullseye. Then the finger curled into the middle one.

The crowd erupted. Heads turned toward Clara Cowley. She wanted to crawl into a hole. It was like the woman had read her mind.

The singer swung again, hair whipping like fire, then snapped upright and dove into another riff—louder, dirtier, sharper.

The guitars dropped out. The redhead handed hers to the Asian woman, who slung her own axe to her back. The drummer and bassist held a tight rhythm that beat into Clara's chest. Sludging start-stop. The drummer's long arms slammed double stick fills down, getting every ounce of sounds she could, but it didn't seem possible to bang with that power and keep it tight. The towering woman did it, anyhow. The soft, pale, platinum bassist faced the drummer, watching every stick strike, timing up every note.

The redhead dropped her arms. The other guitarist took them. They swung back and forth—higher, faster—until the smaller woman launched.

Clara gasped. "Oh my God!"

The woman landed feet from the drum kit, boots sliding across the stage. Before she even stopped sliding, she spun the guitar around, dropped to her back, and tore into a solo straight out of an '80s hair band.

The chaos stopped. Tour shirt man turned.

"Nothing special, huh?"

Clara had no words.

The redhead untangled from the pole. With help from her bandmates, she landed on solid ground. Without a breath, she stepped to the mic.

"Entertained, yet?" she asked, chuckling.

She twisted the knobs on her guitar, picking strings, testing chords.

"You know, life's tough for us women. Barely making ends meet. Men guard all the doors, hold all the keys. Rent went up. I couldn't pay it. You know what the guy said? Told me I could suck his dick to cover the difference."

She strummed the guitar. Clara glanced at the band, expecting cringes—none. They nodded like parishioners in church.

"People look at us and see walking vaginas. Nothing more. Here for their entertainment—until we threaten them with it."

She paused. Pulled back. Then leaned in.

"This one's new. I think it says enough."

She hit a punk riff. No pedals. No effects. Just pick and rage. Her face contorted—not for show but from something burning underneath.

Clara knew that look. She wasn't performing. She was *telling the truth.*

Her truth.

She sang in her raspy, sometimes pitchy voice that seemed almost too deliberate. The tempo was too fast for their typical gymnastics and choreography. Eyes closed and head tilted, she let that imperfect voice and imperfect timing ring out.

Barely got enough for me to eat,
Thinkin' 'bout sellin' pictures of my feet.
Rent man said my check just bounced,
Said I could suck it to even the count.
Girl's gotta do what a girl's gotta do,
But I gotta say, boy—fuck you.
Sex sells, yeah, we know the line,
But here's what I'm sellin' this time:

She hammered the strings as the band crashed in on the chorus:

Fuck your dick, man!
Yeah, I said what I said!
You're such a dick, man!
'Cause I ain't spreadin' my legs!
So fuck your dick, man!
If I had one, I'd rather be dead!
You're such a dick, man!

She screamed into the mic, voice cracking with fury and sadness. No theatrics now. No circus. Just vitriol and pain.

The other woman guitarist ripped a solo so loud and powerful that it made the small woman seem like a giant. As the chorus faded and the next verse loomed, Clara leaned forward on her barstool.

Even from here, she could see the makeup streaking down the redhead's face—sweat, tears, rage.

Played the dive bars, played the shows,
Still they ask me, "How far I'll go?"
He's got a label and a leering grin,
Says, "Give me more," if I wanna win.
He don't hear the song, just the moan,
Thinks my body's what gets me known.
You call it art, they call it luck,
But it's just who they want to fuck.

She stepped back, ready to cue the chorus—but froze. Her whole body trembled.

Then she howled.

She slammed her guitar into the stage.

Again.

And again.

And again.

The only sounds: splintered wood and animal screams.

Then—silence.

She stood over the wreckage, every muscle locked, fists clenched at her sides.

"FUCK! FUCKING FUCK!"

She collapsed to the floor, sobbing.

Only her bandmates moved. They circled around her, easing her up, whispering things no one else could hear.

She resisted at first—then let them guide her offstage, face buried in her hands.

"It's not fuckin' FAIR!"

No one cheered. No one moved.

Tour shirt man turned to Clara.

"What do you think that was all about?"

Her eyes stayed on the stage.

"You wouldn't understand."

Excerpt from "The Voice Was Never Theirs"
BY CLARA COWLEY

"People like to say Kline Thomas was chosen. That fate plucked him out of obscurity and placed him in the shadow of the ghost—and the legend—that was Lloyd Brannon. They call it the easy route.

But that's bullshit.

He was cornered. Pushed. Held up against a dead man's echo and told to sing like it didn't hurt. But it did. Every note, every word, every breath—it cost him something.

The truth is, Kline never wanted to be a singer. Not really. Music was never about fame—it was about escape. The only place he could put his grief. His guilt. The only place he could still feel like something made sense.

And the industry? It never taught him how to survive. Not once. As the pressure built, as the questions piled onto his shoulders, they looked the other way.

Kline—his voice, his pain, his songs—weren't recruited.

He was extracted.

They didn't need him to sing. They needed him to deliver. To satisfy the terms of a contract he didn't sign, built on someone else's legacy. He was a patch on a sinking ship, and they didn't care if he drowned. Just as long as the ship made it to port.

And maybe the saddest part?

He knew. All along."

mondays

05

North Huntsville Industrial Park,
Huntsville, AL

KLINE THOMAS
lifted his head just as Eddie shut the door
behind him and flopped into the conference
room chair.

"Rough night, eh?" Eddie grinned. "You look wrecked, bro."

"Can you not?" Kline muttered, eyes still adjusting to the light. His voice was shot — hungover, and maybe a little ashamed.

Eddie stretched out his long frame and started drumming the table with his fingers.

Kline winced. "Seriously."

Eddie froze mid-rhythm and set his hairy knuckles in his lap. "Alright, alright."

They'd been best friends since college—back when they were broke, lost, and late to class every day. Now they were nearly in their forties, still broke, still working side by side. The only thing that changed was the building—now it was an engine plant instead of a dorm.

Eddie leaned forward, trying to hold back a smirk. "You check our socials yet?"

"Can't think of anything I want less."

"Thought so," Eddie said, already unlocking his phone. "Figured this might help."

Kline rubbed his eyes.

"Normally, our streams get, what, twenty people?"

"Ten, maybe," Kline mumbled.

"Last night, we had ten thousand."

That made him blink.

"Ten. Thousand," Eddie repeated, leaning forward. "Live. Some influencer went viral mid-set. This morning? Over forty thousand views."

Eddie slid the phone across the desk. The video was already playing. Kline's own voice filled the tiny speaker.

He winced. "Jesus. I look wrecked."

"Keep watching."

Kline reached for the phone, but Eddie pulled it back just as the video rewound — the stumble, the bottles, the ramble, all of it.

"Christ. That's awful. Turn it off."

Eddie chuckled. "They think you're a legend. A ghost come back."

Kline groaned. "That wasn't a performance. That was a confession."

"Maybe that's why it worked."

His inbox kept pinging. New emails. Promises. Demands. Too much to wade through, even if he cared.

Eddie cut the video before Kline's rant really began about his wife leaving him after they attended an Aberdeen show. The logistics weren't that simple, but it was all Kline could get out at the time.

Eddie cleared his throat. "So, Humphrey's booked us."

Kline raised an eyebrow.

"Saturday. Prime slot. Good money. And it's already sold out."

"Okay…" Kline said slowly. "What's the catch?"

Eddie hesitated. "They want a Lloyd Brannon tribute. Best-of set. Aberdeen." Eddie's fists were clenched, both raised in excitement while he emphasized the last word.

Kline stared at him.

"It would mean a lot to me," Eddie added quickly. "You crushed it last night. You always do. It sounded… real. Like Lloyd, but not a cheap copy. Not covers." All they played was covers, but Eddie never saw them that way. Not when Kline was singing. He added his own flavor. Even his own lyrics. That had been the biggest surprise of getting him to front Eddie's band.

He couldn't look at Kline, so he looked at the wall. This was a hard conversation to have.

"People are talking again. About Aberdeen. About Lloyd. And no one else can sing that catalog like you."

"And that's all they want?" Kline asked.

Eddie hesitated again. "Well … there's talk of maybe working in one or two originals. Later. Just a track or two to test the waters."

Kline's face hardened. "No."

"Come on—"

"No, Ed."

"It doesn't have to be your stuff. We could co-write or use—"

"I said no." His voice had gone cold.

Eddie backed off, raising a hand. "Okay, okay. Just putting it out there." Eddie would never give up. He didn't know Kline had songs. He suspected.

Kline leaned back, eyes on the screen again. The idea of playing someone else's legacy was one thing. Offering up his own? Letting people hear something real, something that couldn't hide behind nostalgia? That was something else entirely.

Kline leaned back, eyes on the screen again. He'd spent years hiding in covers and irony, trying not to sing anything real. He'd done it before. For her.

The idea of singing his own songs again made his stomach turn. People might not just listen. They might actually hear him.

Excerpt from "The Voice Was Never Theirs"
BY CLARA COWLEY

"There's something uniquely tragic about watching a band try to outlive itself.

Aberdeen wasn't just mourning Lloyd Brannon— they were mourning their own relevance.

The meeting wasn't about healing. It wasn't

about what was right for the music, or for
the people who made it. It was about survival.
Not artistic survival. Financial survival.

They spoke in circles, as they had in the
weeks following Lloyd's death. The truth
is, Aberdeen's creative direction had died
long before. His death didn't kill it—it
just exposed how long they'd been coasting
on fumes.

Up until Lloyd's passing, they clung to
the belief that it wasn't "if" he'd find that
spark again, but "when." And in a twisted way,
he did. Posthumously. And his song—if you
can call it his—was sung by the most unlikely
oracle: Kline Thomas.

The truth? They didn't want a singer.
They wanted a placeholder. A living,
breathing loophole.

The irony? As they discussed bringing in
someone they could manipulate for their own
gain, Pacific Coast Records was already
manipulating them—and had been, all along.

Legacy isn't always earned. Sometimes it's
negotiated in quiet rooms between people who
forgot why they picked up instruments in the
first place.

Aberdeen wasn't trying to move forward.
They were trying not to fall apart."

eveningview

06

Eveningview Mansion, Malibu, CA

It was the first time they'd all stepped into Eveningview since Lloyd died. It was a surreal and very different experience without Lloyd. Like walking into a crypt.

Fitting, in a way. This was where Aberdeen wrote and recorded their breakout album which went double platinum and launched them worldwide. *Eveningview*. Now, two decades later, they sat in cold silence on the same worn furniture, in the same room where they once burned with purpose.

Lloyd Brannon was dead. And with him, the lifeblood of their creativity. In that void, only the wafting weed smoke remained from that past.

They'd avoided this meeting for weeks following Lloyd's death. Avoided each other when the conversations turned grim. But the contract hadn't disappeared. The lawsuits wouldn't wait. Silence wasn't protection anymore.

The band had asked White to let them have a band-only meeting. Since it was progress just getting them in the same room together, White had acquiesced but reminded them that PCR had only paid for so much time, so it should be used constructively.

"Let's forget about the benefit show, for a minute. The LBF is taking care of most of it, and it looks good. We don't need anyone for that. But we do have to come up with something for this record,"

MARKUS KENNEY,

DJ and keyboardist, said finally, voice flat. "If we don't cut this record, we're broke. That's the math, and the clock is ticking."

BEN CANTRELL,

bassist, leaned forward, elbows on knees. Jose Madera, drummer, shifted beside him, already anticipating the next beat. Outside, the Malibu coastline shimmered gold beneath the setting sun.

"So we find someone new," Ben said, as if this were an original thought. But he'd said it in a way differently than before.

Markus raised an eyebrow. "Define 'new.'"

"I don't mean someone from the industry. We've tried that," Ben said. "I mean *new* new. No industry baggage. No label ties."

Mike Kilmore, guitarist, blinked. His dark, nearly black, eyes narrowed. "A person off the street? Who can write songs?"

"They will," Ben said. "Or we will. We've done it before."

Kilmore shook his head. "Lloyd wrote songs because he bled for them. We all chipped in, sure. But none of us carried what he carried. There's a reason he got sole lyrical credit and none of ours was ever used." A sore subject.

JOSE MADERA'S

voice cut through the static. "And none of us *wanted* to." Jose left it at that, but the thoughts still swirled.

Because Lloyd wouldn't let us.

That quiet truth shifted the air.

Markus uncrossed his legs in his tight and tapered jeans and leaned forward, pushed his glasses up on his dark and round face.

Kilmore walked to the bar in the back of the room, poured himself another glass of his failed proprietary brew, and stared out at the water. Another reminder of his failures.

"And what's White's role in this?" Madera asked.

"None. He got us here." Kilmore was still furious with him.

"He didn't kill Lloyd," Ben said.

"No, he killed us," Kilmore replied. No one argued, even though none of them really agreed. Kilmore looked around. No one wanted to talk about that. The contract revisions. The inability to get Lloyd to *do something* other than paint and pontificate about social platforms with podcasters.

"And this person we find …" Ben turned back, raising an eyebrow. "They get the same cut Lloyd did? If we get a new contract?" That was a big *if*. Markus kept his mouth shut. They knew very little about their own contract, other than the label had screwed Aberdeen and then Lloyd, via the LBF, had screwed them all. Markus had asked the right questions and knew. Now was not the time.

Kilmore didn't flinch. "Of course not. That's the point. Cut the album. Do the tour. Who cares if the album is good or not. It doesn't matter. We build this next version on different terms. White can't hand anyone a crown again." Kilmore's hidden message slipped by everyone but Markus.

"We've got this place from Holden for a while. We make as good of an album as we can. We fulfill the contract," Markus said flatly, his eyes on Kilmore. They both knew how Lloyd felt and the culture he'd instilled in this band. Making music for the sake of music wasn't an option. Lloyd would rather not sing a note than force a song, which is why they were here at all.

Well, that and he'd run out of good songs. No one wanted to admit that.

"And that's it," Ben added. "We keep the lights on. One step at a time."

Kilmore started to mention the other option. The one he'd suggested before. But now was not the time, and he could sense the direction his financial advisor had suggested. Sometimes, failure could be successful. If they weren't open to him being the singer, this path was the best option, for him at least.

They drifted into the studio without another word. Quiet agreement.

No one mentioned Lloyd again. Not directly. But every word was haunted by him. Not a man anymore. Just a shadow they could never outrun. The mic still stood at center stage. Set to his height. Too tall for any of them.

Excerpt from "The Voice Was Never Theirs"
BY CLARA COWLEY

"It happened during a panel at USC that I truly didn't want to attend, but I owed Aiesha Holt a favor. I am forever grateful I went. This is truly my entrance into this amazing story.

The moderator asked me about my book and if I thought that rock was still dead. It was the kind of question I've answered a hundred times—always with the same curated, detached insight. A sound bite, not a stance. After all, the book was over a decade old, and nothing had changed. Nothing.

In that moment, I realized something I'd never said out loud—because I hadn't thought it entirely through. I'd asked questions, just not the right ones. It was Markus Kenney, the keyboardist and DJ for Aberdeen, whom I respect thoroughly, who gave an answer that made things click. Now I had the right questions to ask. But where was the answer? Why aren't there more women rockstars in the world?

It was on a bar stage in Hollywood, wearing ripped tights and a chipped manicure,screaming truths I never had the guts to print.

At the same time, the counterpoint was how easy it was for men. That answer was being given across the country on that very night.

It was a soft-spoken engineer trying to sing his way out of grief while the world tried to turn him into a product.

I'd spent years asking the wrong questions. I just hadn't realized it until I was the one being asked."

tupac

07

USC Annenberg School of Communication
and Journalism, Los Angeles, CA

The lecture hall wasn't full. Move-in day was still two weeks out—
but it was fuller than Markus Kenney expected. Graduate students
mostly. A few professors. Some locals with nothing better to do.

Still, it was surreal. He'd sat in those seats once, an older student trying to disappear into the rows. Now he was onstage—panelist, artist, "Doctor Kenney."

He had to remind them: "Just Markus." He never used the title, even if it was earned.

AIESHA HOLT

had volunteered him for this. Publicity move, sure—but he didn't mind. He was proud to be a USC alumnus. So was White, seated beside him in his usual too-expensive blazer. Clara Cowley, on the other hand, looked like she wanted to be anywhere else. Arms folded, flannel shirt rumpled, glasses smudged. A pit bull in the wrong kennel. Clara leaned over to Markus Kenney.

"Remind me to send Aiesha flowers for the cattle prod."

The moderator cleared their throat.

"Markus, you represent a unique generation of artists—those who bridged the analog and digital eras. Could you speak to that experience?"

Markus nodded, thoughtful.

"That's a good question—and probably two questions. One's about tech—Pro Tools, auto-tune, AI, the tools that 'craft sound.' I'll circle back. The other's about the transition—from physical to digital. That's where I'll start."

White shifted slightly in his chair. He already knew where Markus was going.

"Aberdeen bridged that gap. We signed analog contracts. But we live in a digital market. And there've been consequences.

"First? The album died. Not the playlist. Not the singles. I mean the *album*—as a curated experience, as a full artistic statement.

"Everyone blames Spotify, YouTube, TikTok. But it started earlier.

"Vinyl blurred track lines. You heard songs by accident—and sometimes that's how you found your favorite. Tapes sped things up. CDs made it surgical. By then, artists were burying secret tracks—not just to hide their true sound. But, for mystery and desperation. It used to be a way to show fans what could have been, if labels stayed out of the studio. Then? *'Please, just listen to the whole thing.'*

"Singles used to *invite* you in. Now they *replace* the rest. Streaming didn't just support that shift—it mandated it."

He paused to sip water. His voice was holding up better than he expected.

"Why record ten songs when no one will hear past the first? Why build something only die-hard fans will bother finishing? The algorithm doesn't reward patience.

"For newer artists, that's just the game. But for those of us under old contracts? It's a noose.

"We're bound to full-length albums. Full-cycle rollouts. The industry knows this. They use it to trap us—not support us."

White's jaw clenched, but he said nothing.

"Now—tech. I'm not against tools. But they're tools. Not instruments. Not creators. There's a difference. Live music is suffering because of that distinction."

A student raised a hand.

"Isn't that a post-COVID thing? People are still uneasy about crowds."

Markus shook his head.

"No. Coming out of lockdown, shows *boomed*. People were hungry. That was real. But it faded fast. Not because people were scared—because they were disappointed. The experience didn't match the memory."

He scanned the audience. No one challenged him.

"Now with AI creeping in? We're about to find out what happens when creation itself is automated. But here's the bigger question: *What happens to artists when they're no longer needed? What happens when performative art is replaced with a digital construction?*"

Markus kept the last short and to the point, not wanting to get dragged down in the weeds.

"Mister White. Do you have anything to add to Markus's answers?"

"I wouldn't dare challenge him on music creation. But what he said about bridging the analog to digital gap is very, very real." White answered simply.

"In the context of all modern music, Aberdeen is really a small group of bands affected. Isn't that true?" The moderator asked. White considered this.

"Yes, I guess that's true. But, to his point about technology advancing faster than the artists around it, there has to be an entire generation of artists and musicians out there who have spent their entire lives honing a craft that could, ultimately, be replaced." White turned to Markus.

"I think Markus is dead-on about the death of live performances. But he was speaking from the artist perspective. From an industry perspective, are they necessary for selling albums or, in this case, streams? No. And that was the entire purpose of touring. We hate to say it because the performance is for the fan, sure, but it's about tickets, promotion, and merchandise. No way about it. How does that effect bands who focus primarily on performance art? You've answered your own question. Is it disappointing? Of course. Live shows are magic. They make the music breathe." He ended there.

The next question came from a student.

"Miss Cowley. You published a book called *Rock is Dead* over ten years ago, right around the shift into the digital era. Do you still believe that? Do you think it can come back?"

Clara smirked. "First off, just Clara."

She leaned back, arms crossed. "Rock never dies. Every generation thinks they're watching the end of it, and every time, someone finds a pulse. Nirvana didn't invent grunge out of thin air. They were carrying torches from bands no one wanted to hear until suddenly they did. That's how it works."

She leaned forward now, voice hard. "So no, rock isn't dead. But it's in purgatory. Same recycled sounds. Same digital polish. Too easy for artists and for listeners. Live showmanship's gone. There's no way for an audience to call bullshit anymore. And half of you wouldn't notice if there was."

A ripple of laughter died fast when she didn't smile.

"Rock will come back. It always does. But let me leave you with this. Why are there so few women in the story? Not because they don't exist — trust me, I saw one last week who could torch half the bands you worship. The real reason?" She let the silence hang. "Because the industry starves them out before you even get a chance to listen."

She let that hang as she looked around at the wide eyes in the room.

They are thinking. Good.

"So, I saw this band. All women. I'm not saying they're L7 or Hole. But musically? Better than bands I've watched sell out stadiums. Performance, grit, showmanship, heart? Best I've seen."

She swiped her hands, sharp. "And you know what's sad? They'll be noticed for a video of the singer melting down onstage before anyone listens to the songs."

She paused, then slammed her hand once, each word a hammer.

"Because. She's. Fucking. Starving."

Clara wasn't sure if she reached anyone in that auditorium of kids that had to be there. She knew Markus Kenney heard her, but that wasn't a surprise. The man was sharp. In tune with the world, an irony for a musician that never had to tune. So was White. But he was chained by the confines of making money. Still, no one seemed to move. No one spoke. No one seemed to breath. She realized how long she'd spoken. Perhaps she'd gone on her diatribe too long. White and Markus just stared at her.

Clara knew they heard her. Might have even begun to wonder about the truth of her words.

But nothing would change.

She knew this because no one said a word to her when the panel had concluded. She'd picked up her purse, exchanged pleasantries with many people including White and Markus, and had waited for a rideshare.

Clara had stood on the corner and shaken her head.

"What did I expect? To get handed a Nobel for a panel?" On the ride home, she started wondered if it had all been a joke. A simulation. A panel for students when school wasn't even in session. Was it just to check a box for the school? Longer the silent drive went, the more she spiraled.

Clara thanked the driver and pulled herself out.

She opened the door to her tiny home, tossed the keys onto the table. Her cat circled her feet.

"Fell on black days!" Tupac, her parrot, exclaimed. She walked up the cage in the corner, surrounded by framed concert posters of yesteryear.

"Yeah, sweetie. Fell on black days." She sighed. The bird ruffled, shook. The bird squawked.

"Here comes the rooster! Bawk!" She smiled as she made herself a drink, plopped herself into the worn recliner, and kicked the leg rest up in one motion.

"No, he ain't gonna die," she responded back to him. Where was the rooster?

Excerpt from "The Voice Was Never Theirs"
BY CLARA COWLEY

"It's easy to believe Kline Thomas came to Los Angeles for himself.

The timing. The virality. The voice that sounded like resurrection. For fame. For money.

That was the story the industry wanted to sell. It's the kind people want to believe.

The truth is, he came for Eddie Cornell.

It starts as simply as this: Aberdeen was Eddie's favorite band. And Eddie's belief in Kline's voice-that rare, bone-deep kind of belief-was the only reason Ben Cantrell ever reached out.

Then belief turned into weight. He started carrying Eddie's world on his back. When he stumbled-especially by his own hand-it was Eddie's family that made him stand again.

That kind of loyalty doesn't sell. It
doesn't trend. It just costs.

That's the kind of loyalty this industry
doesn't understand. It's too quiet. Too
sacred. There's no angle to sell, no headline
to spin.

And the pressure of trying to live for
someone else's belief in you? Especially when
they die because of you and your choices?

That kind of pressure builds musical genius.
It shapes legacies. It creates legends.

But eventually?

It breaks everything."

god's joke

08

Rosie's Cantina, Huntsville, AL

As part of a long-standing tradition, the group of engineers—once just broke students—met every Friday at a Mexican spot just off campus. The head count varied, but there were always a few. Today, it was just two.

"Are you nervous about tomorrow night?" Kline asked.

Eddie squirmed, wiped condensation off his glass. "No. And yes."

Kline leaned in. "Come on, man. Out with it."

"I've been trying to figure out how to say this." He exhaled hard. "Tomorrow night matters. To all of us. And we are afraid that it just doesn't mean as much to you."

Kline already knew where this was headed. He stayed quiet. He'd heard this one, many times from Eddie. Every time, he'd done right by his band. Well, almost every time.

This was a big show, for them. But it wasn't their first show. Wasn't even the first time at Humphrey's. But, Saturday night with tickets sold? Not just bystanders. People who wanted to see them?

"This is a real opportunity." Eddie hesitated, searching Kline's face, trying to get the words out.

"You want me to keep it together."

That hit the mark. Eddie nodded. But it wasn't just a request—it was a plea.

"For most of us," Eddie said, "this is it. A paying side gig doing what we love. That's the dream. And we're living it."

Kline looked away.

"Songs I'm not interested in playing for a dozen people and a pitcher of light beer," he muttered. It came out too sharp. He winced. "Sorry. You know I love playing with you guys." Eddie knew this to be true. Kline, when he was on? You get the Stovehouse show or the performance at The Camp. As good as it gets. Kline when he was in his feelings? Drunk? Eddie thought back to the 1910 Gin and *Ten Years Gone*.

"You could have way more than this, Kline. Without us. We've got families, mortgages, second jobs. We're landlocked. You're not."

Kline didn't answer. Just stared at the table.

"You know me." Eddie shrugged. "I've always wanted to be a rockstar. God's joke was giving the voice to my best friend instead."

Kline smirked. "You dragged me onstage, remember? Without you, we're not even talking about this." Eddie didn't argue, but it hurt him to hear those words. While he had begged Kline to sing with them for years, it was Chrys who had convinced him by daring him. Eddie knew all about the trip to Atlanta that brought on his first live song with Pearl Temple Garden in Chains at Bishop's Bar and Grill. He tip-toed around it.

Eddie could see Kline weighing it all. The drinking, the weight of the show, the friendship. So, he braced for resistance.

But Kline just nodded. "I hear ya, man. I've got you. Want me to take it easy? I'll take it easy. It's not that hard. Just a few beers, max." But it was. He couldn't admit the real truth because admitting it was admitting he had a problem. That problem wasn't what Eddie knew and saw. It was what he didn't. Eddie saw piles of beer bottles after a show. He didn't see Kline popping anti-depressants. Kline smiled at him.

"We're gonna put on a hell of a show."

Eddie sighed in relief—and guilt crawled up Kline's spine. He'd caused that. Again. But this could be another Stovehouse, just as easy. A framed picture in his guest bathroom held a picture of the two brothers. Eddie ripping Eddie Van Halen, detuned a half step. Kline? Levitating in the air, arms outstretched. If anyone didn't know them. If anyone ignored the tiny stage and envisioned a modern, stadium gig? This would remind them of Mike McCready and Eddie Vedder in 1990.

You just never knew which Kline you would get. You could only hope. The alternative? Eddie had given up the mic to bring Kline in. To save him. To give him a space to share his voice. That pendulum swung both ways. Without him? Eddie still on the mic. Still inside bars where beer bottles hitting the garbage can was the only thing louder than their sound.

Excerpt from "The Voice Was Never Theirs"
BY CLARA COWLEY

"Ben Cantrell didn't mean to choose the worst possible person to replace Lloyd Brannon. But that's exactly what he did.

It was a simple mistake—reaching out to Kline Thomas before consulting Paul White. Had he waited, had the order been different, had one thought arrived a second later, this story might never have been told.

I've said before that the moment in Holden's office was the most pivotal, because it linked everything back to one thing: money. And it did. But this moment? It may have been the most crucial. Because it was the one moment that could've undone the rest—if just one thing had gone differently.

You can't blame Ben Cantrell. I truly believe he's blameless in this—if for no other reason than he was ignorant and simply trying to claim a future he'd never been allowed to imagine. They all looked to Lloyd to lead. When he was gone, Ben just wanted something of his own.

And to his credit, Ben, Jose, and Markus—
especially Markus—stood by Kline from the
moment he arrived, until the moment their
path with him ended.

Still, to Ben, Kline Thomas wasn't a singer.
He was a solution. A shortcut. A commodity.

And while everyone around Kline saw him
through a different prism, they were all
reaching for the same thing.

What fascinates me most about that night
isn't Kline's performance. It isn't Ben's
public outreach or the private DMs that
almost guaranteed Aberdeen and Kline would
cross paths.

It's who was onstage at the same time.

The Painted Queens.

We throw around words like fate and destiny
too easily. But the fact that Rayne Harlow
and the Queens were at Holden's office that
morning could be dismissed as coincidence.
The fact that they were onstage at Harvard and
Stone that night, when I happened to be there?
Or, being at the Whiskey when the call to Kline
went out? That's something else entirely.

At some point, you stop calling it chance.
At some point, you admit the universe meant it.
Destiny Called Today. Some people pick up."

viral

09

Whiskey a Go Go, Los Angeles, CA

Aberdeen were regulars at one of LA's most iconic rock clubs. The music blared, as it had for decades, with hungry young acts clawing for notice. Lights flashed. Drinks spilled. Women and men drifted in and out of the crowd. In the corner horseshoe booth, three Aberdeen bandmates lounged until the fourth arrived, dodging patrons on his way in. Late, as always.

Onstage, four women in fishnets, leather, and vinyl thrashed to a jagged punk riff — half topless, electrical tape across their skin. Too loud. Too heavy. Too erratic. But they could absolutely shred. The set ended with a shriek about biting off a motherfucker's cock and throwing it out a moving car window. Kilmore smirked — Lorena Bobbitt by way of CBGB. On the nose, maybe, but funny in how directly it gutted commodification.

Sweat and paint ran down their faces and onto their chests. They raged as hard on their instruments as they did against the machine they were screaming about.

"God, they'll let anyone onstage now," Kilmore muttered, shaking his head just as Markus slid into the booth. The sound had struck him the moment he opened the door. Bands that played venues like this always seem to sound the same. Poor production. Messy play. Amps cranked and FX set to cover the warts of their play.

Not these women. The sound was meant to sound sludgy. Only a trained ear could pick that out. The convoluted rhythm of start-stops and key shifts? On purpose and very, very clear. Kyuss. Sleep. Early Soundgarden. In the end? Very much Homme in the messy, preciseness that was meant to shock. Never let the listener get comfortable.

The words? Well, that was easy, too. Heavens to Besty, sure. L7 and Bikini Kill. The woman's voice was something closer to Courtney Love. Just enough off key to be unsettling.

Jose caught the jealousy in Kilmore's tone. Some punks only knew three chords. These women? They shined at it. Made a game of it. For all his disdain, Kilmore hadn't looked away. Maybe it was the music. Maybe the leather.

"This sound is at least three generations old, man. Let riot girl punk and proto-grunge sludge die, man. Let it stay dead." Kilmore argued.

"Easy, man. They let us start here," Markus said, eyes locked onstage. "And they aren't bad. Just different. What do you think people thought of our sound, back then?" Kilmore considered it. He knew Markus was right.

Oh, look. Another alt-metal/nu-metal wannabe band. Just a mix of early 311, the Spin Doctors, and the Chili Peppers. Nothing special.

That came easy, since that is exactly what they'd heard back then as they defined their sound from bits and pieces of their heroes into the funk and jazz-driven rhythm with Kilmore's clean, melodic play combined with Markus' overlaid effects layered in. And, of course, Lloyd's unique voice.

Jose had turned to watch the women too, but with a touch of shame. Alejandra would not approve. The women were mesmerizing. Their stage antics looked chaotic, but the longer you stared, the more it felt orchestrated. Not shock value. Strategy. A circus act with teeth. Art in chaos.

"Should've gone to the Rainbow," Kilmore muttered. "At least we could hear ourselves think. Punk died forty years ago. Nobody told those ladies."

No one answered.

Ben and Jose made room for the short, dark-skinned man. Kenney brought up his phone and placed it on top of the table, the fake candle flickering just behind it.

"Hey, guys. Sorry I'm late. I got caught up in something. This. This is our guy," Kenney explained, nearly yelling. He was clearly excited, and that commanded attention from Jose and Ben. Excitement and attention were not his style.

"No business on Saturday nights. You know that. Jose doesn't get out with the boys enough as it is." Kilmore's head was turned, watching the women writhe and play onstage, arm draped on the back of the booth. He never acknowledged Kenney arriving. Jose and Ben showed interest, bending forward.

"We came here to listen to live music, right? Not discuss business." Mike asked, dripping with sarcasm as he patronized. But no one was listening. They were enthralled at what they saw and heard on the phone.

"And this is live?"

"Happening right now," Kenney answered. Mike turned the screen towards him, shot a look over it to Kenney. His lips were screwed into a look of disbelief and confusion.

"Who is this guy and how did you find him?" Mike asked with a raised eyebrow. Even in the raucous environment, what they heard could not be closer to the voice of their deceased friend and frontman, Lloyd Brannon. At least, that's what it sounded like over screeching guitars and screaming voices.

"Okay, so, funny story," Kenney began, recalling the specifics that he'd found. He had to yell to be heard. Kilmore started to point this unfortunate reality out to them again. Stopped.

"There isn't a lot on these guys. Group of middle-aged guys. About our age. Little younger. They're a grunge cover band."

"Gross. Not moving a lot of needles for me, then," Kilmore stated, dismissively. Kenney waved a hand at him while shaking in the negative.

"Not really the point, dude. They play everything. And I mean, everything. From Styx to Cars to Zep and beyond." Kenney adjusted his glasses, fidgeted with the pick in his afro.

"Jack of all. Master of fuck all. The band is terrible," Kilmore added, lackadaisical. Kenney disagreed, again. Kilmore only said that because the lead guitar was good and sounded as good as himself. The bass and drums? Eh.

"You say that about any band that isn't us. Shut up and listen," Kenney ordered, frustrated. From the man's lips came a voice from a ghost. The song concluded, and Kenney set the screen down on the red table, a staple of the bar.

"This guy and his band were performing at some shithole, right? Okay, so at the end of the set, he decided to do an Aberdeen song as a tribute. Apparently, the guitarist is a huge fan and his best friend is the singer. But, before he sings, the singer goes on this diatribe about how his wife left him after one of our concerts, or something like that. Didn't make a lot of sense, and the guy was absolutely wrecked. Some influencer was videoing it and it went viral. Point is, he checks a lot of the boxes we talked about. He sounds just like Lloyd. He has stage presence and experience, and he's not in the industry." Kenney pulled the pick, nervously.

"At least most of the boxes, to be sure. That's a start," Kenney offered. Markus kept talking, almost to himself.

"Even bombed, as soon as the first note hits?" Kenney shrugged. The singer channels and just became someone else.

"He even flubs lyrics. Changes them. But, you'd never know. His lyrics still make sense, like he changed them on purpose." No one was listening. He wasn't trying to preach.

"Okay, so, the band decided to do nothing but Aberdeen songs tonight. Everyone there starts streaming it on socials. Since his whole rant went viral a few days ago, this show goes viral, right?" As they watched, he expounded.

"I went back and watched their other shows. Obviously, not a lot of draw, but the guy can absolutely wail. Not only does he have incredible power and range, but he's also a chameleon. Dude can sound like whoever he wants, and you'd never know the difference. He has great stage presence too. I mean, they aren't usually on a real stage, but he's into it and he owns it. He's fun to watch. And, he can manipulate crowds. I watched this show where he made complete strangers stop what they were doing and start dancing at the stage. And then? He started dancing with them. Shit is unreal." They took his point. This wouldn't be someone that had never been in front of people; of course, he'd never been in front of a stadium full of fans, but everyone had to start somewhere, and he'd already started.

"He makes funny faces," Kilmore joked.

"You can't sing like that without making funny faces, Mike. You obviously never watched Lloyd. Only dudes care about that. Chicks dig it." Cantrell didn't point out that Mike made some pretty stupid faces when he was in a solo, tongue sticking out the side of his mouth, lips working as fast as his fingers on the frets.

"So, you want to hire a singer because his rant on social media went viral and people are watching him sing covers of our songs?" Kilmore began chuckling at his own comment. Markus had expected this question.

"Look at the comments," Markus pressed. "Sure, he went viral for the drunken rant—that's why people pulled their phones out. But what kept them watching was the voice. Our socials got tagged thousands of times. We were trending. People are saying he can sing. That he sounds like Lloyd. That he looks like a frontman."

Kilmore didn't even glance at the phone. Markus had expected that. Had bet on it. Because he'd seen the comments Kilmore would latch onto, the ones waiting to be weaponized.

"There's plenty of negativity too," Markus added evenly, "but it's all about how he looks. Not the voice."

Kilmore smirked, right on cue. "Exactly. Who cares what people think of some pudgy cover-band drunk? They don't know what it takes to be Aberdeen."

Markus didn't flinch. That was the move he'd seen coming. The negativity was real—but it was shallow, and Kilmore had just proved his point by clinging to it. "Fucking listen to this guy, Mike. Be objective, Jesus. If you have a better option, let's hear it," Kenney firmly ordered. The band onstage finished a song just in time for the next Aberdeen cover song began. The tall, skinny man with blue jeans and a flannel shirt opened with the guitar solo.

"Ballsy choice. He can't sing this. Not like Lloyd. No way. Hell, Lloyd couldn't do it live." Kilmore set up what he knew would be a failure.

"Look, if he butchers it, I'll buy the next round," Kenney responded.

"You'll buy the rest of the rounds for wasting my time. This is foolish. Where is this guy from?" Kilmore asked.

"Somewhere in Alabama, I think. At least, that's where the venue that's streaming it says it's from." Markus answered succinctly, as always.

The song drove into its final chorus — the hardest in their catalog. Onstage, the slightly pudgy, bald man screamed the last note, set the mic in its stand, and slipped into the dark alley behind the stage.

The band remained silent, eyes drifting toward the next act setting up at the front of the venue.

Markus had heard enough of this man's voice over dozens of shows to know exactly how it would end. He wasn't listening for the finish. He was watching his bandmates — especially Kilmore.

Cantrell made it only to the pre-chorus before picking up his phone. Markus knew where his thoughts were. He laced his fingers together and glanced at Kilmore, grinding his jaw like it was chewing tin foil.

"Looks like you're buying, eh, Mikey?" Markus jabbed.

Kilmore didn't answer. He shoved his phone aside but kept his eyes locked on the stage.

"Well?" Markus pressed, elbowing Jose.

"Dude can sing," Jose said with a shrug. "Even though he's absolutely bombed. Wrecked. Thing is, it's so good nobody would notice. Nobody that hasn't heard Lloyd sing it lit. Even then, only we could tell. He's that good. It's effortless. Like he's mocking the whole thing. Parroting Lloyd as a joke."

Markus glanced up then, at the band still onstage — their chorus chanting *"Come to My Kitty,"* surely meant as a joke. Just as the man on the screen seemed to be singing like it was a joke. The difference was clear: one was ironic art. The other was a confession. Maybe he was confused on which was which. Maybe both were ironic. Maybe both were confessions.

He chuckled, decades of memory in his tone. Lloyd Brannon, shirtless in those tight jeans, wine bottle in hand. Lloyd could've sung *Mary Had a Little Lamb* in Swahili — badly — and the fans, mostly women, would've screamed like it was gospel.

"Yeah." It was all Kilmore said.

"Yeah, you're buying? Or yeah, he can sing as good as Lloyd, even drunk?" Markus asked.

"Yeah," Kilmore repeated.

Jose elbowed Ben. "Looks like there's blood on the ground."

"It's blood in the water. Check your English, hombre," Ben shot back without looking up.

Ben Cantrell had spent his time thumbing through his phone, seemingly on something completely different, before motioning to the two members between him and the floor. Madera and Kenney slid to let him out.

At that moment, onstage, the band finished what must have been an encore. There was muted applause, but mostly catcalls. The response from the redheaded frontwoman was pure vitriol and middle fingers, but even behind the paint it looked like she loved it. This time the house lights came on, signifying that the show was indeed over. Patrons began filing out of the pit.

"Heading to the bathroom to beat the rush?" Kilmore asked the tall bassist.

"Yeah," Cantrell replied. A lie, but he didn't elaborate.

It felt strange, being proactive. He'd spent most of his life in the background, reacting to cues from Kilmore or Lloyd. But something had shifted. He was done waiting.

This was his moment.

It would piss Kilmore off, no doubt.

Good.

It took just seconds to find the singer's social media accounts. Ben wasn't sure if they were locked down or if the guy just didn't use them much. Either way, he clicked to send a DM.

Then he sent more.

A hand ran through his hair as he tapped out the same message across every platform even from the band's account. He wasn't going to let it get missed. Unless the man never checked socials. Judging by the accounts, that was probably right. Ben frowned.

There was a flicker of doubt. Maybe the message would get buried under the noise. The show had gone viral. Snippets were already surfacing on podcasts and even late-night comedy bits.

Shame if they don't capitalize on this, he thought.

This would've been a dream scenario for Aiesha Holt. Just for a moment, he considered calling her. This was her arena. Ben checked the time. Didn't want that smoke.

Then another stab of doubt—what if the sudden fame made Kline think Aberdeen was beneath him? A bunch of has-beens, washed-up and clinging to relevance and looking for a savior?

Surely not. That was preposterous. He was a cover singer, and they were Aberdeen. Were. That caused some pain.

At the bar, Ben ordered a gin and tonic. It slid his way effortlessly as he stared at the screen of his phone, contemplating the call.

Just as he took a sip, he felt someone step into his personal space. Way inside. Close enough to be intentional.

He turned, out of habit, expecting to look down but found himself almost eye-level with a pair of eyes behind terrifying paint.

What surprised him wasn't the height of the person, nor the sharp face paint but the fact that it was a woman who carried all of it so confidently.

"'Scuse me, big man," she said, reaching across the bar with impossibly long arms to pull a beer from a cooler of ice, as if she owed the joint.

AVA PALATCO monstrous and beautiful drummer for the Painted Queens. Wit that could draw blood, shoulders that carried more than any man. Once a collegiate athlete, now a thunderstorm behind the kit, she leaned over the red-top bar, one stiletto boot kicked into the air.

Ben's gaze drifted upward before meeting her stare again; caught in the mirror behind the bar. She was watching him watch her. She smiled and winked at him.

Embarrassed, he looked away. "Hey, you were just playing, right?"

She twisted off the beer cap, then reached for a bottle of well liquor and poured herself a shot. With a casual flick, she bounced the cap off the bar and into the trash behind it.

"Two points. Crowd goes wild. What was your first clue?" she asked.

Ben couldn't take his eyes off her movements—so smooth, so intentional. They were the same height, maybe, but he moved like an awkward marionette while she floated in grace, beauty, and power. He was constantly aware of how his arms swung, how his head drooped. Not her.

"Playing for the free booze, huh? I get it. Been there." He tried to sound casual but couldn't help noticing her physique—tall, built, muscular. Her stomach rippled beneath a black sports bra, damp with sweat, white salt stains around her arm pits and around the collar.

"Stare any longer and I'm gonna start charging," she snapped, cigarette dangling from her lips, just below a nose that looked much like his own. Ben blinked, shaken from the moment.

"You're just so tall…" he said.

She rolled her eyes. "Sure, sure. Not this huge set of big, beautiful tits and a wagon of an ass, right?" she added, grabbing her chest with one hand and giving her rear a slap with the other. The sound of her huge hand on skin sounded like a rifle going off. Faces turned and he blushed. If she was, no one would see it from the paint. She didn't look like she cared.

He flushed deep red. She smiled, deviously.

"Honestly…" he mumbled. He was used to being talked over by Brannon and Kilmore, but not by women. Truthfully, he wasn't used to talking to women at all.

She stared at him—green eyes sharp, lashes long, smoke curling from one side of her mouth.

Ben realized his mouth was open and snapped it shut. She lightly brought a long finger to his chin, pushed it closed.

"Thought you were tryin' to catch flies there, boss."

They stared at each other in silence until he finally extended a hand.

"Hey. I'm sorry. I'm—"

"Ben Cantrell. I know who you are," she cut in. "You here scouting us? Gonna cut us a record deal?"

"Uh… no?"

"Then what good are you?" she said, turning back to the bar and scanning for an ashtray. Not finding one, she ashed in his drink.

Not just punk on stage. He thought to himself.

Ben stared at the sinking ashes, bewildered.

Then she smiled.

"So, what are you doing out here with the peasants if you're not here to sign us?"

He gushed about the discovery he'd made, proud of himself for once. He'd checked LinkedIn, found the number of a manufacturing manager from Huntsville, Alabama. The picture matched, despite the suit.

"You mind if I make that call?" Ben asked. "Wouldn't it be cool to say you were here when Aberdeen found their new frontman?"

She shrugged, unimpressed. But he could tell she was curious. That was enough.

Ben dialed. She leaned just close enough to glimpse the screen— close enough to memorize the name and number. No one picked up. Ben called another, the first number he should have dialed. Ben cringed as he realized the breach of courtesy. He was just so excited to do something.

"Hey, Paul, it's Ben Cantrell," he said. "I think we've found our guy." Ava Palatco pulled out her own phone, entered both. Saved.

He checked the time. "Sorry for calling this late. But there's this guy... I'll send you the videos. I already contacted him."

The voice on the other end was raised.

"All of them," he said, proudly. But something in White's voice was off.

"Yeah, I guess you're right. I was just trying to be proactive, you know. This guy is it. He's a winner."

More raised voices.

"I understand." Then the voice returned to normal levels as White asked questions.

She was watching him again, eyes sharp, smile amused and calm like a predator waiting for the kill.

"Yeah. Streams. Just... look, you'll hear it. Trying to explain it would sound insane. But he's it. Voice. Knows the songs. Owns the stage. If we're still trying to find Lloyd's voice? This guy has it. I swear."

A pause. His expression dimmed.

"Right. Do what you need to do. But Markus found him, and that should count for something. I'd like to get him out here. This week. Soon as possible. I've got other ideas. He's viral. We collaborate. Aiesha would be proud of me for thinking of that."

The voice on the other end kept going. Ben nodded to no one.

A beat passed. Ben smiled faintly.

"All by myself. Yeah. From Alabama. Huntsville, I think?"

Another pause, this one longer.

"I know. It probably won't work. But it might. It's the best thing we've found so far."

He waited.

"I understand. You and Aiesha should have reached out. Got

it. But White? I'd like to call him." Ben was still proud of himself, despite the browbeating.

Click. The line went dead.

No fanfare. No celebration. Just silence.

"Not the big finish you were hoping for, huh?" she said, grinning.

Ben sighed—but it wasn't defeat. It was satisfaction. Like he'd finally taken a step forward.

"Let me buy you a drink," she said, sweet and savage.

He didn't say no.

She slid a drink his way, smile sharp as glass.

Ben raised it, still flushed with the thrill of being reckless.

For once, he hadn't waited his turn.

Excerpt from "The Voice Was Never Theirs"
BY CLARA COWLEY

"I sometimes wonder what Paul White must have been thinking that night-and into the early morning.

Of course, I've asked. And he's answered. To an extent.

But no one will ever get the full truth. I don't even think Paul knows it anymore. His version changes, day to day, like a tide he refuses to name. And how could it not? The weight of it. The contradiction.

Because yes-he could've stopped it. Right then. Right there. A call. A message. A carefully worded delay. There would've been collateral damage, sure. But nothing worse than what he'd already buried on Aberdeen's behalf. Or, more specifically, for Lloyd Brannon.

So why didn't he?

That's the answer he never gives.

What I do know is this: he sat in his house and watched recording after recording of Kline Thomas performing. Silently. Alone.

And he still let it happen.

He'll tell you the die was cast. That it was inevitable.

I never believed that. Not from Paul White.

He heard Kline. And he gambled.

And that gamble would cost everyone.

distorted

10

Humphrey's Bar and Grill,
Huntsville, AL

Kline collapsed against the brick wall of the narrow alley, slid down, as rain began pelting his head, rolling down his bald skin and into his scruffy beard.

"Don't worry, brother. We'll get all the equipment packed," Eddie joked, lightly. Kline, hands shaking, fished in his pockets for the open pack of cigarettes. He rarely smoked anymore, something he finally learned to give up after she had walked out. He laughed out loud at the irony. Eddie mistook the laugh.

"Dude, I don't know what to say. That was … possessed." Eddie's short, slightly curly hair gathered the rain, shielding his face while the rain dripped down Kline's broad nose. Eddie grabbed the shorter man under his armpits and hoisted him.

"Where did THAT come from?" The cigarette burned, gathered raindrops, and broke in half as Kline flicked its ashes. He tossed it to the side, breathless. Eddie, giddy with excitement and admiration, was juxtaposed against the near lifelessness of his longtime friend.

"What is wrong with you, man? You were an absolute killer up there!"

Kline didn't move. He was physically and emotionally exhausted. Shaking and sweating. But it was the eyes that told him the most. They were tired. Eddie firmly grasped his smaller friend's shoulders and shook him, as if he meant to wake him up.

"Come on. Let's get out of the rain," Eddie offered as he dragged his exhausted friend with shoulders slumping through the throng of patrons.

"You rocked it so hard no one noticed how badly we played," Eddie said sarcastically, trying to lift him up emotionally. He smiled broadly at all the people who showered them with more compliments than raindrops from the sky.

"Y'all played great, man. Made it easy." Kline smiled tiredly. There were pats on the back. Exclamations of admiration and countless offers for drinks to be bought for them. Eddie opened the heavy wooden double doors and crashed the two of them into the first open booth.

"Cheer up, bro. I know that was exhausting, but that was a triumph. It was like watching the real thing, the backing band excluded, of course." Eddie joked as he waved for drinks. Quickly, they were set on the table before them. One set arrived, then another, bought by someone else. First of many. A set of extremely attractive and scantily clad ladies tried to introduce themselves and sit, but Eddie waved one of his rolled-up flannel shirt and hairy arms at them as if they were unwanted. Kline looked up and smiled at them. *Go away, at least for now, but check back*, his eyes said. Eddie passed a napkin to his friend.

"Get that water off your face. I wish Chandra could have heard that. Told her she should have come. Kids, man. They get in the way of all the fun. We are gonna party. Look at these people!" He motioned to the crowd, who started pressing close, while referencing his own wife. Kline's countenance transformed from formless to something Eddie had never seen in his friend. An expression stricken in pain and anger c hanged into something else; he'd made his friend proud, and that meant a lot to him.

1 AM PDT, Sunday, August 14, 2022 Malibu, CA
Sitting in his sprawling L.A. home, a bottle of scotch in hand, Paul White scanned a cluster of video feeds—each capturing the same grainy performance from a different angle. His eyes narrowed. His posture locked. The drink remained untouched.

Most of the clips were easy to dismiss—Kline's band covering grunge-era hits. Decent. Forgettable.

But then one feed stopped him cold.

A close-up. Kline, drenched in sweat. Eyes closed. Every lyric falling out of him like confession.

Eerie. Unnerving. Most important—undeniable.

White watched the entire show, recorded at some place called Humphrey's, in total silence.

He couldn't believe what he was seeing and hearing. The echo of a dead friend and icon.

He closed his eyes and just listened.

It haunted him—not because it sounded like Lloyd, but because it didn't. Not exactly. It was Lloyd's sound, not his spirit. An echo in a winding canyon where all the rough edges, the crags, the switchbacks all distorted the sound, just a bit.

But sound and spirit? He hadn't heard those together in Lloyd Brannon for a long time.

It was sick on that last tour. Dying when Celeste left. Dead when he married the mother of Aria, his only child. Gone the day he signed away his art and legacy—turned it into commodity.

Then let her run it. Cut him out. Divorced him from the need to make music. Why? Did Lloyd not trust White, after all these years, to manage things for himself, his wife, and daughter? Or had she convinced Lloyd that she could do it better? Or was it just a long con?

And then? He died.

He and Aberdeen were marooned, creatively, financially.

Was any of it necessary? If one thing had gone differently, would Lloyd still be here? Still making music?

White's eyes returned to the screen. A man he'd heard of—but didn't know.

More shocking than the sound was the belief. The conviction of someone giving away a soul—not selling it. What the man onstage believed. Who he thought he was.

More importantly—who he knew he wasn't.

But how could he know? He couldn't.

Paul leaned back. Exhaled. And did something he never allowed himself to do. He laughed.

White sat still, breathing slowly, caught in the circular logic that had trapped him:

Why he had to do what he had to do. Why he couldn't. Why he would anyway.

Because fuck her.

History would see him as incompetent. Maybe even evil.

But no one would ever know. He'd never say a word. Let them think he was stupid. Naive. Blind. Let them write it off.

Because the dice were already rolling, and there was no walking it back.

Somewhere in the room, an antique clock rang out a single chime—solemn, low. A reminder: Time had run out.

The pawn had moved forward to start the game—and it had come from the most unexpected of players: Ben Cantrell.

White let out a dry laugh and ran a tired hand over his face. Then, finally, he picked up the tumbler and took a long-overdue sip.

Poor guy. Almost made you feel for him.

After all these years, Ben was finally in the game, and he didn't even know it. None of them did. How could they?

The truth had been buried as deep as it could go. And yet here it was—staring them in the face.

White didn't want to move the next piece. But he had to. White leaned back, glass in hand. Kline wasn't the solution. He was the risk. And Paul knew he was about to bet the house. White picked up the phone. Searched until he found the personal information he needed.

And started drafting an email to Kline Thomas.

He'd twist the knife in Caesar's back—even if no one ever knew he was the one who held it.

On screen, Kline stepped to the mic, sweat gleaming under stage lights. A strange little grin played across his lips.

"I know a lot of you came for this next one. But I always hated it. I don't believe in destiny. Don't believe in cosmic karma or fate deciding who we are. So tonight, I thought we'd do it... a little different." The crowd cheered.

The tall skinny guitarist strummed the intro to an old Aberdeen song. But the lyrics weren't Lloyd Brannon's. And the riff—it wasn't quite Kilmore's either. Something about it had been altered. Distorted. Like a ghost trapped under the surface, clawing to get out.

White looked up when he heard the words, because they weren't Aberdeen lyrics. White recognized it, even though Kline changed them. Bent them. Rage Against the Machine from their song, 'Killing in the Name.'

Kline Thomas held out the mic and the crowd yelled the emphatic anthem's words.

"Yeah! Don't do it!" He gave the call and response. Waved them on. White couldn't believe what he was seeing. Showmanship in front of a few hundred.

The last man on earth who should have replaced Lloyd Brannon was jumping, howling, head whipping side to side. Exploding in defiance—blending Lloyd's reluctant surrender with a heretical thrash. And the crowd? Doing the things that Lloyd wanted but hadn't gotten in the end. Energy. Call and response.

"Fuck you! No! Don't do what they tell us!" White began nodding his head to it. Turned it up. heard himself sing along, but unlike the scream coming from his TV, he whispered it so that only he could hear himself mutter the words. He would be the only one, no matter what, that would ever hear himself say these words and know who he was talking to.

Excerpt from "The Voice Was Never Theirs"
BY CLARA COWLEY

"Rayne Harlow and the Painted Queens had a plan.

And I've often been criticized for romanticizing their role in the manipulation of Kline Thomas, while casting stones at everyone else who did the exact same thing. Maybe that's fair.

But I admit I'm biased. Because to me, the how and why of survival matter.

Rayne takes center stage in this part of the story, but it was Ava Palatco who knew exactly what they needed, what they wanted, and how to get it. Rayne just happened to meet the criteria they believed could trap Kline Thomas.

And as absurd as it sounds, it came down to one thing: her hair color, her height, and her build. She bore a passing resemblance to his ex-wife. And after watching him unravel over Chrys, they postulated that this resemblance might make him vulnerable.

They were right.

Rayne became their siren—not because
she asked to be but because the strategy
made sense.

Was it morally wrong of them to honeypot
Kline? Probably. But do you understand why
they did it?

The industry doesn't starve women by
accident. It starves them on purpose—until
they give up. That's just the ones who fail.

But what about the ones who succeed?

I ask you a simple question: name five
successful female rock artists with staying
power in any ten-year period.

Ask yourself why that is—and you'll
understand the Painted Queens.

Make no mistake. The Queens were starving
for their dream."

pawn

11

Apartments on Fountain Ave.
& Vine St., Hollywood, CA

Rayne guided the tiny fingers on her sweating hand, guiding them from one string to the other.

"Okay. Now strum."

The baby Taylor guitar buzzed with clumsy effort. Rayne smiled anyway—Lanna had come home from a long day of school and *asked* to play.

"Now shift from E to A."

Lanna thought, then moved. Not perfect—but close enough.

They sat cross-legged on the carpet, sheet music and chord diagrams splayed in front of them. Lanna in Rayne's lap. A domestic scene etched in sound.

"If you learn these four chords," Rayne said, "you can play any outlaw country you want."

The door creaked open without a knock. A silhouette swallowed the light.

Ava ducked through the frame out of muscle memory, all limbs and presence, and crossed the living room like she owned it. On the way, she tousled Lanna's hair.

"Hey, peewee. What are we shredding today?"

"Waylon!" Lanna chirped, strumming with renewed vigor.

Ava raised a sculpted eyebrow at Rayne. "Waylon, huh? The Midwest redneckery runs deep in those veins."

She flopped onto the couch with a grunt, massive frame sprawled in leggings and a shredded tank top, sports bra peeking out. Her blonde hair clung to her temple beneath a sweatband.

"I really wish you wouldn't come in here smelling like three-day-old gym towels," Rayne said, all mom-face, zero shock.

"Morning shift. Personal training. Couple hardwood lessons. Then some poor bastard cried after I crushed his PR in front of his girlfriend."

She whipped off her sweatband and let it snap across the

room—hitting Lanna square in the forehead. The girl laughed and flung it back.

Rayne sighed. "There's easier money in S&M." She made sure Lanna didn't pick up on it. The girl's little head bobbed side to side.

"Leather chafes," Ava said, rising to fill a plastic cup with tap water. "These thighs? Fire hazards."

She drained the cup in seconds, refilled it, and leaned on the counter like a lioness in repose.

"At least I'm making use of the athletic scholarship. Basketballs, dumbbells, or whips. Whatever pays the bills."

"Your mom must be so proud," Rayne deadpanned.

"Daddy too. Especially the part where I brought a girlfriend to Thanksgiving. Still waiting on the yearly invite back. Oh well." She shrugged.

Rayne just smiled and shook her head. Silence settled—the familiar kind, thick with shared history.

"You had to do it, didn't you?" Ava said.

Rayne had been waiting for this. She took a breath.

"I held it together last night, didn't I?" she said defensively.

"What? That, I get. I'm just glad it was a cheap Squier. Otherwise, Con might've killed you."

Rayne blinked. "What are you talking about?"

"No, before that. You had to flip her off."

"Who?"

"That woman at the bar. Flannel. Pissed-at-the-world energy."

"Oh—her. Looked like a dy—" She stopped herself.

Ava grinned. "First, not a dyke. Just born in the seventies. Second, she's a beat writer for *Billboard*. Third, no offense taken." She gestured at her statuesque frame. "Some of us redefine the category."

Rayne stared. "Seriously?"

"Deadass. You might've just told the one person who could get us press to go screw herself."

"No such thing as bad press."

"Unless she uses the article she was writing to wipe her ass. Which is likely."

Silence. Lanna plucked her guitar, blissfully unaware. Lanna looked up, seeking validation. Rayne lovingly rubbed her head. So much alike. The young girl beamed and went back to concentrating.

"Then again," Ava said, "maybe someone caught the rest on video. Like you said—no such thing as bad publicity."

Rayne frowned. "Did it work for us?"

Ava didn't answer right away.

"Well," she said finally, "no one cares. Woman falls apart over real shit like rent, groceries, survival? Doesn't trend. Doesn't sell. You know that."

Rayne did.

She kissed her daughter's head and gently nudged her toward her bedroom.

Once the door clicked shut, Ava rolled off the couch and stretched out on the floor, head landing in Rayne's lap like it belonged there. She twisted so she could see her best friend's face.

"Listen, no one likes talking about it, okay? I get it. But if you're struggling, you could have—hell, you *should* have talked to us, Rayne. I appreciate that you live your music and that was real punk rock, rebel girl shit. And the song is incredible. But no one's gonna listen to it, as true as it may be, and help. *We* can."

Rayne looked up, trying to keep the tears from falling. She sniffed and wiped them away.

"That's the problem, Ava. I *know* you guys would help. The last people that should be. The poor leading the poor or some shit."

She sniffed again.

"I've asked so much of you guys over the years. You took me in when I was pregnant, when I had nowhere to go. You left this apartment so I could be the mother to Lanna that mine never was to me. I can't keep asking."

Ava's words cut to the bone. "You're so afraid of being your mother that you forget to be hers."

Rayne knew she meant it to help. Even if it didn't feel that way. She was right, though. Rayne thought back to ripping the notice from Lanna's hand. She'd done it to protect, but never explained. Never apologized. Protection came naturally. Affection did not.

"I didn't come to insult your marketing or your parenting," Ava said, eyes on the ceiling. "I have news." Rayne raised a brow but didn't speak. Just combed her fingers through Ava's damp hair.

"Aberdeen found their guy."

Rayne froze.

"You were actually serious about that?" she asked, voice soft and skeptical.

Ava smirked, her grin full of teeth and ego. "I told you Cantrell would be there. I may have overheard a conversation. Seen a profile. Stole a phone number. Got a name. Did a little stalking"

Rayne leaned in, their noses nearly touching. "You conniving bitch. Don't do that to me."

"You? Please. You're boring. Jen, though?" She laughed. "That woman's browser history belongs in a museum. The nudes she sends? Whoof. Both in content and number."

Rayne didn't want to know.

"So," she sighed. "What's the play?"

Ava didn't miss a beat. "You. You're the play, doll parts."

8 PM PDT, August 14, 2022 Los Angeles, CA

Headlights pulled up to the corner store.

Rayne had been watching the man outside, trying to hustle. She hadn't given him anything when she went inside for a drink. She didn't listen to his story when she came back out.

The car pulled up next to her. She stepped off the curb, eyes flicking to the camera under the overhang. It comforted her—somewhat.

A more-than-middle-aged man stepped out.

Rayne wore sweatpants, a loose t-shirt, her hair pulled up. No makeup. As unattractive as she could make herself.

"Hey, Cherie!" the man called.

She waved. He didn't make a big deal of it—just handed her a roll of hundreds.

"Fuckin' Rams, man. Am I right?"

She painted on a smile, nodded.

"It was a bad beat for the Chargers, for sure. Bad luck. Get 'em next time," she said, tossing it out like change. The man laughed.

"Nah. Getting to meet you in person? Worth the money."

Uncomfortable silence. She tried never to meet customers in person—whether for making book, or her content creation. Especially the last. Always the last.

But this time? Three thousand dollars was worth it. The bills were piling up.

"This might sound... perverted. But I appreciated the custom content you made me."

Rayne cursed herself. She hadn't cross-checked her subs carefully enough. She slipped into the mask, didn't flinch.

"Yeah, I enjoy it too. Especially when it brings my customers joy." She lied. Doubled down.

The balding man smiled. No ill intent, she could tell. Still, her eyes went back to the security camera.

He moved to get back in his car, then paused. Hands braced on the roof of his Benz.

"Don't take this the wrong way. I know it sounds creepy. But I know you sometimes play down at the Rainbow. I hear you're really good."

That was common knowledge. She was. But she stayed away from the sharks.

"There's a guy who owns a studio. He's playing tonight. The reason I asked to meet in person is because I wanted to tell you that. Didn't really have another way."

She held up a hand. "No, I appreciate it."

"I mean, they're looking for another player. Normally I sit in, but I figured you could. And maybe you could—"

"Yeah. For sure." She was suddenly interested.

"Just don't forget who let you know."

Rayne was already in her beat-up car, heading for the Rainbow.

There was a line out front. She walked up to the security guard. He knew her—but still waited for the password.

"Black Dog."

He wasn't going to stop her anyway.

The big man with the earpiece stepped aside, to the dismay of dozens waiting behind the rope. Past the skinny bar. Past the booths and stools. Past Mike Kilmore, staring into a drink as a woman pressed against him. She smirked. He'd probably learned his lesson with working women.

A man stood at the last booth before the back room. She flashed a hundred and whispered the other password.

"Maroon."

In she went.

The sound of chips shuffling met her. Eyes lifted. She cursed herself—amateur mistake—not asking who the mark was.

There was a seat open. She took it. Threw the wad of hundreds on the table. The dealer counted them out, took twenty percent, and handed her the chips.

Cherie played. Mask on. For hours.

Dead & Company flickered on the TV—live from the Las Vegas Sphere. Rayne appreciated it but felt for the men still standing, having to fill in for Jerry. What must that even feel like?

She pulled herself back to the now. She had rehearsal. But she was up doing what she did best. Beating men out of money. The only honest trade she'd ever learned.

Her mark had a mouth. Couldn't shut it. Bragged about his bankroll, his tells, his luck. They called that a bounty. Cherie called it blood in the water.

And now? It was feeding time. Time to make rent. Time to get signed. Time to be a Queen.

He was in the small blind. She was big. A couple of calls. A couple of folds. She hadn't looked at her cards. She never did—not in hands like this. It wasn't about the hole cards. Not yet.

He called. She peeled the corners. Bullets. Spade. Club.

She raised a thousand. Smooth. No splash.

Everyone folded but him. He called.

Cherie turned to him.

"You want to wager some studio time?"

The man laughed. She didn't react.

"I'm dead serious." Flat. Cold.

He looked at his cards again, sat back like his vision was failing.

"Let's see how the flop goes."

Cherie nodded.

The dealer tapped the felt twice. A hush fell over the backroom. Only the sound of cigars puffing and ice against glass.

She knew she was outgunned. All she had was what she brought in—and that included her wits.

Ace of diamonds.

Five of hearts.

Six of hearts.

He checked to her, watching every move.

She didn't hesitate. "All in."

His arms threaded behind his head.

"What you got over there? Big slick?"

She didn't react. Never show emotion. Not in the face of a man. Momma never did. Not till she got home. Rayne couldn't wait to win this hand, get out of this building. She'd show it, then. Her mother never came home smiling. Tonight, she would.

Stone face. Always.

She folded her arms across her chest.

"Call and find out," she dared.

"I put you on big slick. Maybe pocket Queens." He picked up his tumbler. "I've heard about you. How you make your money. You think gambling's an honest trade? I've heard that's what you've said."

She shrugged. Picked up her cheap beer, a contrast to the high-end whiskey around her.

"No. I said poker's an honest trade. Only suckers buck the tiger. Odds are all on the house."

He laughed. Knew the quote.

"Well, I suppose I'm deranged. I guess I'll just have to call." He echoed back. She grinned.

He flicked in his chips.

Four of spades. Seven of hearts.

"Four-seven," he said casually. "Madison County, Alabama. That's where I'm from. I always play it."

He watched her for a reaction. But she couldn't know.

"Never, ever discount anything from the four-seven. Most educated city in the U.S. Birthplace of flight. Space and Missile Defense Command. Marshall Space Flight Center."

He turned to the player beside him, smirking.

"Oh—and me. No big deal."

He had outs. She had the set. Fuck. He had a lot of life left in those cards, even though she was dominating.

She flipped her cards over. Delicately. Deliberate. An audible gasp followed. She smiled. She tapped the cards, played the movie quote back to him as he chewed the cigar.

"Does this mean we're not friends anymore? You know, if I thought you weren't my friend? I don't think I could bear it." She waited for a response. He chewed away.

The dealer tapped twice.

Turn: Queen of spades. Safe.

"You sure you want to do this?" the man asked.

"Tell you what. Walk away now, and I'll listen to a demo. No promises. But I'll listen."

Cherie shook her head.

"All or nothing. I don't believe in surrender. If I did, I wouldn't still be here."

She took a pull from the beer, then pulled the other half of the wad she kept back. Her rent money. Everything she had. All her book from this weekend that would keep her above water for another week.

She tapped it on the table.

"A demo means nothing. Let's go for broke. Sign us if I win."

He drew on his cigar. Didn't flinch. That's when she knew she'd made a mistake.

Didn't matter what she put on the table. He wasn't going to fold. He wasn't going anywhere. Three grand meant nothing to this man. It was his world.

"Deal."

She already knew what would happen. The story of her life.

The dealer tapped. Slid the river.

Eight of clubs.

He didn't react, didn't need to. It was impossible.

"FUCK!" Rayne shouted as she stood, chair crashing behind her. Her hands went to her hair, rustling it. It was a terrible play, but not for her. He played shitty cards. Done what every man with money could do: play every hand. No concern about what could happen after the cards were dealt.

The dealer slid the chips and the cash to the man.

He laughed, shook his head.

"But feel free to come by sometime."

He looked her over. Not like a poker player. Not like a competitor. Like prey.

"Come on in sometime. I'll see what I can do. Maybe put on some makeup next time. Maybe a skirt. Who knows?"

Rayne didn't blink.

"Fuck your dick, asshole."

And she walked herself out.

It was a long road to the Hotbox. She'd missed most of rehearsal. Already rehearsing the apology in her head.

Didn't matter. She had bills to pay. And nothing left of value but her skin and her guitars.

She couldn't sell her body anymore.

The roll-up door was open.

"Well, look who it is," Ava joked. It didn't land.

Rayne didn't react. She walked to the corner and picked up a guitar case. The Gibson SG with worn finish and custom pickups.

She turned to leave.

CONNIE GYUEN

lead guitarist for the Painted Queens. World-class musician. Quiet with wisdom that hit like a ten-pound hammer. Stoic, long black hair cascading down her back, expression carved from stillness. She turned on her stool, presence heavy enough to quiet the room without a word.

"Where you going with that?"

"Don't worry about it."

"Look, I'm sorry I missed rehearsals, okay? I don't want to hear any questions. It's been a shitty night." Rayne kicked around the Hotbox. As if her bandmates weren't playing without her.

"I'm asking questions." It wasn't the voice she expected. Not the former child star—polished, always professional. Not the giant Barbie doll—loud, used to being heard.

It came from the smallest one in the room. The quiet one. The one no one ever saw coming.

Connie.

Rayne stopped at the edge of the roll-up door. Connie strummed, didn't look up.

"I don't need questions, Con."

"And yet, here we are."

She stopped strumming. Finally looked up.

"I asked, where are you going with that?"

"I've got to sell it. Pay bills."

"No, you don't."

"Yes, I do."

"No. You don't."

Connie stood. Placed her guitar in its case.

"You don't just sell that guitar. And by sell, I'm guessing you mean pawn."

Rayne shifted.

"So what if I do?"

She set the case down.

"Then you're an idiot."

"The fuck you know about it, Con? You've got a trust fund to fall back on, even if you don't want to admit it."

Connie chuckled. Shook her head.

"I know what that guitar is. And I know where you got it. You're not pawning it."

"Oh? You going to buy it from me?"

"If that's what it takes—yeah."

JEN HARLOW

recruited singer, former country star, rhythm guitarist, the soft counterpoint to Ava's muscle and Rayne's edge. Short and rounded, platinum glints in her blonde hair, face open and unreadable. She stayed quiet, and the song seemed to bend around her silence.

Connie walked to the edge of the Hotbox and pulled out her phone.

"How much do you need?"

Rayne softened.

"I had a bad night. I don't want to talk about it, okay? I was gambling for studio time. Shit went south." She didn't tell her what it had cost her. She didn't have to.

She held her arms out. "I'm not an addict. I'm good at this."

She heard herself. Realized she'd heard those same words before, almost daily, growing up.

No one said anything.

"It was a bad beat, okay? I thought I had something. It didn't work out."

"How much?" Connie asked.

"Four."

Connie froze. Stood straighter. All four-foot-eleven.

"Jesus, Rayne."

But she already knew what she had to do.

The guitar wasn't worth that. Maybe half. But she couldn't see it go—not with its past.

With a huff, Connie pulled up an app and sent the money. No one knew if she had enough for rent. Or groceries. Didn't matter. It meant that much to her. And that was enough.

All eyes went to Rayne.

Who was really making the hard choices, when it came to art? It didn't matter. None of these women would dare question each other—not out loud.

But still—Who would burn and scream for mercy? Who would burn and smile, singing a funeral dirge? All witches on a stake. Who gets the last laugh? This was something they'd done together.

And suddenly, Rayne saw it.

Maybe she wasn't as hard as she thought she was. Maybe that was the lesson.

Connie opened the case, pulled out the guitar, hooked it to the amp, tuned it, then strummed. She looked up with pure disappointment. A look Rayne had never seen.

"Missing rehearsal is one thing. I don't like it, but I understand. At least with you."

That caveat carried the weight of the Stones' "Wild Horses" as she looked at the case.

"But gambling away rent money? Pawning an icon? That? I cannot understand. Maybe one day you'll get it. Really understand this life."

Rayne—and the part of her that still answered to Cherie—looked at her, confused. If anyone understood this life, wasn't it Connie?

But then she looked around the room. At Ava. At Jen. And she saw it.

No story was more dire than the next. Whatever the past had been—they'd been here.

Rayne hadn't. But something shifted. A thought. A lyric. One that didn't sound like her. Not yet.

Some of us will scream.

Some of us will sing.

All of us will burn.

One of us will laugh.

If only someone could write the rest of the song. It didn't sound like her. She didn't have the voice. Cherie found herself thinking back to another game. Aberdeen. Possibilities. Poker faces. She heard Lady Gaga.

"My Poker Face."

If that's what it took?

But Rayne couldn't believe that's what it would take. It took lyrics. Real lyrics. Her own. But, she had nowhere to put them.

Rayne walked outside, back to her car. She heard the sound of size eleven shoes pounding behind her.

"Hey?" Ava asked, effortlessly.

"I don't want to hear it, Ava." Rayne held a hand up, black fingernails just shadows in the dark.

"What happened?"

"I had a shot. For all of us. I took it. It didn't work out, okay?" Rayne offered.

"But what does that mean? Not for us. For you." Ava asked, concerned. Rayne turned around, saw Connie looking over the guitar, knowing she knew it just as intimately as she knew it. Knew she was just holding it for Rayne to pay her back. And Jen? Oblivious, as always.

"It means I've got to find another way to pay my fuckin' bills. But what else is new? I'll pay it the same way we always pay bills. I'll spread my legs, light myself up like I'm made of stars. Dance around like I care. Spread my cheeks. You know the drill." She pretended that it didn't bother her, like it didn't bother her sisters. But it did because she knew that a little girl would find out, one day.

"But why?" Ava asked. Ava's strong hands grabbed Rayne's smaller, but muscular arms. Rayne wheeled around.

"Because what were my options, Ava?"

"You could have walked away. You could have stuck to the game plan." Ava offered. Rayne laughed.

"The game plan? Seduce some asshole from Alabama? Come on. Be serious. I am a good player. This was far more lucrative than that." Ava's eyebrow raised.

"Is it? What about now?" she asked.

"That's not fair." Rayne answered.

"Of course it is. Because it just happened. It's real. As real as the guitar you just tried to pawn. As real as your bandmate trading everything she has to keep it." She jabbed a finger into Rayne's small breasts.

"That's real. This is real. This is life. It's all women like us have."

"Is that so? I don't recall walking away from a WNBA contract to play drums for a shitty punk band. Was that real?" Ava took a step back, her shadow looking large over the pavement of the storage facility.

"You know why I walked away," she answered.

"Then you know why I played cards, tonight. This shit with the new Aberdeen guy ain't real. Cards are real. Dollars are real. Don't test me, Ava."

"You're not made of stars, Rayne. You're made of fire. Burn smart." Rayne didn't hear her.

She closed the door to her car and drove away. Ava walked back to the storage facility where two other women waited for her.

"She's had a rough night. Let's go over it again." They pretended it didn't matter. Ava counted them in as the sweat flowed.

Rayne drove away with a line she couldn't shake.

All of us will burn.

10 PM CDT, August 14, 2022 Huntsville, AL

Kline felt something in his soul, but he couldn't define it. He was hurting, and no one could hear it. There was an emptiness he just couldn't fill—not tonight.

It was out there, somewhere. Where? He didn't know. But it wasn't here. Not in this hollow house, not in this space that still reeked of Chrys. For moments, their shows filled that emptiness. It helped that more and more people were coming and enjoying it.

More and more venues were asking for them and the dates were filling up. Once again, this weekend was booked.

The rec room upstairs was gathering cobwebs—left untouched since Destin. That tiny explosion of self-expression, gone the moment she walked out to become the woman she was meant to be, leaving Kline exactly where she'd found him.

But… there was that memory. A flicker. A moment he'd felt true.

Stovehouse. It wasn't the only time. He'd had more, especially lately.

But like these notebooks, he'd buried them. Covered them up by telling everyone else that what he made was for someone else.

What was it Chrys had said? *Be somebody else, or find somebody else.* He'd sung those words. No one heard.

He couldn't sleep. He couldn't write. He went for a drive, beer in hand, because he had nowhere to be and no one to see. He wasn't out of beer. He just didn't want to run out. Better to buy now than then. He knew what that could look like, even on these backroads. He may not hit a car. May not hit a mailbox. He'd keep it between the lines.

Sometimes, that wasn't good enough and he'd learned that lesson.

Kline pulled up to the corner store. There was a vagrant outside.

"Hey, man, can you help a brother out?" the Black man with a shopping cart asked. Kline looked down on him, something he was unfamiliar with. He could have offered money. He could have offered food. But he knew why he was there and why that man might be there. Kline didn't judge.

"What do you want?" Kline asked, at first. But he cut to it. "Don't say money or food, if you don't really want those. Say what you want. Say what you feel." The man looked up at him, surprised.

"I'd have a beer."

Kline nodded.

He entered the store, picked up two cases of beer. It meant nothing to him. Kline wasn't rich, but $12.99 meant nothing to him. He walked back outside, half-drunk.

Fully drunk.

Kline set the case next to the man and sat down on the curb. He had nowhere to be. Nowhere to go. He'd felt this before. About the time he'd met Destiny.

Kline ripped the cardboard side of the box, pulled out a beer. Handed it to the man. Pulled out his own. The man took it, but with questions. Kline laughed.

"I know this may be a surprise, man, but I got nowhere to be. Nowhere but here." He cracked the top. The man did the same. Kline turned to him.

"Can I ask you something? And it's not a trick question, okay? I'm not here to judge, God knows." Kline took a sip of the foaming beer. The man, never taking his eyes from Kline, did the same. He drank from it as if he were Moses in Midian. The man looked up to the stars.

"No one has ever asked me that before. Just looked at me and walked away."

Kline, with a beer between his knees, looked up at the same stars. "Well, here I am. Asking you." The man pondered it.

"I guess I was born to push away."

Kline listened to the man's story, dug in his wallet, and left the man with every cent he had. He went home, climbed the stairs to his makeshift studio, pulled out a notebook and scribbled furiously.

"I was born to wander. I was born to wonder. I was born to push away."

Kline went back the next day and didn't find the man. He returned to the same notebook.

"What did his words mean about me? What's the real price of being free? Did he vanish into the gray? Was he here or just walked away?"

"Yeah, yeah. I was born to wander.

Yeah, yeah I was born to wonder.

I was born to push away."

As he drove away from the store, two cases of beer in hand and only one meant for him, the radio sang out. It didn't matter what band sang about cold black clouds and heaven's door.

He didn't know why, but he felt it. He belted it. He nailed it. That's what he could do. Cigarette between his lips, beer in the console, and windows down. Nobody heard him. Nobody ever would.

Still, Kline did the only thing he knew to express himself. He kept singing.

Excerpt from "The Voice Was Never Theirs"
BY CLARA COWLEY

It's fascinating to me how the members of Aberdeen—Mike Kilmore aside—never put it all together. All the information was there, right from the start.

But I think it's as simple as this: they just didn't care who Kline was or where he came from. Because to them, he was a pawn. Always had been.

And pawns don't take down kings.

It would be easy to say they were just self-absorbed. But that wouldn't be fair.
They were trapped, too. Grinding beneath the same wheel they once thought they'd been steering. And people in survival mode rarely make room for anyone else's story.

I've often wondered when Mike Kilmore knew. Not when he was told—we know he was the first to be informed of Kline's history.

But the how, the why, the when—those are the things that will define how history judges his role. Because what happened in Kansas City was evil. And nothing will ever change that.

But whether it was planned—or a reaction—does change the lens, at least a little.

Meanwhile, we know this much: Paul White, Aiesha Holt, and the Lloyd Brannon Foundation knew the truth from the beginning. From the very beginning.

If even one of them had taken a hard stance before the live streamed show, it would've ended there. If they had stepped in before Kansas City, it would've never happened.

They knew. And they let it happen.

Why?

History might suggest that they believed in Kline. That they were swayed by the virality. By the voice. That somewhere in

the echo of Lloyd Brannon, they heard a
second chance and said: Fuck it.

But I don't buy that. Not for a second.

These are some of the most intelligent,
calculating people I've ever met in this
business. And that's saying something.

No.

They didn't see salvation. They saw
dollars. They saw a martyr.

They saw a way out."

karma

12

Paul White's Office, Century City,
Los Angeles, CA

"And you came up with this plan all on your own? The other night, at a bar?" Paul White looked up from his notepad, his voice balanced right on the edge between sarcasm and sincerity. Just enough of each to keep them unsure. Markus was easily the most forward-thinking member of the band. Kilmore, the most ambitious. Jose was the most down-to-earth. Ben? Ben came up with this? Last one he expected. But perhaps the one with the most to gain by becoming proactive.

Ben Cantrell sat forward slightly, trying not to look too eager. "What do you think?"

Paul placed his pen—custom, heavy, and absurdly expensive—carefully on the pad. He looked over the four faces in front of him, then leaned back in his chair, letting it rock as he considered how to respond.

"It's… something."

He had, of course, already done the work. As soon as Ben called him that night, Paul had gone digging. The videos. The voice. The name. And then the *last name*. It didn't take long before everything came together—just not in a way these guys were prepared for.

"You want to bring in a cover band singer," he said, slowly, "from Alabama. A guy with zero real frontman experience. Because he went viral?"

Markus Kenney shifted in his seat, arms crossed, glasses perched on the bridge of his nose. "Every frontman starts somewhere, Paul. You know that."

Paul's own glasses slipped down slightly. He adjusted them out of reflex, not from comfort. Markus's tone had weight. Quiet, steady disappointment. That cut deeper than outrage.

"He's got the voice. The showmanship," Markus continued. "And yeah, the following. Numbers don't lie. Our streams spiked after that video—nearly the same bump we saw after Lloyd passed. If we don't act, someone else will." Paul considered what he meant.

That's exactly what he'd rather happen. Keep him as far from here as possible. And yet, to deny the logic would add water to the waning confidence the band already had in him. Without this, there may not be an Aberdeen. Or revenge

Markus jumped back in. "Honestly, Paul, I'm surprised you're pushing back. You and the label have been grinding us nonstop since Lloyd's funeral. Now we're trying to make a move, and suddenly it's a bad idea?" That stung White, coming from Markus, with whom he had such respect and kinship.

Paul bit the inside of his cheek. He couldn't tell them why this was a bad idea. Not yet. Not until he figured out whom he'd rather disappoint—the band... or her.

"I think bringing him in for a streaming event could work," Paul said carefully. "It'd buy you some breathing room with the label. Ride the wave while it's hot. Could be a smart short-term play."

Ben nodded, encouraged. Markus remained still. Jose hadn't said a word the entire meeting.

Paul turned to Mike Kilmore, who sat in a chair across the room like he'd rather be anywhere else.

"Mike? What do you think?" He needed Mike's voice here.

Kilmore shrugged, rubbed his hands together. His long hair hung in front of his eyes as he leaned forward.

"I think it's a terrible idea."

Ben deflated. Paul tried not to show relief.

"But," Kilmore added, "Ben's right. We're off the map right now, and that's not where we need to be. Truth is, I want to play again. Badly. So yeah—fuck it. Let's see what the guy's got. Doesn't mean we have to commit." Such a combination of complex feelings was rarely sensed from Kilmore.

All three heads on the couch turned to him. Even Paul's stomach tightened a little at the honesty in Kilmore's voice. It was rare. He meant it.

Ben clapped once, loud and sharp. Paul flinched.

"Alright," Paul said, tone final. "I'll see what I can do."

Ben, Markus, and Jose stood and filed out. Kilmore lingered in the doorway.

"I want you to look into him," he said, quiet but firm. "Everything. Just in case."

Paul nodded, but he didn't need to investigate anything. He already knew. He had a call to make. And if he didn't do it now, he wasn't sure he'd find the nerve to do it at all.

Paul picked up the phone, looked up the number, and tapped it before he could change his mind.

She answered immediately.

"Paul."

He opened his mouth. Nothing came. The words jammed in his throat, dry and weightless. Finally, he forced them out.

"Aberdeen thinks they've found their new frontman."

Saying it aloud chilled him. Not because Lloyd was being replaced—but because of *who* was doing the replacing. Because of who would be hearing it.

There was a beat of silence on the other end. Then:

"Well. That's good news, right? Does that mean Aberdeen's locked for the benefit concert?"

Of course. She went straight to business. The Lloyd Brannon Foundation benefit was *her* stage now, and Aberdeen's involvement was leverage. Legacy. Optics. Money.

"It's … news," Paul said flatly.

"You sound glum." A sigh, soft. She shifted the phone.

"I know it's hard. You were close to Lloyd. You *found* him. You shaped that band."

Paul let her fill the silence because he couldn't.

"That's true," he said quietly. "And I appreciate you saying it. We all lost him."

"But that's not what this is really about, is it?"

"No."

She waited.

"The guy they've found..." He hesitated.

"Who?"

He closed his eyes. "Kline. Kline Thomas."

Nothing. Not a breath, not a word. Then finally, a slow, shaky inhale. Paul could picture her now—stone-still, not blinking.

"You're protected," he rushed. "The foundation. The label. All of us, legally."

He didn't need to say what *she* already knew.

"We both know it's going to come out," she said. Her voice was low, tired. "It always does."

He stayed silent.

"Tell me this makes sense, Paul." Now her tone had changed. Not angry. It was resigned. "Tell me this *has* to happen."

"I can't," he said. "I can't promise anything. I don't know how this plays out."

And they both knew—he wasn't talking about album sales or tour dates, which should have been the conversation.

"Then tell me why."

"Because he has the voice. Because he has the presence. And because—right now—he has the eyes of the world."

Paul let that hang and braced for the impact of her voice. Nothing. Then, more carefully: "But we haven't made contact. I wanted to call you first."

Another silence. This one long.

"I appreciate that," she said finally. "I guess karma's a bitch."

Then a pause.

"But I don't want to see him. Ever."

She hung up.

Paul stared at the phone.

She didn't scream. Didn't threaten. Didn't ask for time. She just folded. Instantly.

And somehow, that scared him more than if she'd fought.

Excerpt from "The Voice Was Never Theirs"
BY CLARA COWLEY

"When Ben Cantrell called, I don't think Kline saw it as an opportunity. I think he saw it as a way out.

Not of pain. Not of grief. But of the version of himself he was tired of carrying.

Even as ridiculous as it must have sounded— and it had to sound ridiculous—there was the slightest flicker of change. And that was exactly what Kline Thomas needed.

For that matter, so did Aberdeen. Though I'd wager what "change" meant for them now is almost certainly not what Ben Cantrell imagined when he placed that call.

It's worth mentioning: Ben really did believe in Kline. And his eagerness—reaching out that night, and then cold-calling him days later—proves it.

He didn't have to do that. From what I've heard, Ben was adamant that Paul White let him be the one to make contact. You could say it was ego—that Ben wanted credit for trying to fix Aberdeen.

But I prefer to believe it's because he
saw something in Kline. Something he couldn't
ignore.

And Kline? He jumped at the chance. Which—if
you knew him—wasn't like him at all.

But when you already believe you're the
mistake in every story, all it takes is someone
from the myth to call you by name.

A name like Ben Cantrell."

call

13

Thomas Residence, Madison, AL

Kline was woken from oblivion by the phone ringing. In his stupor, he realized that it wasn't the first time that it had rung itself silent this morning. Next to him, sheets shifted slightly and a warm foot grazed his ankle. The shades were closed with only the barest amount of sunlight peeking through, not enough to see clearly.

What time is it?

Didn't matter. Sunday. It was Sunday. They'd been invited back for another Saturday evening show. It had been even better, both in the performance aspect and the viewership. The warm body next to him reminded him that fame had its perks, at least.

He rolled to his side, fumbled for the phone, and lifted it to his ear as his head hit the pillow.

"This is Kline," he grumbled out, running one palm over his forehead and over the back of his skull.

"Kline. This is Ben Cantrell." The voice on the other side was unknown, but the name was familiar, though he couldn't place it immediately.

"Who?"

The voice laughed, not surprised in the slightest.

"From the band Aberdeen. Bassist. I left you some voicemails last week? I know it was late and all. And, reached out to your socials." Ben should have been used to adding that caveat to explain who he was.

Kline sighed, mightily, as his head tried to make sense of that. The name rang a bell. Last night. Worrisome butterflies replaced nausea and a brutal headache.

"Shit." He planted his elbows on the mattress and sat up against the headboard. "Look, I don't want any problems. I don't check voicemails or social media. Sorry. If singing your music is some sort of copyright infringement..." Kline began apologizing. The voice on the other end laughed, raspy but heartily.

"No. Nothing like that. Singing cover songs isn't...." Silence, momentarily. The voice sighed before it continued.

"That's beside the point. So, check it. We watched your videos. Watched it live last night. Been watching the last few shows, actually."

"Glad you're a fan," Kline responded sarcastically, cotton mouthed. He leaned to the bedside table, picked up a half-full glass of water, and finished it. His head pounded. The body next to him turned towards him.

"Can you hang that up? Go back to sleep," the contralto voice whispered from a mass of long, straight, black hair. It wasn't her. Kline's face scrunched in a combination of disapproval and surprise. He turned on his side.

"Funny guy. I like that." Ben chuckled as he spoke.

"Look, Mister Cantrell—" Kline began.

"Ben," he said simply.

"Ben. Sure. I'm flattered, really. I'm a fan. But I don't see you calling every jerk-off that covers your songs. I never thought this would happen. To be honest, I'm a bit hungover."

"And straight to the point, I see."

Silence. Wind could be heard from the other side of the call, rushing, and the sound of waves. The sounds cut with the sound of a sliding door closing. It struck Kline that he should be happy about this. For some unknown reason, he wasn't.

"I'll get straight to it. Kline, we were all really impressed with your...performances. So much obvious feeling and energy. It's the closest we've seen to Lloyd since..." He trailed off.

"Since he died?"

"Yeah. Exactly. And then, there's the singing. Where did you learn to sing? How long have you been singing? Can you play? Do you write songs?"

"Slow down, partner. It's been...." He looked at his phone to see the time.

"...a rough morning." That elicited another chuckle.

"Brother, I know all about those. Weed helps. Thank God for

California, right?" The strange woman turned towards him.

"Who *is* that?" the woman asked.

"Shut up a minute, would you?" Kline shifted the phone to the other ear. She shot him a hurt look, but he didn't know her, didn't owe her anything. Still, he stood up, navigated the unkempt room, naked, suddenly self-conscious. Kline donned one of the two matching blue robes from the door and entered the light of his living room, started a single cup of coffee, and swallowed a handful of pills that resided in a prescription bottle by the coffee maker that didn't bear his name, a routine. The voice on the other side remained quiet as he sat down in a well-worn chair.

"Grew up taking singing lessons, thanks, Mom. Took guitar lessons for a while. Wasn't very good. Couple of years with the band," Kline offered, simply and concisely. It wasn't a complicated thing to fully explain that he came from a musical family, and he'd been singing his entire life, just not with a band. He didn't have the energy to talk about church choirs, school chorus, and endless nights of karaoke.

"Really?" Cantrell asked, surprised.

"We all need hobbies, man," Kline added flatly. His eyes went to the empty bottle he and the woman shared, once they'd made it in the door.

"That's a *hobby*?" Cantrell exclaimed, sounding amazed.

"A recent development." Kline bristled at the thought of trying to say more. He wasn't in a place to go into why he had joined Pearl Temple Garden in Chains and not just because he was hungover.

"Sure, sure. Again, I'll get right to it. We'd like to fly you over to LA." At this point, Kline was the one chuckling.

"For what? Sign my band? I don't really think they'd—"

"Well, no. Not your band. I mean, they aren't *bad*. But they aren't exactly *good* either. The guy who plays guitar? The guy you harmonize with, he's okay. Actually, he's more than okay. We want to see if you'd be a good fit as our new frontman." Kline's chuckle turned into a full laugh.

"Alright, whoever you are. Good joke. Had me going. Who is this? How did you get my number?" Another drawn-out silence.

"You aren't that hard to find." He said it so simply, though he didn't know. "Okay, so, look. Check your inbox. We reached out from our official band account yesterday on social, but it doesn't appear you do the social media thing, anyway. Well, you just said that. And you don't check voicemails. Right." Kline set the phone on a coffee table, put it on speaker, and thumbed to his email and socials. He rarely checked social media and posted even less. There wasn't much in his life worth posting about, he felt. Although, over the last week, he'd had to turn off the notifications because of the flood of messages he'd been receiving. It was more an aggravation than anything to hear his phone constantly beeping for something he didn't think mattered. Admiration wasn't why he sang. Sure enough, they'd been trying to reach out to him for over a week.

"For someone with a viral presence, you don't spend a lot of time online."

Kline found the email.

"Yeah, okay. Found it."

"Alright, you need to get in touch with Paul White. He's CC'd. He wants to set up a flight for tomorrow morning. All expenses paid. But we can change that if it's too soon. He just needs some basic information to book it."

"Ben, I have a job. I have … a lot … going on in my life. And can we just talk about how easily you found this information?" Kline was still stuck on that, but he guessed it wasn't that hard to find for someone who was motivated.

"I don't know, man. White's a bad dude. He always knows what we're up to, where we are. Anyway, we completely understand that. We can shift it if you need some time." Ben waited for him to respond but got nothing. He implored on.

"Just give us the benefit of the doubt. Just a couple of days. And, if it doesn't work, well, you got to see LA. Got to hang out with us, do a little singing, have a few laughs and drinks. We'll show you around. That's all we ask." Cantrell had clearly practiced for this possible eventuality.

"But, if it does work out, we were thinking of teaming up with you for a live stream show. You know, like people were doing during the lockdown? We think it would be huge for all of us. For you." Kline was listening and thinking.

"It'll pay," Ben added, but Kline wasn't really motivated by that.

"I want Eddie to come. I'm not that good, by myself. We complement each other well. That's what makes us sound so good. Plus, he's the one who really loves you guys, not me. It would mean the world to him." There was some truth to it, but Kline found that he had answered because he simply didn't want to go alone; besides, Aberdeen was Eddie's favorite band, not Kline's. He certainly wasn't going to go into why he secretly despised Aberdeen. Lloyd Brannon. Kline found himself thinking about Bishop's, an eternity ago. First time he'd sang with a band. Aberdeen songs. Her impetuous reaction, almost anger, that he'd shown greatness at something. It still didn't make sense

On the other side of the country, Ben Cantrell looked at White, who was letting Ben take a more active role in this. He was proud to see the growth and initiative, even if it had taken Ben thirty years.

White shrugged, as if to say, whatever made him get on the plane.

"White will set it up. I assume you will reach out to your bandmate?"

Kline sipped the hot, black coffee as the thin, naked, and much younger woman paraded past him, looking at his cup of coffee. Without vocalizing a word, she conveyed her dismay that he hadn't also made her a cup. He pointed to the machine in the next room. He hadn't shared a cup of coffee in this home since? His attention snapped back to the call, but not before a single word echoed through his head.

Destiny. Destin.

"No promises. He has a family. A career. But it would make me more comfortable, and he will love it. I owe him that," Kline whispered around the rim of the mug. All of this was factual.

"If he doesn't, fine. But we hope to see you both, tomorrow afternoon. If not, maybe a few days after."

Kline didn't respond.

"We are really, really excited about working with you, Kline."

He ended the call.

Excerpt from "The Voice Was Never Theirs"
BY CLARA COWLEY

"The story of Aberdeen and the Painted Queens does have its happy moments. But I think this might have been the purest of them all.

And I hate that I wasn't there to see it—especially knowing what I know now.

That's when he went to see Eddie.

Not to celebrate. To sell it. And maybe not even to Eddie, really. But to Chandra.

Eddie had been the one steady voice through all of it. The one who told Kline the music still mattered. That he still mattered. The one who saw something worth saving in him long after Kline stopped looking.

So, Kline framed it like hope. Like maybe this could be real. Like maybe he was ready.

And Eddie believed him. Because of course he did.

That's what makes it so hard to talk about now. Chandra, as you will learn through this book, was very guarded in when and what she would talk about. This was one of the few things she would discuss. Certainly, she didn't discuss her anger that Eddie was far more involved in raising Kline than his own son. But none of us are perfect. Not even Steady Eddie.

I once asked Chandra what she remembered about that visit—what Kline said, what Eddie heard.

She smiled. The kind of smile that only lives halfway between love and regret.

"He told Eddie this was his shot. That he wasn't going to waste it. That it finally felt like something was happening for him, not to him."

What struck me was how Chandra remembered what Kline said—but not what Eddie felt.

Because Eddie never talked about himself. Not even then.

That was just who he was. Kline had invited him to share the moment—because he knew Eddie was such an Aberdeen fan. But Eddie? He saw it as something else entirely.

A chance for Kline to escape.

As for Chandra... Chandra's a silent voice in all of this. She won't talk about the conversations they shared when Kline started unraveling—melting down and seemingly self-destructing everything they'd all sacrificed for.

But we know Eddie carried that weight. And it could only have come from one place. You can't blame her a bit."

catastrophe

14

Cornell Residence, New Market, AL

Kline had made the half-hour trip to his friend's house shortly after disposing of the young woman, then pounding electrolytes and medication. That had taken just minutes. The sheer absurdity of the idea. His mind circled the potential pain like a predator, but a sudden, piercing clarity struck him.

The sunny, ride, windows down ride cut the edge and Kline slowly felt human. The tall boy 24-ounce beer helped. So did driving the drop-top Camaro that once belonged to his ex-wife that he so rarely drove, left behind and discarded like him.

It was a perfect day for it all.

"Must be pretty important if you want to discuss this in person." The two friends were in Eddie's shop, where he maintained his other hobbies. A weird mixture of sports cars, engines, guns, and fishing equipment occupied different corners of the shop, which was larger than his own home. Where Kline had just two hobbies, Eddie had dozens, and he was just as good at them as Kline was drinking and singing.

"It is." Kline pulled the cork from a bottle of whiskey, poured two shots. He picked one up, snuffed it, and pointed Eddie to the other.

"You're going to want that," Kline said.

"You're just saying that because you need the hair of the dog," Eddie pointed out.

"You're damn right about that. Killer hangover. You could have stopped the free drinks at some point, if you cared for me at all." Eddie looked him over. He did look rough. Eddie also knew he didn't leave alone and that was a good thing. As far as he was concerned, that was only the second woman he'd seen Kline truly interact with since that short fling, right after COVID. Kline had refused to discuss that, even now.

"Either really good news, or really bad news, eh?" Eddie asked, his glasses trained on the job he was working on. He knew it must be good news.

"It's definitely good news." With a nod, Eddie clinked his glass against Kline's empty one and drank his.

"Give it to me, then." Eddie crossed his hairy arms, waiting.

"Ben Cantrell called me this morning. Well, called me a bunch. But I finally answered this morning."

"The bassist from Aberdeen?" Eddie sat down on a stool, fingering a piece of hardware. Twisting it, flipping it, as if he had never seen it before.

"The very same. He wants us to come to LA. Tomorrow." Kline waited for Eddie to erupt.

"For what?" Eddie still never looked up, even as he questioned, but he couldn't hide his excitement.

"To try out for being their two singers." At this statement by Kline, Eddie carefully laid the hardware down and looked up. Kline had expected much more of a positive response. The tall, rail thin man said nothing as Mad Season's "Wake Up" played in the background. Layne Staley's voice echoed off the tin walls and roof. Eddie turned down the volume.

"Fuck off." A look of complete disbelief, shock, but excitement.

Eddie poured another drink and shot it. Watched Kline stand there, arms crossed, serious.

"You're actually serious?" Eddie questioned.

"Do I look serious?" Kline responded, in turn.

"Yeah. A little too serious." Eddie returned his gaze to the remaining pistol parts lying on a piece of cloth, which he had been meticulously cleaning. He began reassembling them without looking up.

"Jeez, Kline. There's a midlife crisis and then there's a midlife *catastrophe*." Eddie motioned with an open hand and then with the other.

"I guess I had an epiphany this morning when I got the call and kicked this strange chick out of the bed."

"Sounds awful," Eddie joked as he slid pistol parts together.

"I'm serious. There's nothing more for me here, Eddie. I've worked my entire life to support something that doesn't exist anymore. And, honestly, I don't even like my job that much. If I am being honest," Kline continued. Eddie frowned at that. Kline made really, really good money as his boss. He knew there was a lot of stress in it, and he didn't envy Kline for that. But the pay made it worth it. Now, Kline seemed to look to the open garage door and pontificate.

"Haven't you ever wanted something more? Something worth doing? Besides *this*?" Kline pressed on.

"No offense, bro. But two years ago, you wouldn't have even *considered* something like this. Hell, you didn't even want to come sing for us."

Eddie avoided his gaze. There was more that Eddie was going to tack on to the end of that sentence but wasn't going there. Too good of a friend. He recalled the last he had seen of Kline, last night. How had that person become this person? Maybe the desire was there, all along, but Kline didn't have the out until the call this morning. What a call to get. Maybe that was why. When destiny calls, you don't let it ring.

Eddie realized that might be happening to him, too.

"A lot has changed in two years." Kline's voice grew dark. Sensing it, Eddie looked up, his bright, naturally inquisitive eyes throwing an apology.

"I'm sorry. That's not what I meant. A year. Two years. Some span of time ago. I didn't mean to..." Eddie tried to walk it back.

"I know. Forget it. The truth is, you're right. Now I'm playing two or three times a week with my friends in a shitty cover band." Eddie smiled at Kline's half-serious derogatory remark.

"And, the thing is, I love it. It gives me something to look forward to." Kline realized that this was something that he had never actually said to his best friend.

"I never thanked you for that, by the way. For making me do it. So, this is my way of thanking you," Kline offered, kindly.

"It was always there, man. I just didn't want to see it wasted," Eddie pointed out. Understatement. Once Eddie had drug Kline on stage, he had become a different person. Sometimes happy, sometimes not. But entertaining? Hell, yes. As long as he was on the stage.

"So, you'll do it? Come with me? We've got nothing to lose," Kline asked, hopeful.

"Gotta run it by the boss. But, yeah. I'd be nuts not to." Kline wasn't sure if he meant his boss or wife. Eddie scanned around the room thoughtfully, as if looking for the words to string together from the corners of the shop.

"You've always been good, you know. It's always been there. But the last few shows? That was *real shit*. Rockstar shit." Eddie found that he couldn't expound with any other adjectives, though they were so deserved. Nor did he want to tackle the comedown effect, afterwards.

"I love playing with you, Kline. More than you will know. Wish we'd been doing it a long time ago. Maybe we could have done something big, like Aberdeen." He let the thought die. The gun now complete, he pulled on the slide, thumbed the hammer down. Eddie laid the stainless piece down, wrapped the rag around it, crossed the concrete floor, and deposited it in the safe next to the dozens of others. He selected a long rifle next, slid the bolt up, pulled back while holding the trigger, and removed it.

"But, and this is what bothers me, Kline. What scares me,

You have those moments where you are happier than you've ever been." He trailed off for a second, searched his friend's face for warning signs, continued.

"But afterwards, it's like all that positivity pulls in the darkness like a vacuum. It's like you have only so much happiness in you at a time, and when it's gone, it leaves a space that only hate and fear and despair can fill. And it just floods in." He made a rushing motion with his hands, like water flooding an empty space.

"I think I need this. Hope, I mean. If only for a few days." Eddie saw the desperation on his friend's face.

"To hell with it. Why not?"

Kline slapped him hard on the back.

"That's the spirit! I'm happy to give you the days off," Kline practically yelled.

"You're not the boss I was talking about, but thanks," Eddie finished.

The small talk continued. Drinks were poured, and the two enjoyed the rest of the afternoon of guns and cars, but Eddie's head was somewhere else. The next conversation. Frankly, he was shocked she hadn't come out to check on them. He envisioned her in the kitchen, waiting. Knowing what they were likely up to. Eddie wasn't sure how it would go, but he wanted to try for Kline.

Kline had left. Eddie stayed back, needing a few minutes to breathe before walking into the house—before having *the talk*. The only one that really mattered. At least it might dissuade her from another argument about the use of his free time not being used in changing diapers.

He was buzzed, maybe more than he intended. A few drinks with Kline, then a few more after. Trying to calm his nerves, but the more he drank, the more the emotions came up instead.

He threw back one last shot, flicked off the lights to his massive shop, and stepped through the gate into the backyard. His shop was easily twice the size of their house. Probably more. Inside waited questions.

CHANDRA CORNELL

> Midnight skin. Runner's build. Patient, logical, steady from years of teaching. Eddie's wife heard the back door open.

She was at the dishwasher, methodically putting away the last few clean dishes.

"Was that Kline I saw?" she called, without turning.

"Yeah." Eddie's voice was measured.

One of her dark brows lifted. "Y'all do a little day drinking?"

He looked down, already guilty.

"You know how I feel about letting your friends drive after they've been drinking," she said, that firm but loving tone kicking in. "You know he's not *fine* just because he says he is."

"I know," Eddie said quietly. "But he was okay. I swear."

Chandra didn't answer. She didn't need to.

"Where's the baby?" he asked, shifting the subject, but regretted it.

"Napping. You'll be next, if you've had as much as you sound like." She said it with a smirk, wiping her hands on her apron. He relaxed a bit. There wasn't the accusation he expected or the scolding he'd become used to.

Eddie crossed the hardwood, past the fireplace, and slid onto one of the kitchen stools. She kept working, back to him.

"Haven't seen him just stop by in a while. What's he up to?"

Eddie took a breath. "No way to ease into this. So I'll just say it."

That got her attention. She turned and untied her apron.

"Kline got a call from Ben Cantrell this morning. From Aberdeen."

"Okay..." she said, unsure where this was going.

"They want him to be their new frontman."

She blinked. Crossed her arms. "Ben Cantrell from *Aberdeen* called *Kline* and wants *him* to be their new singer?"

Eddie nodded slowly.

"Are you messing with me, or did *he* mess with *you*?" Thin-lipped, Eddie shook his head.

"Kline showed me the messages. The interest is real. And they want me to come along, too. I think he swindled them a bit. I'm not going to argue with it."

She absorbed that, trying to wrap her head around it.

"Is this something *you* want to do?"

"Baby... when I was a kid, I didn't say I wanted to be a fireman or astronaut. I said I wanted to be a rockstar."

She smiled. She'd heard him say it a hundred times, but it hit different now because it was *real*.

"Sounds like they want Kline. You're just along for the ride."

"Oh, no doubt. He had to convince them to bring me out too, but he said that they liked our sound. Anyway, might not be anything more than a couple days out there. Maybe a streaming show. There's talk that we'd get paid for that, too. But yeah... I want it to be more. How could I not?" Now, he spoke to the air.

She caught the hope in his voice. Even if he was trying to hide it.

"Think he asked to bring me because he knew I'd love it," Eddie said.

"And that's the kind of friend he is," Chandra replied honestly.

"Yeah." Eddie nodded. "But sometimes I wonder if he sees me as a safety net… or a sidekick."

"Getting to meet, hang out, *play* with your favorite band? You'd be insane to pass that up. I'd be a bitch not to say I support it." She leaned over the counter and kissed him.

"I love you," he said. "Thank you."

"I'm happy for you," she said, genuinely. But her hands were already moving—wiping down the stove that was already spotless. She couldn't sit still.

"Couple other things," he said.

She leaned against the counter. "Go on."

"I'm worried about Kline."

"His drinking?"

"Well, yeah. But not just that. I'm worried about *him*. Especially if this thing takes off."

She frowned. "How do you mean?"

"Getting him to play with us was like pulling teeth. But he did it—and he was *incredible*. The talent's there. Maybe more than he knows. But I don't think he wants it. Or maybe he doesn't think he deserves it. Or he's scared of doing it in fear of failure. I don't know. I'd be over the moon. Hell, I already am. But Kline?" He shrugged as if to say that it was no more to Kline than cashing in a ten-dollar scratcher for a hundred up on the state line. Then the familiar question. How was Kline incredible? It didn't build over the last two years. It wasn't there, per se, that first night at Bishop's or The Camp, before COVID. By the time they played at 1910 Gin? Stovehouse? Boom. No denying it.

She raised an eyebrow. "Kline? The rockstar? Now *that's* a thought."

Eddie misread her tone.

"I *know* he doesn't look like one. Not like Lloyd Brannon."

At that, Chandra's eyes went wide, and she smirked. "Tell me about it…"

Eddie pointed at her, mock accusatory. "See? That's exactly what I'm talking about. And you *like* him. Imagine what the world's gonna do when they see that voice come out of *that* guy." Eddie envisioned it, and it hurt him. He had another thought.

"And he's in the shadow of Lloyd Brannon? That's not starting from zero," Eddie said quietly. "Kline's starting from six feet under." He hadn't meant to say it like that. It surprised even him. He wasn't a poetic guy—but it felt true.

She nodded, sobered now. She saw what he meant.

"That's a powerful thing. And a very real thing." She let the thought breathe.

"So you're not just chasing your own dream," she said. "You're trying to protect your friend."

"Yeah," Eddie admitted. "But… I don't want to be a bad husband or dad. It's a risk. And I've never been—"

She nearly choked on a laugh. "Baby, please. You've flown down drag strips with duct tape holding things in place. You're not risk-averse—you're just *comfortable*. There's a difference.

"You're not a bad husband or father for wanting something for yourself. You think I stayed home just for the groceries and naptimes?"

She moved behind him and began rubbing his shoulders. He melted under her touch.

"Ed," she said softly, "I know men hate hearing this, so just bear with me, okay? Because I see you struggling with something you shouldn't be."

He didn't say anything, but he didn't pull away either.

"When Kline got the promotion—did that bother you?"

"No," he said plainly.

"Why? Was he a better engineer than you?"

Even Kline would've laughed at that. Without Eddie, he might not have graduated.

"I could've done the job," Eddie said. "But he had the better skill set for it."

"Exactly. And a rising tide lifts all ships, right?"

He nodded. That part was true. Kline's promotion had opened doors for both he and Eddie. Just meant not *that* one for Eddie.

"Would Kline have gotten the job without you?"

"No."

"There you go." She leaned in closer. "Don't think of it as second fiddle. Think of it as first fiddle… in a different row.

"Besides, we're lucky, Ed. Most people move three, four times in their lives for work. We never had to. But we always *could have*. So how is this any different?"

He covered her hand with his.

"You've always told me to do what I want. But I wasn't sure if you meant it outside the garage."

She leaned close to his ear. "If you wanted to change jobs? I'd support you. Start a speed shop? I'd support you. A band? Still support you. I stayed home so that you could chase whatever dreams you had, and, honestly, this has far greater potential to make it worth it."

She grinned. "But just know—I'll be keeping a very close eye on you… and them groupies." Her arms looped around his neck, and she gave him a playful shake. "You hear me, rockstar?"

Excerpt from "The Voice Was Never Theirs"
BY CLARA COWLEY

"I often think about that flight. Kline in the window seat. Eddie beside him. Two people heading toward something they didn't have the language for yet.

What were they thinking?

Kline was probably rehearsing. Not music. Not lyrics. The version of himself he'd have to become.

The way he'd smile. The way he'd shake hands. The way he'd make sure no one could see how scared he was.

Because you can't show up trembling when you're stepping into a legend's shoes. And you can't sound like Lloyd Brannon without pretending not to hear the echo.

He probably stared out the window and wondered who he'd need to be to survive it. Because he knew exactly what he was leaving behind.

And he wasn't going back.

What we do know is this: Kline took the trip seriously, from the very beginning. By most accounts, he was the most sober that week than at any other time during his run with Aberdeen.

And Eddie? Eddie was probably just trying to believe. That this was going to be something good. Something fun—for however long it lasted. And he was okay with that.

That they'd meet Aberdeen. Maybe even
like them. That they wouldn't be just relics,
or assholes, or cautionary tales. He would've
told himself it didn't matter if they were
kind—just that they were real.

He grew up with those posters on his wall.
Learned Mike's guitar riffs from old videos
and tabs from Guitar One's October 2004
edition. Meeting them was like opening
a door to his own past.

But I don't think Eddie was nervous. I think
he was trying to remember every second.

That's the difference between them."

mimosa

15

Somewhere over the Midwest

It had been a quiet flight from Huntsville to Atlanta, then on to LAX. First class—Aberdeen footing the bill. A big step up from the usual business class grind Eddie and Kline were used to.

They hadn't talked much. Too early. Eddie noticed Kline's untouched mimosa and elbowed him.

"You gonna drink that?"

Kline slid it over without a word.

Eddie raised an eyebrow. "You ordered it."

Kline popped out one earbud. "Figure I shouldn't drink before an interview."

His voice wasn't judgy. He wasn't pointing fingers at Eddie. He was pointing the finger at himself. That nailed down if Kline were taking this seriously or not, Eddie realized.

Eddie wanted to ask a dozen things, but Kline spoke first.

"I haven't really listened to their newer stuff. Just singles. They're good, but the albums…" He trailed off with a shrug.

"You haven't missed much," Eddie replied. "Lloyd wrote and produced almost everything. It got repetitive. I don't even listen to full albums anymore. Just playlists."

Kline nodded, earbuds halfway back in.

Eddie leaned in. "I've got questions."

Kline smiled, a little tired. "Shoot."

"First off, thanks for bringing me." Kline smiled warmly at him.

Kline looked at him. "Dude, of course. I've dragged you on way more pointless business trips. Least this one might mean something." Absolutely true. The benefits of being the best friend of the boss.

Eddie chuckled, then shifted, serious again.

"I gotta ask… why'd you jump on this? It's not like you've ever chased industry jobs, and this—this is a big shift."

Kline turned to face him fully.

"It's not just me. It's *we*. I thought about how much you'd love this, and yeah, that was the first push. But the more I sat with it, the more I realized I need this too. You've been pushing me for years. Without you, I'm not on this plane."

Eddie nodded, absorbing that.

Kline looked back out the window. "I need a change, man. I've been stuck on the same loop my whole life. Even when Chrys left. Everything changed—but I didn't. And nothing ever got better." Mostly true. He'd gotten better and happier for a very small period.

Silence. Heavy, even up here above the clouds.

Then Kline shifted, lighter.

"Okay—my turn. Why do you think they're even considering us? We're not the only Aberdeen cover band out there."

"You fishing for compliments, or you actually want an answer?" Eddie asked.

Kline smirked. "Surprise me."

Eddie shrugged. "Lloyd is gone. Their relevance tanked. Then suddenly, streams spike like ten times over. Hits back in the top ten. But they can't tour. Can't sell out venues. Lloyd checked out years ago—more into painting and mushrooms than singing."

Kline winced, remembering the last show he'd seen. Despite the bad memories, one thing he did remember was how off Lloyd had sounded.

Eddie continued, "You sound just like him. That's rare. And the viral clip? That's marketing gold. If it works, they get attention. If it doesn't, they still get buzz. Win-win."

He popped his earbuds back in, grinning. "So, y'know—no pressure."

Kline laughed. "You're in this too, buddy. Don't dump all the weight on me."

"I just wanted to hear Aberdeen from a good seat," Eddie shot back with a wink.

Kline grinned, then turned back to his playlist, picking apart every nuance of Lloyd's voice. He'd made a list of songs for the audition, but now he wasn't sure he could breathe, let alone sing.

Just pretend no one's watching.

Even as his phone kept blowing up—DMs, tags, shares, messages from people he hadn't talked to in years—he forced himself to mute notifications.

He'd never cared about being famous.

But now? Now, the whole damn world was watching.

Excerpt from "The Voice Was Never Theirs"
BY CLARA COWLEY

"The focus on that fateful day will always be about Aberdeen, Kline, and Eddie. But there's another story about that day that happened hours earlier. Even earlier than the car ride where Aiesha Holt and Paul White built up the legal walls of contracts and NDAs to protect the LBF and Aberdeen from this man they'd just met, who was blissfully unaware of what they were trying to and ultimately failing to protect.

No, it would seem as innocent a story that would seem not worth mentioning. On their way to baggage claim, Kline was bumped into by a woman, who spilled a drink all over him. It led to a conversation and the passing of a small trinket that carried the weight of the

world for that woman and, ultimately,
for Kline as well. It was a gamble. A bet.
It would pay off, but not at first and not
without a lot of pain. Her name? Rayne
Harlow. That wasn't how she introduced
herself. She introduced herself by her
stage name. Her mask. Cherie Antoinette."

bracelet

16

LAX, Los Angeles, CA

The plane landed smoothly, and the two made their way to baggage claim after grabbing energy drinks from a vendor. Kline hadn't taken two steps from the escalator when someone barreled into him. He hit the floor, drink spilling down his chest and soaking his shirt.

"Jesus Christ, lady!" Eddie barked as a chorus of gasps rippled through the baggage claim. Kline lay sprawled on the cold tiles, pinned under the weight of whoever had slammed into him. Eddie helped pull the woman off and hoisted Kline up by the armpits.

"Oh my God, I am so sorry!" a contralto voice said. Kline brushed himself off and turned to see the assailant.

It wasn't what he expected, considering it felt like he had been run over by a linebacker.

The woman, about his height, had hazel eyes with flickering yellow flecks that should have been captivating, but her attempt to hide them was painfully clear. Her deep auburn hair was cropped unevenly, buzzed on one side, and jagged tattoos climbed from her wrists to the edges of her black, long-sleeve shirt. They peeked out like secrets she wanted others to see—but only on her terms. Even her impressive physique, her powerful legs accentuated by tight yoga pants, felt like armor rather than a celebration of herself. It was as if she were trying to distract from the parts of her she feared people might find too raw, too real.

"I am so sorry," she repeated, hands darting to smooth his shirt. "Are you okay?"

"I'm fine," Kline replied, still shaken. He glanced down at his drenched shirt. "The shirt? Not so much."

She winced. "Sticky rides suck. Let me fix this. I'll buy you a new one."

Kline started to refuse, but she had already grabbed his arm and dragged him toward a souvenir kiosk. Eddie, meanwhile, flagged down their waiting chauffeur.

"Sports or tourism?" she asked, holding up a shirt with a local football logo and another featuring a California bear.

"Sports," Kline muttered, still unsure how this whirlwind of a woman had overtaken him.

What is happening?

"What are you? A medium?" she asked, grinning, sliding the shirts around on the rack.

"Not in twenty years. Large."

She handed him the shirt and smiled, brushing her hair behind her ear. A flash of piercings and dimples caught Kline's eye. As she held the shirt up to his chest, her fingers brushed his shoulder, sending an unexpected thrill through him.

"Here on business?" she asked, casually.

"Sorta."

"Where to?"

"Malibu, I think."

She cocked her head. "You think? Friends?" Her teasing tone disarmed him.

"I don't know anyone there," Kline said simply, trying to survive this awkward encounter.

"Now you do." She stuck out her hand. "Cherie."

"Kline." They shook hands, her grip firm and calloused.

As they talked, Kline's eyes flicked back to the bracelet on her wrist. The charm was shaped like a small apple tree, its trunk and branches intricately etched. It looked worn, like something personal.

"That's an interesting bracelet," he said, gesturing to her wrist.

Her face softened. "This? It's my good luck charm. My mom gave it to me when I moved out here. She told me, 'No matter how hard the wind blows or how heavy the fruit gets, as long as the roots stay strong, the tree doesn't fall.'" She smiled wistfully, twisting the charm between her fingers. "It's gotten me through a lot."

Kline's brow furrowed as he nodded. "Sounds like it means a lot to you."

"It does," she admitted, but with a painful sigh. She looked him up and down, as if she could see his soul, then placed her hands on her hips. "But today, I think you need it more than I do."

Before he could protest, she slipped the bracelet off her wrist and pressed it into his hand.

"I can't take this," Kline said, trying to hand it back.

Cherie shook her head firmly. "You can, and you will. You've got a big tryout, right? You'll need all the luck you can get."

"But—"

Wait, what?

"No buts. There's just one rule." She leaned in until her chest brushed his, close enough that her breath warmed his ear, as if she were whispering a secret only for him. Her hand pressed flat against his sternum, pinning his attention. Her voice softened. "You have to bring it back to me after. Deal?"

Kline stared at her, stunned by her earnestness and stirred by her touch. The bracelet was warm in his palm, the cord fraying slightly at the edges. Finally, he nodded. "It's a date, I guess."

"Good." Her smile returned, brighter than before. "Come by my bar. I'll buy you a drink to celebrate—when you're done blowing everyone away, of course."

She scribbled an address on the back of a receipt and handed it to him. As he tucked it into his pocket, she added, "Don't forget. I'm serious about getting that bracelet back."

"I won't forget," Kline promised, a grin tugging at the corners of his mouth. He hadn't been a rockstar for a day and already was capitalizing.

"Sooner rather than later," she murmured, her voice almost a purr as she brushed past him to pay the vendor, her hand caught his and she traced her fingers down his palm. He watched her walk away. Eddie looked to his friend with a smile, shook his head.

Some things never change. Eddie thought to himself. Kline had always been a sucker for red heads. Several in college, including his now ex-wife.

"You lucky bastard! Things are looking up already. What is it with you and red heads?" Kline said nothing as he went to the nearest restroom and changed.

Kline spent the walk to the airport's exit thinking about the serendipity of the moment. Just ahead stood two men. One held a sign and wore a cheap suit. The sign had their names on it. The other man, a bit under average height, deep dark skin, and a warm smile, wore a much more expensive suit. He stepped towards them and held out his hand.

"Kline. Eddie. Welcome to LA. My name is Paul White. I am the agent and manager of Aberdeen. Very pleased to meet you. Hope the flight was good to you." They exchanged handshakes. The man motioned towards the exit where a limo was waiting.

"Right this way."

⋮

Ava was waiting in the cell phone lot when she got the call.

"Success?" she asked.

"Yep. Even if I didn't know what he looked like, they had a big sign for him. But that black manager of theirs was waiting. So, I intercepted them before they made it that far. Made it easy. Poured a drink all over him." Rayne looked both ways before crossing the lanes of traffic. People clustered around for rental car shuttles.

"Ha! Bet that was fun. Come up with that on the fly?" Ava chuckled. Rayne nodded.

"Yeah, well, cost me twenty-five bucks to buy him a new T-shirt. And I about messed up. Let him know that I knew why he was here." Cherie scowled.

"I doubt he caught it. Write it off as a business expense," Ava joked, apparently missed that she'd nearly screwed it all up from the first. Rayne still wasn't sure how and why that had happened and was ashamed of it. Luckily, Ava didn't press her on it.

"And… I gave him Mom's bracelet."

"Why would you do that?" Ava barked.

"This plan's flimsy enough. I had to rope him in somehow. I don't know. I thought giving him something with real meaning to me might convince him to see me again."

"Hope you're willing to kiss that bracelet goodbye, sweetie pie." Ava backed out of the parking spot, still laughing.

"Wasn't this your idea? To meet him, seduce him, and parlay that into studio time or a deal?" The word *parlay* jogged her memory. She pulled out her phone to check her illegal bookie app. Parlays were a big money maker for her — sucker bets, until one hit. Luckily, none of the amounts wagered were big enough to scare her off.

"It was our idea, but your ideals, founder. If the world sees us as sexual objects, why not use that as a weapon instead of a crutch, right? And I have faith in your charming personality and that red-hot hair. Better looking than his ex-wife, too. You'll rope him in far better than a wooden bracelet your mother gave you. Newsflash, Rayne: if that bracelet had any real value, your mom would've pawned it years ago."

"It has meaning to me, you heartless bitch." Rayne shot back.

"No, just a sociopathic lesbian. And in this world? That's basically the same thing. I couldn't do it. Not just because I play for the other team. I'm a foot taller than him. Connie? We both know her trauma. Sending an asexual to do a sexual job?" Ava spotted Rayne up ahead, hung up, and pulled to the curb.

Rayne slid into the passenger seat. Ava sped off. They drove in silence for a few seconds. Ava checked the rearview, merged into traffic, headed toward Hollywood.

"And Jen?" Rayne asked, though she knew the answer.

"Jen could fuck up a wet dream. You know that."

"Look, if nothing comes from it? Then it was an hour wasted and an overpriced T-shirt. At least it'll make a good story for Lanna someday — if he makes it. Who knows? Maybe he writes a song about that bracelet. And you can sue his ass." Ava smirked toward her.

"But if it does? If he calls you?" She switched lanes again.

"Well, then you do your thing. Use that thing between your legs." Ava pointed a long finger at Rayne's crotch. "Get your claws in. Manipulate him. Get us what we deserve."

Cherie heard her words, but Rayne hated how her own band-mate commodified her the way men always had. And yet Cherie understood why. Because wielding sexuality had become a blade — the only way she could survive and chase her dreams.

The man she met, though — even in a few minutes — wasn't what she expected. She'd felt an instant connection, and the mask she tried to wear had never fit right. Then again, that had always been her problem with men, hadn't it? They all felt like saviors in the moment. They never were.

Growing up, they came and went. No one saw the collateral damage left behind in Rayne. How those men looked at her. How they touched her. How all of it shaped her views on men.

Kline Thomas felt different. But then, she'd said that before.

Excerpt from "The Voice Was Never Theirs"
BY CLARA COWLEY

"While Kline was still figuring out why
he was drenched in someone else's drink and
wearing a new shirt from the airport, and Eddie
was grinning like he'd just won the lottery,
Paul White and Aiesha Holt were three steps
ahead. The machine never stops.

They'd already outlined contingencies.
NDA frameworks. Contract addendums.
Recoupment. Who needed to know—and who
needed to never know. That's how the industry
works, and artists, God love them, are never
prepared. Even the good ones in the business
only explain so much, because they know
survival pressure falls squarely on the
artist. If you're worried about tonight's
meal, you can't plan for two months from now.

When you're dying of thirst and someone
offers a glass of water, you don't ask where
it came from—or what it will cost. You just
sign and hope it's enough. No one asks how many
points get shaved off the back end—because if
you're dead, it doesn't matter.

I've heard the door to the limo wasn't even
fully closed before a pen was pressed into
Kline's and Eddie's hands and the papers
shoved across their laps.

I've also heard White was ready to pull the limo over on I-10 and leave them by the side of the road if they didn't sign.

That doesn't sound like the Paul White I know. I may paint him in a certain light for his role in all of this, but he's a thoughtful man. Calculating, yes. Cold, sometimes. But never cruel.

Aiesha Holt? I'm not so sure. I say that in love and truth, having known her for so long, knowing how important her faith in Kline would ultimately become.

And truth be told, I can't say I would've blamed them. If Kline and Eddie hadn't signed, that's all they needed to shut it down—quietly, legally, without anyone ever asking why but having an answer if they did.

Maybe they truly believed there was a chance those boys would walk. We'll never know.

But what happened in that limo wasn't planning. It wasn't celebration. It was insulation. Damage control.

They weren't building a future. They were building a firewall.

This was the moment the business side of the story took over.

And Kline?

He wasn't an artist anymore.

He was already a product. He was inventory. Tagged. Boxed. Already on the shelf."

weight

17

I-10/Highway 1

The limo pulled away from LAX.

Already seated was a tall, striking Black woman in a black-on-black tailored suit. Natural curls swept into a high bun, skin smooth and deep brown, posture sharp enough to cut. She looked up from her tablet just long enough to acknowledge them—then back down, as if the rest could wait.

"Kline, Eddie," White said. "This is Aiesha Holt—Aberdeen's publicist."

"Among other ventures," she added coolly, shaking hands—limp, perfunctory. "But yes. Aberdeen."

"She's sharp," White said. "Politics, D.C., campaign management. Turned to the music industry once she realized artists lie less than senators."

Aiesha gave a subtle smile. That look between her and White had history.

She's still pissed, he thought. She'd been brought in to modernize Aberdeen's image. What she couldn't control—Lloyd Brannon's death—had derailed everything.

"You mentioned other ventures?" Eddie asked, curiously but mostly as small talk.

Aiesha crossed her legs, flipping open an expensive leather notebook.

"Other bands. Some actors. Most aren't household names—some are. But that's not relevant. Every job is unique and different from the last. Everyone equally important," she said, flipping a page in her notebook.

"Because, you never know. Who is big today might be little tomorrow. And who is little today may be big tomorrow," she said with practiced ease.

Kline gave White a glance. "So, we're in good company, huh?"

"Let's say you're a new project," White replied.

It was meant to be light, but Kline heard the edge. So did Eddie.

"For the next few days, you'll be getting to know the band. Ben Cantrell may have mentioned a possible live streamed performance. To prep for that, I've got a few asks. Eddie—you've got barely any social media. Kline—you've got none. I can fix that. But until we see how things go? I need you to stay off platforms entirely. Or better yet? Let me manage it for you."

She looked up, lashes low, tone measured. "Questions?"

Kline leaned forward. "Yeah. Why does that matter?"

Her smile was like glass—polished, cold, and sharp.

"To protect Aberdeen. And to protect you. We've already seen what's publicly available on you, Mr. Thomas. And we'd rather not have anything else surface unintentionally."

Kline blinked. That wasn't a threat. But it was close enough to make the air feel thinner.

"Like what?"

"Old tweets. Bad opinions. Private matters made public." Her voice never changed. "We've already reviewed what's out there. We're not saying you'd live stream yourself snorting coke off a stripper's ass—but we've seen worse." Now Kline shifted uncomfortably.

Eddie cracked up. White didn't. He knew she was serious.

"We've seen a few things," she repeated. "It's L.A."

A quiet beat passed. Kline didn't move, but something behind his eyes shifted.

She handed them each a contract. "Temporary agreement. Covers media access, image rights, streaming. All standard."

White glanced at Kline. Too casually.

"Just a precaution. And you'll find information on what the streaming show will pay, if it happens."

Kline didn't bite. He nodded and scanned the contract, but the line about *relationships* stuck in his brain like a splinter.

"So…" White said, shifting tone. "Long flight?"

"Uneventful," Kline said. "Didn't touch my mimosa. Figured I should show up clear. It's an interview, right? Just because it is music doesn't make it any less important. So, that sucked."

White chuckled as he nodded. "Practical. Some guys would've hit the minibar before the gate."

"I've done that too," Kline said, not missing the implication. "But not today."

White smirked. "You always this self-aware?"

"Not always. Working on it."

White let that hang, then tapped the seat's armrest idly, recalling the small talk they'd shared. Eddie had gone quiet—not checked out, but watching. Letting Kline speak, even if it scared him. That was Eddie's faith, in its own way. He wasn't built for business talk and hadn't considered what any of this meant beyond the thrill of meeting Aberdeen. Kline, though—he had a plan. Or at least it looked that way. That was different. Refreshing. Odd. Very not like Kline, but welcomed.

"You know, Eddie mentioned it was your idea to pursue this. That you were the one who pulled the trigger." Kline nodded once. "We've been playing Aberdeen songs for years. The moment came, I took it. Not just for me. For both of us." Not a lie. Not really true. They played everything, when the mood suited.

White studied him. "But *why* you?"

"Because I don't want to be stuck anymore," Kline said, steady. "I've done the same thing for a long time. It stopped being enough. I want something harder. Something real. I've never been great at anything. Good, sure. But this guy has convinced me that I'm great."

Aiesha didn't look up, but her pen had stopped moving.

White nodded. "You know the pressure this brings, right? People will hate you on principle. Lloyd fans. Hardcore loyalists. Hell, even some of the band."

"I'm not here to replace Lloyd. I'm here to sing. Let's be perfectly clear."

That made White pause. Not defensive. Not desperate. Just... sure. Or, aware. Eddie turned in his seat, surprised. There was a resolve in Kline's voice he'd never heard.

Aiesha smiled slightly—maybe the first real one.

"You think you can carry the weight?" White asked.

Kline met his gaze. "I'm already carrying worse." He thought some more. "I'm already carrying it." White could tell that he spoke the truth, at least from his point of view. Yet, Kline couldn't know. The weight Kline referred to was certainly real to him, but what he really had on his shoulders, unknowingly?

Silence. No one moved. Then Eddie cleared his throat and grabbed a pen.

"Pro bono?" he asked, shifting the energy.

"For now," Aiesha replied, flipping the mood like a switch. "Sign it, and I build the brand. Don't sign, and you're just two guys with a decent cover band playing for free beer and discount wings. No harm. No foul." White watched impassively as she tossed down the gauntlet.

She's so damn good.

She watched them mull it over.

"Yeah, I know—I look like a hard-ass. Six-foot Black woman in a $3,000 power suit and $1,400 sneakers. That intimidates people. Good. But you sign that paper, and I'm a dog on your side. That's a dog you want in your kennel, not on the other side of it." Neither of the men budged. She sat forward.

"Look, I know this is all coming fast. Maybe you're thinking, *nothing's gonna happen*. And maybe you're right. But what if you're wrong? This streaming show, for example, is going to pay."

"How much?" Eddie asked, finally getting involved. Aiesha had made a note of how Eddie had become very quiet when Kline began talking. Could be a concern that they weren't on the same page. But it also could be that Eddie trusted Kline, implicitly.

"Vast majority is based on streams. Pacific Coast Records gets a healthy cut. Like almost all deals between artists and the industry, the industry gets their money back first. But it won't be a problem. Band gets a lot. The VIPtix sales, if it's a go, will easily pocket you a few grand if it sells out, which it will. Hardcore fans will pay whatever we want just to be inside Eveningview. But in the room, with that band? Playing? Hard to put numbers on, but I guarantee it will be more than you'd make in a month of sawdust floor, beer joint shows. That's not really my point." Kline wasn't listening; his mind was on the wording, still.

Kline narrowed his eyes. "You saying you'll work against us if we don't sign?"

A silence. Then Aiesha laughed, pointed at him. Eddie seemed concerned at Kline's directness.

"I like you. You ask the hard questions. Don't scare easy." He didn't ask about the logistics of getting paid after the recoupment. None of them ever did. Not until it was too late.

White filed that away. Aiesha was rarely wrong about people.

"To answer—no. I'm *always* on Aberdeen's side. That doesn't make outsiders enemies. I build. I don't destroy."

White relaxed. Just a touch. Aiesha passed the pens forward.

Kline signed. So did Eddie.

And as the limo rolled into the city, White sat back—still unsure if Kline was a miracle or a mistake but knowing damn well: *he was something.* White had the revelation that he was rooting against this man because of the threats. For all intents and purposes, he had passed the first test. But just the first of many. What if he kept passing them? What then?

Excerpt from "The Voice Was Never Theirs"
BY CLARA COWLEY

"The thing people never understand about meeting their heroes is how small it feels.

You don't walk into greatness. You walk into a conference room. Or a rehearsal space. Or, in Kline's case, the legendary Eveningview Mansion. Talk about a space overshadowing a moment.

By all accounts, no one knew how to act that first day.

Kline was polite. Quiet. Uncharacteristically sober. And everyone—Ben, Markus, Jose—was trying too hard to be normal people to two normal guys. Now, I think it's fair to say that Ben, Markus, and Jose are lovable and normal guys, and making Kline and Eddie feel at home is genuinely who they are. But to pretend this moment wasn't intimidating is folly.

They did their best.

And, we have to be fair that no one thought anything would come of this moment.

Mike Kilmore didn't say much. He stared. Not aggressively. Just long enough to try and make Kline nervous. Again, by all accounts, that never happened. It was the other way around. One was intimidated. One did the intimidating. One had the world in front of him and the other had financial ruin and hard choices on his shoulders like Atlas.

And Eddie? He was the only one in that room not pretending. He didn't hide his emotions.

The legend goes that Kline had selected the hardest song Lloyd had ever written and performed, at least to that moment, and slayed it. When he was asked why, he'd simply said that he wanted to get his bad performances out of the way early. There's a story people tell about that day—that Kline held his own. All day and all night. Markus will tell you, as an observer, that Kline simply blew them away. Not just in his demeanor, but when the moment counted. At the mic.

And, speaking of that mic, from the very beginning, from the very first note, Kline had made it clear that he wasn't going to live in anyone's shadow."

18

Eveningview Mansion, Malibu, CA

White opened the limo door for the two Alabamians, who exited after the hour-and-a-half ride. The driver set their luggage out, the most important piece being Eddie's guitar. On the steps waited four men with familiar faces.

"It was good to meet you two, and I look forward to working with you. I will be in touch very soon." Aiesha leaned out the door and shook their hands again.

"Thanks, Aiesha. Have a great day." White and Aiesha exchanged a look that no one else could see. Both said the same thing without speaking.

We've got a long road ahead of us, don't we?

The limo eased across the driveway of the iconic mansion.

"Jesus Christ! This is Eveningview!" Eddie exclaimed, hands on his hips as he surveyed the property. Eddie realized that in all the business and small talk, they'd never asked where they were going, though Aiesha had mentioned it in passing. It shouldn't be a surprise that Eddie didn't know where they were headed, much less mention it. Chandra always planned trips; he just showed up. Same with business trips with Kline. White grinned at him and leaned close.

"I figured you'd like that surprise," White said, warmly. "We've got it for a few months, courtesy of PCR, to cut this next record."

"The one and only!" The voice came from the first one down the steps. Ben Cantrell grabbed Eddie's hand with one of his long, skinny hands. The other picked up Eddie's guitar case, Telecaster tucked safely inside.

"Ben. You must be Eddie." Eddie, a tall and skinny man himself, had to crane his neck up to see the long-black-haired man peering down at him. Cantrell moved a step to the side, a full stride for anyone else.

"And you are Kline. We spoke on the phone. Jeez, just yesterday." He pumped Kline's hand. White was shocked to see Ben leading the way, but it was a welcome surprise.

"Eddie, Kline. Mike Kilmore, Jose Madera, and Markus Kenney." There were introductions and handshakes all around.

"Welcome to Eveningview." Ben stretched out his long arm over the property. Eddie couldn't contain his awe, and he looked to Kline, who seemed to be a passive observer.

"Eveningview, Kline! Don't you know what this place is? What it's meant?" There were now several sets of eyes on Kline.

If he doesn't know what this place is, how could he be our new singer? several of them seemed to say to one another.

"No, I know what it is. The album was made here."

"THE album," Eddie said excitedly but realized that might have been a bit offensive and looked for disappointment from the band. None was there.

"Are you not excited?" Eddie almost whispered.

"No. I'm just hungry," Kline said, flatly. Laughs.

"I bet. Come on in. Let's get some food. Some drinks!" The band picked up their suitcases and ushered them inside where catering awaited.

Their tour of Eveningview ended in the studio. Foam-padded walls, rug-covered floors, and the haze of weed smoke gave it a worn-in charm. Bottles of water, soda, and liquor littered the space. What there wasn't was notebooks and pages of songs.

Kline Thomas had impressed Kilmore immediately—not by what he said but by what he didn't. He didn't ask for pictures. Didn't fawn. It was the band who asked *him* for a photo. Even knowing it was for PR, it still bruised Kilmore's ego.

Kline introduced himself like he was walking into a boardroom, not a sacred temple of rock. It rubbed Kilmore the wrong way.

Eddie, meanwhile, was a wreck. Sweating, jittery, pounding drinks just to slow his heart rate. Mike found it fascinating: Eddie couldn't shut up, while Kline said nothing.

"You always this quiet, Kline?" Kilmore finally asked.

Kline didn't answer right away. Just scanned the room like it bored him.

"Eveningview is awesome. Always wondered how you wrote the Eveningview album in a place like this."

"That's why we're here," Kenney said, belching after a sip of dark liquor. "Try to recreate it."

Kline cut in. "Shall we get started?"

The band exchanged looks.

"Usually, we bullshit first. Drinks, stories, loosen up a little. Get to know ya," Kenney said.

White watched. Aberdeen were clearly Eddie's heroes. Kline's foot hadn't stopped bouncing.

If we just get started, maybe I'll calm down, Kline thought. *I must nail this.*

"If it's all the same, I'd like to jump in."

The urgency in his voice didn't go unnoticed. Eddie shifted, uneasy. White studied everyone's reactions.

Kline stood, pulled a folded paper from his pocket, and smiled tightly at the seated band. A version of himself was emerging— blunt, determined, teetering on unstable.

"They've come a long way. Let them play," Madera said, sliding onto the drum stool and adjusting his kit. A quick rap. "Besides," he added, raising a bottle, "we can drink on the job."

Kilmore tipped his beer and took the paper from Kline. Eddie opened his mouth to say something—then stopped.

I've never heard him sing stone sober.

The thought stopped him cold. On the flight, Kline had refused to drink, making a whole point of it. Now it made sense.

He thinks it's the right call, Eddie decided. *So do I.*

"Figured we'd start with these," Kline said.

Cantrell slung on his bass, scanning the list.

"'Last Night'? That's a tough one to open with."

Eddie tensed. *Why that one?*

"Why not something easier? Lloyd used to open with 'Echoes' when he could. Layup song."

Without looking up, Kline responded: "Last show I saw, Lloyd took three songs to find his groove. I always wondered, why butcher three good ones when you can just butcher one?"

Kilmore nodded, amused. *Not wrong. But this guy has no idea how hard this is going to be.*

It was the first song he ever sang with us, Eddie remembered. *A dare. A betrayal. A knife to the ribs weeks before she left him. It mattered.*

Kilmore spoke before Eddie could: "Can't fault that logic. Why didn't we ever think of that?" He struck the opening chord. Sarcasm. Or maybe not.

"Don't let him be modest. Kline slays this song," Eddie said.

Cantrell caught the tension. *He wants Kline to fail.* White saw it too.

But what if he didn't?

"You wanna lead, Eddie?"

"Wouldn't dream of it. I've only dabbled with Aberdeen rhythm stuff. Might sound rough."

"Now who's being modest?" Kline smirked.

Kilmore's eyes went to Eddie's Strat. Eddie could feel the judgment from the wall of guitars behind Mike.

"You guys mind if I hit the head first?" Kline asked.

"There's the nerves," Kilmore muttered.

"Up the steps, on the left," Jose said, pointing with a drumstick.

Kline locked the bathroom door, turned the faucet, splashed water on his shaved head, then stared into the mirror.

"Did you stand here?" he whispered. "What did you see?" He pictured Lloyd. The legend. The voice. He could almost see the reflection beside his own. He was not praying for success. He was asking permission. "Fuck it."

He stepped out and strode past White, who gave a small nod. Kline stopped at the iconic mic stand. He adjusted it, then froze. Its shadow reached across the rug. The imagery couldn't be denied, White realized. He wondered if Kline felt it.

He lifted the stand.

"NO!"

The shout was instant. Unified. Raw.

Kline let the stand drop. Around its base the carpet was bright, untouched by time. A perfect circle.

"Lloyd thing," Kilmore said. "That mic is dead center. Everything in here was placed around it. No one moves it. Not even the owners."

Kline started to put it back, then didn't.

"Let's see what happens," he said.

The air dropped out, a vacuum. No one moved. The last time they tried out a new member, they were kids in a garage.

Kilmore hit the opening riff.

Kline turned off-axis from the mic and threw the opening into the room, all chest. No wobble. No nerves.

"Hey, momma. Momma, hey!" He held the last word until the control-room glass hummed.

"Whoa." Markus pressed two fingers to the bridge of his glasses and scratched at his afro. On the board the meters maxed, the preamps clipped. White looked up. Markus reached for Kline's fader. White gripped his shoulder.

"No. See if they will follow," White said. Markus slid Kline's fader back up.

Kline's eyes swept the line of players as they played the intro.

"You even trying?" he snapped. "Come on. This isn't karaoke night. Send it. If I have to impress you, you need to impress me."

Jose flinched, jarred back to attention. Ben glanced over, startled, then laughed and straightened. The pocket tightened.

Then the harmony. "How could I ever deserve your love?" Eddie found him on the third. Their voices wrapped like cable. Kline turned. "Come on, Jose. Play the fills right."

Jose locked in, trying not to listen how good the two voices sounded or how the two guitars now matched the same energy and instead hear his cues.

Ben nodded along, recognizing the moment. Not just power. Not just precision. Recognition. It wasn't just Kline singing.

No, an echo. A different energy.

Kline skipped the next line and barked a wake-up instead, then hit the entrance on time.

"Let's go down to the shore without a care. Who cares if we go in our underwear. Walk the beach of sand so white. Make love like we did last night."

Markus blinked. Out of Lloyd's mouth those words had always played like a wink, a sunlit strut down the shoreline. Anyone could picture Lloyd traipsing the beach in his underwear without a care. Of course they could, with that face, that body, that myth. Out of Kline's mouth the rhyme bent into something else. It became an indictment. A reminder of the man he could never be.

Their voices wrapped again. White listened for what was the same and what was different. The second real guitar, not a loop, gave the sound a new edge.

He watched the way everyone moved. Then Kline began to move. Swaying. Stalking. He leaned into Eddie as Eddie played.

The tall, skinny man transformed from tagalong to stand-alone in front of them. Eyes closed. Smile set. His long, callused fingers raced Kilmore. Kilmore shifted down a key.

Everyone played harder. Even Kilmore. Especially Kilmore.

Eddie was playing his ass off, even on rhythm, and White could see how badly he wanted to rip the solos. Kilmore stopped mailing it in and started playing. Eddie was not competent. He was not just good. He was great.

The room changed shape. A new sound. A new intensity.

Eddie took the lead for the break. Kilmore answered. They pushed each other until the song opened into something else. Something new. It became a jam.

White wanted to believe it was just the hunger to be challenged again. It probably was for Kilmore. The other three felt different. White looked to the glass. Markus was already nodding. He had started recording the moment Kline opened his mouth.

Something was back. Or it was born. Something dangerous.

•

"It was pretty good, eh?" Kilmore muttered; arms crossed as he stared at the monitors.

Kenney pulled the headphones from his head, the plastic leaving a slight impression in his hair. Only the two of them remained in the booth—Kilmore had bailed as soon as the others started fawning over the new guys. He didn't come for the feelings. He came for facts.

"Were you not listening?" Kenney asked, incredulous.

"I was playing. Hard to analyze and perform at the same time," Kilmore deflected.

Kenney raised an eyebrow, almost smirking. "Funny, it took the amateur to remind us all to actually play."

Kilmore didn't respond.

"It sounded… okay?" he said, but it came out too forced. He was trying not to give it away.

Kenney's hands flew over the keyboard, summoning graphs, overlays, waveforms. "This is the Lloyd master. Notice the jagged-ness in his peaks? Struggles at high strain. Slight flat notes here, sharp ones there. We boosted the gain, smoothed things out in post. Overdub. We always did."

He clicked a few buttons. "Now this… this is Kline. One take. No sweetening."

Kilmore leaned in, scanning. He rubbed his goatee, trying to find something wrong. "He's pitchy in the verses. Struggles with mid-range."

"Yeah. He hunts on the flats. But only when it's static. Ask him to climb or descend and he's flawless. Harder and faster, the better. You know what that tells me?" Kenney paused. "He tunes out when it's too easy. His mind's already ahead, bracing for the hard stuff."

Kilmore didn't respond. Kenney let the silence sit. "I know it's just one take. But listen to the vibrato on the high deltas, and it isn't intrinsic in his voice, it's controlled. You aren't supposed to be able to control that. Nailed every major leap with force and sustain. That's something that made Lloyd so special. Dude just climbs or descends octaves with ease, and you must start perfectly to do that. Most live singers would play it safe. Not him. And it's not just natural—he's choosing it."

He hit play. The last verse boomed through the speakers, louder than intended. Out in the studio, the others turned, caught off guard.

Kenney winced, but Kilmore was watching the band. Smiles. Nods. Heads bobbing.

Kilmore's frown deepened.

"This time," he muttered. "He's been rehearsing this song non-stop. He picked it."

"Sure. Wouldn't you?" Kenney shrugged. "But—"

"But?"

"I think he could do it better—if he wasn't trying to sound like anyone but himself. But he knows that's not why he's here."

That made Kilmore laugh, short and sharp. "You think he's holding back?"

"I think he's trying to sound like Lloyd. Too much. Because he thinks that's what *we* want. But it's not a natural cadence for him. Yes, he sounds like Lloyd. No, he doesn't want to sing like Lloyd. He was nervous. Rushed. I don't even think he *likes* singing Lloyd's stuff." Kilmore knew not to question Doctor Markus Kenney. He may not play a conventional instrument, but his knowledge on music production and theory was beyond reproach.

"If we asked him what he really wanted to sing? Now that would be something. I can make some guesses. Somehow, I think the tables would turn real quick on who can do what." Markus seemed lost in thought on this.

Kenney turned back to the board. "But this… this is what I want to show you."

A few more keystrokes. The screens lit up again.

"Kline and Eddie. Their pitches align—imperfectly. But beautifully. Unconventional harmonies that *work*. We never had that. You and Lloyd? It was passable. We buried your backing vocals because we had to. Same way we pushed Ben's bass and pulled Jose's drums. We managed balance. But this?"

He pointed to the screen.

"This is something new. Something we never had. They've created a harmony that makes the original sound outdated. No offense."

Kilmore stared at the waveform like it had insulted him.

"I was rocking out in here. Not just impressed. I was *into* it. And the crazy part?" Kenney leaned in. "Kline uses Eddie's voice to settle himself. When he gets pitchy? He finds Eddie. Lines up with him. Then launches. You've got to start in the right spot, on the right note or it's all off. I think that's how he climbs the ladder so well on those big dynamic deltas."

A long pause. Kilmore didn't move.

"And Eddie's guitar work? It's clean. Steady. Doesn't try to steal the spotlight. But it fills the gaps we've *never* been able to fill. Not backing tracks. Not overdubs. Real rhythm. Real bones. That's new too."

Kilmore grimaced.

Kenney sighed, rubbed his face. "Maybe my expectations were just low. But I don't think that's it. I've been thinking…"

Kilmore didn't look at him. "What?"

"All these artists re-recording their catalogs—taking back control after getting screwed in their early contracts. I think we came in here trying to sound like we always did. But that's not what happened."

Kilmore turned slowly.

"And I keep thinking… could we do that?"

Kenney let the question hang. Lloyd had always been the wall. No re-records. No re-imaginings. But Lloyd wasn't here anymore.

It would sell, he knew.

That would be a problem.

"We aren't doing that to Lloyd's legacy." Kilmore offered with finality. The two of them stared out the glass.

Kilmore finally spoke. "Let's see what else they've got before we anoint them the second coming."

Kenney frowned, already imagining the possibilities.

Kilmore saw it too—possibility turning into temptation.

And that was the danger.

Excerpt from "The Voice Was Never Theirs"
BY CLARA COWLEY

"I think people forget that Eddie Cornell had a family.

Because in every version of this story, he's framed as Kline's right hand. The grounding force. The harmony to Kline's melody-the part that made Aberdeen's new sound so strange, so different.

And for about six weeks, Eddie Cornell was the rock star. The frontman.

But the truth is, Eddie was a husband. A father. A provider.

The legend of Eddie and Kline says it was Eddie-not Kline-who always wanted to be the star.

And, Eddie being who he was, he didn't care in the slightest that Kline took the spotlight he never wanted.

Now here he was. In Los Angeles. In Eveningview. Eating catered meals and walking the halls of a mansion where a platinum record was nailed into the drywall like an afterthought.

For the first time in years, Eddie didn't have to clock in. Didn't have to answer to anyone.

He was with his best friend. Watching him do something impossible.

And he was, for lack of a better word, glowing.

Was he homesick? Of course. Did he miss Chandra? Constantly. But did the guilt ever outweigh the joy? I don't think so.

I don't think we talk enough about what those days must've felt like for him. Not in hindsight. Not through tragedy.

But in the moment. When the lights were soft. And the music was just beginning. For once, Eddie wasn't holding the spotlight.

He was standing in it. And he looked like he belonged there.

boots

19

Moonshadows, Malibu, CA

The days blurred together. By Thursday evening, the exhaustion had finally caught up with Eddie. After another whirlwind of rehearsals and city tours courtesy of Aberdeen, he called it an early night. Slightly drunk for the fourth night in a row, he collapsed onto his hotel bed just as his phone rang.

"Hey, baby!" he answered, voice still flushed with adrenaline.

"I was starting to wonder if you even missed me," she said—equal parts teasing and hurt. She wasn't wrong. He'd been reduced to quick texts and half-hearted check-ins.

"You know I do. But… I'd be lying if I said I'm not having the time of my life."

"Well, you deserve it," she said softly. "What are you up to?"

"Just got back to the hotel from the Rainbow. The Rainbow! That's where Alice Cooper, Ringo, GNR and Mötley Crüe hung out! I was there! As a band member of Aberdeen!" Chandra didn't have a clue what any of that meant, but he was obviously excited. Eddie realized that wasn't what she wanted to hear about.

"That sounds like an adventure."

"Yeah. We've been rehearsing like our lives depend on it, though."

He kicked off his boots, peeled off his sweat-soaked flannel, and dropped onto the couch in his boxers. He'd already had to buy new clothes mid-week. White overheard and offered to comp the cost, clearly not thrilled Eddie hadn't come to him about it.

"Practicing? For what?"

Eddie grinned. "Big news. We're doing a live stream tomorrow night—YouTube, Twitch, socials, everything. Real-time performance!"

"Seriously? That's amazing!"

"Yeah, but hush-hush. It's not public for another twenty minutes. We go live at ten your time. Think you'll make it?"

"I'll chug coffee. Are they really paying you?"

"Are you kidding? I'd pay *them*." He laughed.

"I bet you would." She paused. "So, how's the band?"

"They're cool. Markus is reserved but wicked smart on theory and stuff. Cantrell's weird, in a lovable way. Jose feels like a Hispanic version of me. Kilmore's… standoffish. I don't think he wants us there. Or maybe that's just how lead guitarists are wired."

"And Kline?"

Eddie hesitated. Her tone had shifted—guarded, careful. She didn't ask like a casual observer. She asked like someone bracing for impact.

"Actually? That's the crazy part. He's barely drinking. Couple nights he even left early. He's serious. Like, *locked in* serious."

"That's… surprising."

But was it? Kline always took his performances seriously. It's when it was too serious that things went sideways. When the music started to seep from him like a cut vein.

"Yeah. And he's killing it. I've never heard him sing sober. But now? He's got control, power—hell, *presence*. I think this is going to happen for him."

"That's good. But what about *you*?"

He paused. She was the only person who'd asked.

"I think I bring something to their sound—especially when I'm harmonizing with Kline. But there's still tension. Kilmore wants the old Aberdeen. But they *need* to evolve. I think even he knows that. The rest seem to think so. But, Kilmore is in charge."

There was a beat of silence before she spoke again.

"So, what does Kline think?"

Eddie blinked. "What do you mean?"

"I mean… about replacing Lloyd Brannon. About becoming the *face* of the band. About whether he wants to carry *that* kind of weight. Are you sure he can? More importantly, does *he* think he can? Does he want to?"

He didn't have an answer. For the first time all week, Eddie's certainty cracked. "If he's doing it, he thinks he can handle it."

But even as he said it, he wasn't sure. Chandra noticed Eddie hadn't asked how she was doing. Or how their child was. She didn't want to dampen the moment for him — or start another fight, especially long-distance.

It wasn't that he didn't care, she knew. He just didn't know how to be a father. Not yet, anyway. For men like him, fatherhood didn't begin until the kids were fun.

Just a floor up, a few rooms down, Kline Thomas rested his forehead against the cool porcelain of the toilet bowl. His face was slick with sweat and vomit.

He lifted his head slowly, wiped his mouth on his forearm, flushed, and reached for the half-empty bottle perched on the tank. He drained it. Then stumbled back into the living room, collapsed onto the couch, and stared at the ceiling in silence.

Same ritual. Every night.

Excerpt from "The Voice Was Never Theirs"
BY CLARA COWLEY

"While Aberdeen was performing at Eveningview-raking in money from a live streamed show viewed by over a million people, with dozens of fans spending thousands on ticket packages-Rayne Harlow and the Painted Queens were rehearsing in a sweltering storage unit.

This, I think, is where the echo starts to be heard-at least for me.

Their histories didn't align. Their scars weren't the same. Kline's voice was always an

echo of someone else—and he knew it.
Rayne and the Queens weren't echoing
anyone. They were clawing for their own
sound, their own survival.

Neither was being heard. Not truly.

I spoke to Kline an hour or so before
that show. I'd seen something in Rayne days
earlier—and now I saw it in him, too.

So, I asked.

He wasn't ready to answer. Either because
he didn't know the answer or because he was
afraid of it.

Minutes later, I watched the Queens' Full-
Frontal Friday stream.

They weren't just rehearsing. They were
selling the clips. The songs. The commentary.
The nudity.

Not because they wanted to. Because they
had to.

Because female artists don't get industry
backing. They get content platforms. They
don't get handlers. They get OnlyFans.

While Kline—dropped into legacy like a
parachute he didn't pack—was being reluctantly
escorted from VIP lounges to label reps to
industry men, Rayne was paying overdue bills
with her band by performing completely nude
for a few dozen viewers, still trying to break
through. Those were her good days. The bad
days? Those cost her subs more.

Kline woke to find his nudes splashed across social media, posted by an influencer. He raged. Aiesha scrambled to bury it before it buried them.

Rayne woke to check how much her nudes had brought in—and whether she was collecting illegal book money or handing it out. Never about the fact that her body would live online forever, or how that might one day scar a young artist named Anna Molly.

One was born into echo. The other into silence.

Wildly different scenarios. The same hollow feeling.

Kline had it rough, replacing Lloyd Brannon with everything that followed. No question. But Rayne Harlow was trying to survive. Which is why this book is ultimately about her. It won't seem that way for a while, I know. Just trust me.

I'm not a chess player, but certain pieces are always on the move. Knights keep the board shifting, tricking novices into thinking the game is about them. But when the Queen moves, you realize it always was about her.

Both hated it. Neither knew how to fight it. Not yet.

And that's the part no one wants to talk about.

full frontal friday

20

The Hotbox, Santa Monica, CA

In a rental storage unit, Jen Farrow led the drums of Ava Palatco. Sweat poured down her face, from her shoulders, down her armpits, between her breasts. Her jean shorts were drenched in the sweat of over a hundred degrees' worth of practice space in the only place they could afford to rehearse.

Badda boo da baaa dum! The bass kick and the snare beat together. *Badda boo da baaa daaahhh!* Drum fill finished with another double punch of bass kick and snare. *Daddaa dooo da dooo dum!* Jen's tongue was in the corner of her mouth, just barely peeking out, her fingers pirouetting across the four strings. She nailed it. "Good!" Connie exclaimed. "Yeah, girl!" came Rayne's exclamation. It echoed off the aluminum door and walls of the twenty-by-twenty space.

Jen's head dropped in exhaustion. She'd been trying to master the riff that Connie Gyuen had written for half an hour. She turned to face the other half of the rhythm section. Behind her, Ava twirled a drumstick. She was already down to her biker shorts and sports bra, her long hair pulled into a ponytail to keep it off her shoulders. Jen's own blonde hair with her signature platinum tips was stuck to her face. She blew out a breath to push it from her eyes, reached into the cooler, pulled out a can of beer from the ice, and popped it open.

"Was that it?" she asked, seeking approval from her bandmates.

"Uh, yeah, baby doll. That was it." Ava pulled the earplugs from her ears. The soft and round artist from Nashville beamed. Connie gave her a brush over her back.

"That's not an easy bass lick, Jen. Good job." That was high praise from the classically trained musician who outclassed them all. The storage space was sweltering. No A/C. No ventilation. That meant the smell of weeks and months of sweat built up. But it was the only place they could afford to keep their stuff set up between gigs. An oscillating fan broke the silence as it pushed in air from the open door.

"What did you think, Franky?" Ava pointed a stick at the sixty-year-old man that sat in a folding chair. "I think the Kim Gordon would be proud of Jen's bass work," he responded—high praise from the facility's owner and manager, who had heard them once at a gig and offered them a comped space to rehearse. He'd been their staunchest fan since that day. No one wanted to address what would happen next, so Ava did what she always did and took the fall.

"Alright, ladies. We ready to do this?" It was a Friday night tradition and always their number-one seller. They all knew why.

"Yeah, I think the sound is tight," Connie answered, music always on her mind. But that's not what Ava referred to. Rayne looked down at her phone that sat on the plain concrete floor. "Four and a half minutes. Smoke 'em if ya got 'em." She pulled at a vape pen. Ava reached to the floor for a pack of smokes. The other two retrieved cheap beers from the soft-sided cooler that rested against the corrugated wall of their cell and passed them out.

"Brought a little something to set the mood," Jen offered as she reached into a backpack and pulled out a bottle of tequila. She took a pull, shook her head as she swallowed it down, and passed it to Ava behind the drum kit.

Ava took a massive pull, as only she would do, and offered it to Connie, who shook her head. "Come on, man. Live a little," the drummer implored her. But she knew it wouldn't do any good. Connie would cut loose any day that didn't start or end with a guitar around her neck—which was practically none. She was a perfectionist in every sense of the word. Always had been, from the very day they'd recruited her. Rayne sometimes wondered what the elite musician saw in them. She could play for anyone, anywhere.

Connie saw that familiar look in Rayne's eyes and smiled. Because she wanted to be here. To be in the shit. The sweat. The gutters.

"After the show," Connie answered to placate her friends. Ava looked at Rayne with curious eyes.

"Are you still hardcore about streaming the Aberdeen show?" she asked her best friend. Rayne hit the bottle of tequila, knowing she'd be leaving her beat-up car in the lot and taking a rideshare home—a few bucks she really didn't have to spend. Rayne swished the golden liquid back and forth.

"Hell yeah, I'm watching it. I want to see what the dude can do. Call it research and development," Rayne answered, and Ava laughed.

"Should be a tax write-off, right, Frank?" she asked the man she was pretty sure was laundering drug money through his storage facility. The old codger lifted a skinny arm with a smoke in his fingers.

"Absolutely." Rayne passed the old man the bottle, and he hit it harder than the rest of them combined.

Rayne found herself wondering what Kline was thinking right about now. What kind of nerves he had. What it had been like practicing in Eveningview all week—a far cry from what she was used to, here in the Hotbox, as they called it. On one hand, she was fascinated with what must be going through his mind, being dropped into this. And, on the other, so frustrated that he fell from the sky to land this gig while the Queens struggled, selling content in the context of music when it really wasn't. Meanwhile, she'd spent the better part of a decade honing her craft in such conditions to be here, still. Naked. Sweating. Starving.

"Alright, ladies. Pants down, tits up." It had become their motto. Connie, the artistic director for the Painted Queens, made her way to the open door near where Frank was sitting and started the live recording. She checked the WiFi connection—another bonus he'd given for letting them rehearse, but truly a payment for letting him watch. It was good. The counter showed a few dozen people already waiting. Connie gave the thumbs-up as she walked, topless, back to her spot to Rayne's left.

Rayne squeezed the sweat from her face down her neck to her bare chest. She knew it would make a sheen that would light up on camera. *Like she was made of stars.* She did it without feeling.

"Hey, everybody! Painted Queens, here! It's Friday night from the Hotbox. And you know what that means." She pointed at the camera; her guitar slung behind her back.

"It's Full-Frontal Friday!" She feigned excitement. In unison, all four members peeled off sweaty panties in front of the camera and tossed them just short of it.

"Let's go, Jen! Take it away!" Jen's country, singsong voice came in right on time with her bass and Ava's drums, just as they'd rehearsed.

I make me.
I break me.
I buy me.
I save me.

Her beautiful country voice rang out. Then Rayne joined, the two singing and screaming together.

I am, I want, I sell, I'm starving.
I think I should find this alarming.
I stand in front of this mirror,
Just ain't coming clearer.

The music slowed. Jen closed her eyes and went back to her singsong voice. She sighed.

Who I am?
What I want?

She ended the chorus with a scream.

I don't know!

They raged into Connie's solo. Connie stepped toward the camera, Flying V raised, her fingers a blur on the neck. She leaned back, giving the viewers their money's worth. Connie may not play that game offstage, but on it she knew exactly how being an Asian woman could be sold — and she sold it on her own terms. She sneered into the lens, black studded strap biting across her chest.

Jen circled her, mic in one hand, yanking the camera close with the other. Platinum hair whipped across the lens as she shook her head violently. She spat the refrain like a curse:

"I am. I want. I sell. I'm starving. I think I should find this alarming. I stand in front of this mirror— Just ain't coming clearer. AAHHH!"

Her scream shredded into Connie's solo, the camera catching every frantic note before Jen leaned in, pressing herself against Connie's back, sweat and ink colliding — a shot staged for the feed as much as the crowd.

The frame jerked to Ava, her sticks flying, bouncing, caught midair before she slammed them into another violent fill. She froze, tips grazing her cheeks, eyes smoldering. Then she sneered and went right back to pounding.

Rayne came in low, bass slung like a weapon, jaw clenched as sweat-matted red hair veiled her eyes.

"I am, I want, I sell, I'm starving. I think I should find this alarming! Alarming! Alarming!"

The music cut. Silence.

"I think I should find this alarming," she whispered, breathless, as the last notes reverberated off the tin walls.

Connie raked her pick down the Flying V in a shriek of feedback, a final slash of sound that left the room ringing, again. Just to remind their viewers who owned perception.

Excerpt from "The Voice Was Never Theirs"
BY CLARA COWLEY

"Sometimes the hardest lyrics to sing…
are the ones you put on paper.

A great artist said that, once. Never
said it again, I imagine. He didn't believe
in repeating things.

I heard a rumor, once. Filed it away.
I didn't think about it, again, until putting
all the pieces of this story together. I may
have said it before. Perhaps many times.
Perhaps too often. Nothing Kline did, when
it came to music, was not saying something
profound. When thinking about this moment
in time, I recalled the songs that were
played on that live stream. I had forgotten
about the song that was not played live,

but it was played. I did a search for Aberdeen and/or Kline setlist. Sure enough, one came up with an affidavit that could be believed. There it was, in black and white. Last song on the setlist? Temple of the Dog, "Pushin' Forward Back." Under that song? Encore: STP, "Piece of Pie." With a line through it.

Scribbled in its place? STP, "Only Dying." Make no mistake, "Pushin" had meaning. Good God, to hear Kline and Eddie shred "Piece of Pie"? Of course, they did with PTGiC. But, they didn't have Ben Cantrell and Jose Madera to back them and, well, that's important. Still, the videos exist. Videos of it can't put you in the sonic space. Phone pickups weren't what they are, now. I tried, so hard, to blast those videos. To hear Kline's full-frontal assault of prime Scott Weiland. To hear the mix of blues and explosion of Dean DeLeo's solos. Things we miss. Just like the meaning of this song.

So, I called Ben Cantrell. "Yeah, it was a bit of a disappointment. We'd practiced both songs, but 'Only Dying' is a demo they put on the remaster of Core. The sound quality? Well, it was from 1990. What can you expect? It's hard to nail it down. Of course Eddie knew it. None of us did. 'Piece of Pie'? I was dying to play this song. Robert DeLeo is such an underrated bassist. And that song?

Led by his bass, all the way through. I'd
never had the opportunity, up until Kline
showed up, to showcase my play. Much less
lead. This song, it felt like at the time, was
a segway for what I hoped would happen, and it
did. Just not right then. And we'd practiced
it. Kilmore wasn't opposed to playing Dean's
part, up until Kline said that Mikey wouldn't
be playing it at all. Eddie would. Even then?
It wasn't until those two ripped it that we
saw and heard what their performance art could
look like. Kline had tried to mimic Lloyd, up
until that moment. But when Kline was Kline?
Whoa." Cantrell would take a breath here; you
could hear him think. Remember.

"Looking back, I'm not sure it was because
STP was so far from Aberdeen, or because Kline
wanted to play it. Sometimes, I think it's
because that song is led entirely by bass and
drums. And when Kline came in with the pre-
chorus? Me slapping and Jose playing just fill
with no cymbals? Duh-duh-duh duhduh duh duh,
Yeah. Duh-duh-duh duhduh duh duh, Yeah! Duh-
duh-duh duhduh duh duh, YEAH!" Ben stopped,
thought about the lyrics. "Starin' me down,
duh duhduh duh" He slapped his knees in rhythm,
and I could feel him realize it.

I didn't think that was the whole story,
so I called Mike Kilmore. "Temple of the Dog
is so much closer to Aberdeen's sound. I love

that record, so when Kline suggested it? I was all in. Did I expect all the other stuff that happened? No." And STP? "He outplayed me on that one. I'll admit it. It was always going to be 'Only Dying,' but he pitched 'Piece of Pie' as the song and 'Only Dying' as a distant second option. Hell, I thought it was a joke. Considering the other songs he wanted to play, though? 'Only Dying' felt safe because no one knows it. No one has anything to compare it to. So, if we butchered it? No one would care because no one would know."

And Rayne Harlow?

"No fuckin' way." She leaned forward.

"'Only Dying'?" Her hands crossed in the air, swiftly. Laughing.

"Didn't happen." I told her I saw it with my own old eyes.

"So, I think we were watching from the Hotbox. I remember Ava and I saying that 'Pushin' Forward Back' was a message. I thought to myself, it was more of a rhetorical question with an answer. But the feed cut. I had no idea." She turned to her husband, in that moment, as we all shared a drink as we frequently do when we feel nostalgic after all these years.

"Fucking ballsy-ass Kline Thomas. Messages within messages. None of us peasants would ever have known what it meant." She tried to

remember the lines. Hummed it. Until
she could remember the lyrics and then she
sang the chorus in her contralto voice,
played the drums with the palms of her hands.
Hummed the bassline.

"Dum, dum," her husband had hummed.

"And where I'm going, I don't know now.
Did he know where he was going? I guess he
does, now. But I don't think I can give him
that kind of credit" Rayne finished the lyric,
laughed, and shook her head as she turned to
her husband, who just shrugged.

"And to have the stones to do that song,
that night? Wow. I had a new appreciation,
which I didn't think was possible."

Regardless of what happened, whether
Kilmore vetoed it, or Kline called an audible
and went with a song that doesn't even qualify
as a deep cut. Because he could. Because
every song meant something. Anyway. I bought
that setlist. It cost me a lot. Not as much as
forgetting the memory and why it meant so much.
I'd tell you what that song says and what it
means, both for Scott and for Kline. Do it for
yourself. But ask yourself, why wasn't it on
Core? What was Scott saying, way back then?
What he's currently telling us, now?

Sometimes the hardest lyrics to sing… are
the ones you put on paper."

bleeds

21

Eveningview Mansion, Malibu, CA

The studio was spotless. Lights rigged, cameras placed, cables taped down tight. A professional setup—expensive and overkill, in White's opinion—but he paid the invoices anyway. Because for once, Aberdeen was doing *something*.

Kline and Eddie watched from the edge of the set, freshened up and nervous.

"This is going to be, like, a real show," Eddie breathed. "With Aberdeen, man. Can you believe it?"

"I can't believe this is happening," he added, slinging an arm around Kline.

Kline, unusually still, let him. He pressed the cold beer to his forehead for the grounding sensation more than the drink. This wasn't a bar crowd. This was *their* turf—the real thing. And he still didn't know if he belonged.

Upstairs, the band was fraternizing with the dozens of fans who had bought the VIP tickets to be right there, in the room, watching the show. Eddie could almost sense what Kline was thinking.

"Reminds me of the Eveningview sessions. Hell, that's exactly what this is! Holy shit! We're doing our own Eveningview session!" He looked around, picturing the grainy digital images from his DVD that had been packaged with the collector's edition of the Eveningview album.

"You mean people are going to be right here? In this room?" Eddie didn't realize that Kline was talking in jest. Sarcasm was his defense against nervousness. So was what was in his pocket.

"Where else would they be, man? Yeah! They'll be lining the walls. Man, there's no telling how much those tickets went for. Bet it was a lot, considering the food they're serving them upstairs. Have you seen that spread?" Kline shook his head no. The last thing he wanted was to get mixed up in all that. The temptation was strong enough, as it was. Up there? He knew where he'd end up. It was the focus that mattered, and he didn't need to hear about expectations. Nor did he need to hear about how good he was. That set a bar and that's where he struggled in life.

"VIPtix charges three hundred a head just to get thirty seconds and a photo with them at their shows. It's gotta be thousands for this," Eddie pontificated.

When no one was watching, Kline slipped a pill from his pocket and swallowed it. The label warned against mixing with alcohol. He did it anyway. It wasn't nerves. It was something deeper.

He walked to the mic stand, now returned to its original spot—as if he'd never touched it. A glossy setlist sat on the floor by the teleprompter. All Aberdeen songs. Except two. The last two. His pick.

They'd resisted at first, especially Kilmore. But Ben and Jose backed him. "Fair's fair," Ben had said. "He sings our songs. Let him end the show with his."

Kline looked up to see a middle-aged, heavyset woman skulking around. He wasn't sure how she got past the ropes and guards. She looked around the studio, then settled her eyes on him.

"Kline, I presume?" the woman asked, extending a hand.

He raised an eyebrow. She didn't look like the people upstairs, though he hadn't paid much attention.

"Yeah?"

"Clara Cowley. I'm a rock journalist." She offered her hand like the name should mean something.

When she realized it didn't, a half-smile tugged at her mouth.

"Oh. Cool. Are we on or off the record?' he joked, like he understood what that meant.

She gave a full smile now. "Very off. Did a favor for Aiesha a few days ago—panel at USC with Markus and White. She owed me one. This is it." She reached into a large burlap purse, brought out a pack of smokes, offered him one. Kline looked around, saw no one looking, and took one. She lit hers, then lit his. They enjoyed the silence in the smoke. She felt obligated to tell him the breadth and scope of what that meant but didn't.

Clara poked the cigarette at him, smoke snaking from the side of her mouth.

"I went back and watched your videos," she said. "Aiesha made sure they floated to the top. Smart. Anyway, I saw a lot of grunge. Why?"

"Well… I love grunge. Grew up with it."

"Do you sing it because you grew up with it? Or because you *mean* it?"

He considered. "Mostly because it's hard. I like pushing myself. Cornell, Staley, Weiland. Legends."

She nodded. It was a good answer, but not quite the one she was chasing.

"Do you identify with what they were trying to say?"

He paused. "Never been addicted to heroin, if that's what you mean. But the rest? Yeah. Alienation. Self-deprecation. The internal stuff. That kind of awareness? I get it."

"Do you think *you* could go there? And I don't mean literally die—I mean metaphorically. Sacrifice. Bleed for it. Most people want to live off their music. They don't want to die in it." She got right to it.

"I don't care about the money," he said without hesitation.

She let that sit. He meant it. She got a push notification on her phone and looked down at it. The Painted Queens were about to go live. She didn't know what that meant, but she'd set it up to let her know. It made her think.

"Could you starve for it, though?" she asked. He didn't follow.

"Let me give you an example I witnessed the other night," she said. "I watched an artist come completely undone. Onstage.

Smashed her guitar in a fit of rage. People thought it was performative—maybe even calculated. But it wasn't. She's broke. Starving. No one is watching. And still, she destroyed something she couldn't afford to lose. Why?"

Kline didn't say anything. He didn't know where she was going. He couldn't possibly understand.

"She did it because she *bleeds* for it," Clara continued. "That's the difference. She believes she's starving—and that belief is real. You could feel it. She felt it so much that it overcame her." He didn't have an answer.

Then came the pivot.

"What I will leave you with is this, because it factors into that conversation. Are you here to replace or are you here to carry forward? Are you here because you *can* be? Or are you here because you *should* be? Would you bleed? Would you starve like her?" Kline couldn't fathom where this came from, why, or how he was the focus of it. He couldn't answer. He wasn't sure he had to answer or could answer. He was simply *here.*

And that's exactly my point. She could see it in his face.

"Well," she said, patting her stomach. "Free food upstairs too good to waste on people who won't touch it. I'm past the point of caring. Think about what I asked."

She turned and walked away.

Kline watched her go.

What a weird fucking exchange.

But something about it stuck.

Am I here because I can *be? Or am I here because I* should *be?* That line wouldn't let go. It echoed louder than the crowd, louder than the setlist, louder than anything he'd rehearsed.

He hadn't earned this. He knew that. He didn't fight for it—he landed in it.

But was that all it was?

Purpose had always been an abstract idea to him. Everyone else seemed born with one. He wasn't.

Until now.

Because tonight—for the first time—he knew why he was here.

Clara stuffed a plate of food and found a corner. She pulled out her phone and clicked on the notification where she watched four talented, female artists strip off their clothes for clicks and then started to play. Clara looked at her bank account balance. She had seventy-eight bucks.

She sent it all.

⋄

Kenney took center stage for the intro, calm and composed. The perfect emcee. The dozens of fans circled the room. Tape had been laid down to establish boundaries, but in the dark, the cameras wouldn't show it to those watching the streams. The fans had been more than respectful to the band. Other than a few handshakes, the fans had barely acknowledged Eddie and Kline's presence. It wasn't them that they'd come to see.

"Welcome, Aberdeenians. It's been too long. I'm Markus Kenney, and we are Aberdeen. Tonight, we're streaming live across platforms and grateful to all of them—and to you—for tuning in."

He gestured wide. "You know Mike, Ben, and Jose. But tonight, we welcome two new voices: Eddie Cornell on rhythm guitar and backing vocals. And Kline Thomas on lead vocals."

Kenney paused. "Lloyd Brannon can never be replaced. But

what you're about to hear is, we believe, the closest thing to hearing his soul again."

Lights down. Kenney disappeared stage right. Spotlights hit Kline. He gripped the mic stand, smiling faintly. Reverent. But the snicker came anyway. He knew what the stand meant. And what it didn't.

Kilmore watched from the corner. His expression unreadable. Tribute or takeover?

And then it started with *Last Night*. The crowd didn't expect it. Their response was instant, palpable, from the first iconic note out of Mike Kilmore's PRS Custom 24.

Kline didn't just sing — he ripped. Forty-five minutes of fire. Like he'd always belonged. Every word landed heavy. Every note commanded. And when he sang their hits? He sounded like Lloyd. The crowd didn't warm up to him. He forced them to.

Sun Machine. Gravity High. Drift. Static Summer.

Eyes closed; Eddie couldn't tell Kline from Lloyd's mastered recordings. Eyes open, the difference was stark. Lloyd stood still. Kline moved. Reached for people. Drew them in.

At one point he held hands with a girl near the front. She glowed; unaware this was a replacement. He passed her the mic, and when her voice cracked, he leaned in, coaxing her to take the line. She did — both hands gripping his — and the crowd roared when she belted it back.

"Pretty awesome, little lady!" Kline shouted, grinning, before slamming into the chorus again.

Summer machine's gonna take me home,
Down the 10 where I belong.
Summer machine's gonna let me roam,

Another endless verse in my song.
Hey, hey, hey —
Another endless verse in my song!

He had the room in call-and-response, sweat flying, turning a cramped venue into something bigger. The crowd danced, swayed, shouted the words back. Kline conducted it all with ease.

Lloyd would never. He'd always played to the band, like it was still Kilmore's garage in the mid-90s. The crowd was background noise.

But Aberdeen's founders played to impress. Even Kilmore, smiling now, trying to outplay Eddie's rhythm guitar. The twin guitars gave the songs new life. Fuller. Real. Comments lit up Aiesha's feed: *Better sound. New sound. Finally alive.*

White forced himself not to watch the numbers climbing, just listened. He heard it too. The resonance. The interplay. Two guitars grinning at each other in sound.

Kline never paused, never sermonized between songs. He waited for the band's nod and drove straight on. And when it ended — too fast, Eddie thought — Kline stood shirtless and glowing, joy radiating off him. Swagger in his step, smiles between lines.

By the last song, Eddie knew. Kline was finally happy. For now.

"This has been… unreal," Kline said into the mic, voice still catching his breath. "I wish you all could feel the energy in here. But I *feel* you."

Kilmore stepped forward.

"And I know Lloyd can feel you too."

The comment lingered. Kline's jaw clenched. Cameras missed it, but Eddie didn't.

"That man," Kilmore continued, "could never be replaced."

Kline's eyes went cold. A beat passed.

"Maybe. Maybe not," he said. His voice calm, but sharp enough to cut.

Ben smirked. Jose grunted in approval. Eddie braced himself.

"This next song isn't an Aberdeen track. It's a favorite of mine. One that honors legends like Lloyd, and the many incredible artists who died too soon. Artists like Scott, Layne, and Chris. Just to name a few. It's called 'Pushing Forward Back' by Temple of the Dog. Thank you for this chance to add my flavor to this set."

Eddie smiled and shook his head. It was one of Kline's favorite songs because it would absolutely push him to his limits. If he could nail this…

He watched the smug look on Kline's face as they had to de-tune.

In the booth, White stared at the viewer counter.

1M.

A million. In real time. It had to be a glitch. But it wasn't. The chat exploded.

"Aberdeen is back." "This is magic." "Who IS this guy?" "Put your shirt back on, dude." "Not Lloyd." "Came here to see a rock God. Got a rock Dog."

White's gut tightened. This wasn't just a performance. This was a turning point. He glanced at Aiesha. She raised her brows, then smiled. Even she hadn't expected this. She was already extrapolating the dollar signs. She was already doing the math. Every note Kline sang, she heard as money hitting the account. The final song began. Tight, clean, driven. It started with Eddie playing a driven guitar riff before a staccato of snare drums came in. The drums were so simple. No fills. No intricate and multiple snares. So unlike Jose's typical work. But Kline turned to watch the pure enjoyment of Jose get to wail on the snare and bass kick.

Then Ben's simple, repetitive, and grinding bassline kicked in. Kilmore wailed on the lead. The band nailed it—but Kline soared above them. For the first time, Aberdeen felt like *his* band. The words hit differently now. Not just lyrics. A challenge. A mission.

White wasn't sure how this song would do. It was way out of scope for Aberdeen, but they owed it to Kline and Eddie. He checked the comments.

"Who sings this song?" "This song absolutely slaps!" "This ain't Aberdeen WTF?" "Rock has missed this." "My dude out here killin' TotD!" "World needed Kline, even if it didn't know it."

As the last chorus rang out, Kline stepped forward. Gripped the mic stand. Thought of every side comment, every look, every reminder of what he *wasn't*. He turned to Kilmore and smirked.

Then he shoved the stand.

It crashed to the floor, a loud metallic clang echoing through the studio. The last note died. Silence held.

Kline loomed over it, chest heaving, eyes on the nearest camera, staring. At who, he didn't know. And then—he smiled.

◊
◊
◊

10 PM PDT Friday, August 26, 2022
Storage Unit, Santa Monica, CA
The four of them had wished Frank good night and settled in front of the TV, resting it on a milk crate.

"What a creep," Connie said, tugging her shirt back on over her bare chest.

"Small price to pay," Ava muttered, pulling her sports bra down over her massive chest. Connie shot her a disapproving look. Just a game they played. She'd never minded her small chest.

"Jesus, Ava. Do you just sit up all night thinking up this shit?" Jen asked, wriggling back into her soaked jean shorts.

"No, sometimes I think about you riding my face. But other times..." Ava turned toward Rayne and raised her eyebrows. "Rayne's the headliner."

Rayne stopped mid-motion and stared.

"Jesus Christ, you're foul."

Ava grinned, sliding around in a pool of her own sweat, tongue out, wagging like a child dared to go too far.

"Rayne, are the fires still burning in Santa Monica, or did you raze the fields?"

"The hell are you talking about, you sick fuck?" Connie asked.

"She's asking if I shaved," Rayne muttered to Connie, "because she can't see it from the back forty of this massive studio."

"You two are sick." Connie shook her head and latched a guitar case.

"But did you?" Ava pressed, smiling.

Rayne turned toward her and bowed. Ava slow clapped with a pair of drumsticks.

Rayne synced her phone to the TV.

"I can't believe you're actually paying for this drivel, Rayne Rain Go Away. Besides, better check the time. Babysitter gonna get out of Dodge if you don't get home." Ava cracked. Rayne frowned. She was right, as usual.

The screen flickered. Kline Thomas appeared after Markus Kenney's intro. Connie was still scrolling through her phone when the first notes hit—Kline, pitch-perfect. She froze. Set her phone down.

"What's the damage?" Jen asked.

"Seven seventy-eight in tips. Two new subs," Connie called out, still watching the screen.

"Hell yeah. Solid night." Ava elbowed Rayne and raised her beer.

"Who sends seventy-eight bucks?" Jen asked.

"Some chick named CC? Who knows. Who cares? Spends the same."

"Subtract the Squier incident, and we had a win." Ava belched, crushed her can on her head, and tossed it in the general direction of a dozen others that Jen would collect for scrap.

Jen watched the can roll. "How do you drink that many? I can't even"—she jiggled her soft tummy, "fit half of what you drink, even with this gut."

Ava laughed. "Gotta burn calories to drink calories, babe. Been telling you."

She flexed, then killed the last of the tequila.

"Ow. Firewater bad for figure. Must pound iron," Jen said, posing in a fake accent. "Says Scandinavian Valkyrie with superior genetics."

They cracked up.

The song kept playing.

"Dude can sing," Jen admitted. "Swagger. Voice. But not the look. Just so… plain. Not Lloyd Brannon."

Rayne tilted her head. Jen had a point. But how did Kline have that presence? It didn't add up. He looked and sounded like a veteran, but from everything she'd seen, he'd fallen out of the sky. Sure didn't look like it. And she would know.

Ava leaned in over Rayne's shoulder. "That's why we put *her* on him, not you."

Jen blinked. Rayne and Connie watched her for a reaction.

"I thought it was because he liked redheads?"

Connie looked to Ava. Ava looked to Rayne.

Just a grin and a shrug.

They kept watching. Commentary flowed—missed cues, sloppy timing, loose transitions. They weren't tight. How could they be? Aberdeen hadn't played live in years.

"Your guy's outclassing them, Rayne. You should beat feet to Eveningview—flies will be on him like stink on shit in fifteen minutes," Ava said.

Rayne considered it. And the plan.

Ava wasn't wrong.

The new sound—Kline's weight, the guitarist's sharpness—was something Lloyd never had. But it was Lloyd's voice. His ghost. His absence. That's what gave the set depth.

Then Kline's moment came.

Rayne lifted a hand. "Shut up. I want to hear this."

It was between songs. Nearly over. Kline stepped forward.

"'Pushin' Forward Back'?" Connie squinted. "How does that fit the Aberdeen motif?"

Rayne hushed her again. *It doesn't, and that is exactly the point.*

Of course Connie recognized the song. But did she get what it meant?

Rayne did.

She glanced at Ava. Ava's face said the same.

Then silence—almost holy.

And then Kline destroyed the song. Kilmore looked like he was chewing glass trying to keep up. The new guitarist carried the weight.

Rayne sat cross-legged on the floor, humming, swaying side to side.

Then it happened. Kline shoved the mic stand over and stared into the camera. Not a pose. Not a stunt.

Rayne felt it in her chest.

"What was that?" Jen asked.

"That," Ava said, pointing with her beer, "was a message." Yet, it only felt like half a message. It said, we are going somewhere, but didn't say where we were going.

Rayne's phone buzzed. The sitter.

How much longer? Guilt cut through her. Not just for the sitter money she couldn't afford. She had convinced herself this was acceptable parenting — her own mother would have left her alone in the dark for far less. Presence mattered more than responsibility. Ava's eyes, steady on her, said the same without a word. Only now—when it couldn't matter—did she feel the truth press in. She didn't answer as she packed her things. Ava's words came back to her: So afraid of being your mother that you forget to be hers.

Markus Kenney picked up the mic stand as Kline wiped sweat from his face and drank from a water bottle.

"Thank you for such a great show," Markus said. "You've been a beautiful crowd. That concludes our live stream. We can't wait to see you all in Kansas City!"

The crowd cheered, but it died quickly. The cameras shut off. No one moved.

Not the production crew. Not the band. Not the fans.

They knew.

Encore.

A modest cheer rose from the small crowd. Dozens, not hundreds. But even they could feel it—something was still coming.

Markus didn't leave the stage. He looked to Kline. Gave him a nod. Then stepped back.

Kline moved to center.

"I sang that last song for a lot of reasons," he said, breath shallow.

"All my kings have fallen down. Fallen heroes feed the ground. And I appreciate the hell out of Aberdeen for letting Eddie and me sing one of our favorites. I know it wasn't an Aberdeen song, but it mattered to us."

Sure as shit it did, Clara thought. She glanced around, searching faces for recognition. Some got it. She wasn't sure she did.

Kings and heroes—but no mention of Lloyd Brannon. Which would've been expected. Maybe necessary. But Kline hadn't said his name.

What did that say?

He let it hang. The crowd murmured. They thought he meant Lloyd.

Maybe he did.

"How about one more?" he said.

The crowd's energy surged back. Kline smirked.

"This one's unreleased. By one of my heroes." He let them clap, then added, "A fallen hero." He looked around. "A different fallen hero."

Now they knew.

They still hoped.

Then Eddie began to play. A clean jazz riff—smug in its smoothness. Something you'd hear in a hotel lobby or the martini room of a slowly failing resort. It didn't fit. That was the point.

Clara froze.

She knew this game. She'd searched thousands of songs. Deep cuts. Covers. B-sides.

She couldn't place it.

Kline looked out at the crowd. "It's called 'Only Dying.'"

Oh. *Oh.*

Eddie ended the lounge riff, stomped his pedal, and turned to face Ben and Jose. A breath. Kline smiled, hands behind his back as he leaned towards the mic.

"Let us show you how we do it down in Bama."

Then, chaos.He dragged the strings through gravel. Jose hit. Ben locked in.

He opened with a confession that his life had ended the night she died. The last word snapped the air like a wet sheet in wind.

Eddie slid in on harmony. Kline answered alone, stretching the line until it scraped, every vowel a wound. He said it would not change anything now.

He followed with the only way out he could see. Eddie came back in. Their voices collided, not blended.

The crowd did not know what they were hearing. It was not Lloyd. It was not Aberdeen.

Markus dragged a stick down the chimes. Ben hit two notes. Dum dum. Jose added the kick-snare. Dum dum. Dum. Snap. Dum dum. Dum. Snap.

His snare cut against their pattern, leaving everything unmoored, off-kilter, like a séance disguised as a song.

Eddie launched into the solo. He stepped forward. Claimed it. Kline stepped back. He swayed. He let Eddie shine.

When the final note rang out, almost too late, Kline pulled the mic from its stand, leaned on Eddie's shoulder, and poured out the last plea: shattered and begging for help. Then he screamed the refrain about dying, again and again, until his voice cracked.

Silence.

No cheers. No clapping. Just a room full of people trying to understand what they had witnessed.

Kline stepped back toward the mic, quieter now. "Thank you for that moment. Scott and STP never performed that song live—and that's a shame. I like to think he's out there somewhere, hearing it now.

"Hearing someone sing the words he wrote but maybe couldn't face."

He let that sit.

"Sometimes," he said, voice thinning, "the hardest lyrics to sing... are the ones you put on paper."

Eddie turned toward him, just for a second. A breath hitched. A flash of something—not just recognition. Realization.

He's not talking about Scott.

Kline winked. Just once. Eddie saw it. Understood it.

Then it was gone.

Kilmore smirked. But when he turned to the others, their faces didn't show confusion or embarrassment—what he had been bracing for. What he hoped to see. Something he could explain to the VIPs.

They showed respect.

They showed vision.

Then the clapping started. Slow. Unsure.

But it built. It grew. Not loud—just real. Like a sound learning to believe itself.

Clara was compelled by that line. She wrote it down.

Sometimes the hardest lyrics to sing... are the ones you put on paper.

Kline woke to the rustling of a woman beside him. She smelled just as good as she had when he took her to bed at the end of the after-party. There had nearly been fights among the women—he didn't even know who to pick. By the end of the night, he wasn't sure he had to pick at all. Perhaps he shouldn't have picked anyone.

He felt almost guilty about it. Like he was taking advantage. But every time he turned one away, the look on their face told him the only thing he was doing wrong was saying no.

Eventually, he'd picked one.

He rolled over just in time to see the flash of a camera. She was already halfway out of bed, smiling into her phone.

Before he could say a word, she was pulling her panties back on. He watched her from the plush mattress of one of Eveningview's many too-lavish rooms, propped on an elbow.

"Hey," he said, struggling to remember her name. "Where are you going?"

She turned. There was something in her face he couldn't quite read. He rubbed his aching head.

"Not going. Leaving," she said, picking up her purse and heels.

"You're not coming back to bed? Maybe we could…"

"Nah. Got what I needed for the 'gram. Thanks, though. It was fun." She shrugged, stepping toward the door.

"Wait—that's it? Are you… a starfucker?"

Her laugh was cruel and honest.

"Sweetie, you gotta be a star to get starfucked."

She reached for the doorknob, then paused. Turned back.

"I'm sorry, I didn't mean it like that. Look—you're trending right now, okay? It wasn't just about the hits. I like you. We had fun. But…"

She trailed off as she shrugged. As if he should understand.

He could've followed her down a dozen different paths. But his brain locked on to one.

"But I'm no Lloyd Brannon?"

She must have thought he was joking. She dropped her shoulders.

Tilted her head.

"Baby, come on. You know what this is all about, right? You didn't really think…."

He didn't.

"Oh. You did," she said, sly smile on her face.

She saw it in his face—how lost he looked. Her expression scrunched up, hesitated, then—

"You mind if I tag you?"

He just stared at her.

Something hot bubbled in his chest.

"Fuck you, bitch."

He tore the covers off and launched himself out of bed, naked. For a second, even he didn't know what he was about to do. Then he froze, mid-step.

She watched him, expression unreadable. Calculating.

"This is the part where I run screaming, right?"

He stood there, bare, heaving.

She lifted her phone.

Snap.

"Told you that you were trending."

She turned and left him there, naked, and alone.

‡

"No, you did the right thing. That's on me—not making sure you had my number."

Aiesha kept her voice even, despite the string of curse words exploding from Kline's end of the call. White, sitting a few feet away with his coffee, could hear every single one. Kline couldn't have been more than a hundred yards away, still unraveling.

They'd been enjoying the morning cleanup when the woman breezed by—heels in hand, feet plodding on the tile, eyes forward, expression unreadable. She climbed into a rideshare and vanished. Nothing had seemed off. Until Kline found Aiesha's number. Then came the meltdown.

"Welcome to L.A., Kline," Aiesha said, rolling her eyes at White. "Look—I handled it. She's a small-timer. Easy-peasy."

It took her seconds to find the post. One report, one content violation. Suspended—for now. It'd pop back up eventually. She'd be ready.

"Yeah, I get it. Believe me. You've got to be more careful. Did you use protection?"

She waited.

"What do you mean 'you think you did'? Either you did or you didn't."

Beat.

"Did it come off?"

White sipped his coffee, face unreadable as Kline screamed through the speaker.

"I mean, I'd think you'd know. Did you come in her?"

Kline's voice cracked through loud enough to make White flinch. Aiesha pulled the phone away from her ear. She got more truth about him than she'd expected.

"Look, I know who she is. I'll handle it. Just give me time. We'll suppress it. Legal action if we must."

More yelling. She sighed.

"No, I get it. It's your body."

Even she couldn't believe she was saying that. To a man.

"Kline. Chill out. Let me do my job, okay?"

She waited for his nod and hung up.

"Jesus," she muttered. "You'd think I was the one fucking groupies."

She dropped the phone into her clutch.

"You got it under control?" White asked calmly.

"Yeah. But it's going to be a learning moment."

"Only if you let it be. If you handle everything for him, he never has to."

Aiesha set her porcelain cup down on the table. The same table where a million career decisions had been made—some fatal.

"I don't let men off the hook, Paul. Especially not for shit like this. But let's be honest—what did you expect? Or better yet, did you expect anything at all?"

White looked toward the ocean. Didn't answer.

"I didn't even have time to vet the VIP ticket buyers," she said. "No time to flag names. Not enough staff to filter the leeches. And that's exactly what they are."

She paused.

"Call it luck if you want, but his fixation with redheads saved us. There were at least six influencers here last night who would've wrecked him harder. We got out clean."

"You don't usually give grace," White said.

"No. I don't."

She studied him.

"You thought he'd fail."

He didn't answer. He didn't have to.

Aiesha leaned forward.

"Paul, I grew up in Memphis. Three 6 Mafia. Project Pat. That was my music world. This? Grunge? Heavy metal? Alt-rock? Whatever all of that even means." She shrugged but stared at him, and a long finger came his way.

"And I'm telling you—you've got something here. He's it. He's the voice."

White raised an eyebrow. She meant more than the voice. Or maybe that was his projection. Those two last songs were nukes wrapped into a teddy bear. He'd gotten an earful from Mike Kilmore, but Mike hadn't cared enough to look at lyrics when Kline had asked for the songs. White wish he had.

"He's going to be a disaster," he said. Even then, White realized that he was basing this on everything around Kline, not Kline himself, and certainly not about the music. Well, maybe the music, if Kline were truly sending messages coded in dead men's songs.

That one hit close to home.

But how could he? This was no Prince or Bowie. Reznor nor Keenan.

"Yeah. Like every man I've worked with. Always sticking their dick in crazy."

She didn't blink.

"And that's not giving him a pass, just so we're clear.

"He's raw. He's reckless, and who can blame him? He doesn't know how this will turn out. But you're not protecting him. You're measuring him against a dead man with unrealistic expectations. You're playing defense. He's not Lloyd. He's never going to be Lloyd. And that's the point. He's far more. Play offense."

A beat.

"He wants to push this. Past what Lloyd could. It's right there. I don't know what he's capable of, but he wants it. No matter what he says."

White said nothing. Aiesha thought about something she'd spent some time researching. Something she'd found odd and out of place but was sure it meant something. Turned out, it had made perfect sense.

"Have you even looked up the last songs he sang?" she asked.

"No." But Kilmore had explained, in detail.

"He told you everything you need to know by choosing them. Even without the vocals. You think he's here for a day trade—for clicks, for clout. That song, 'Pushing Forward Back,' was his message. So was, whatever that other song as. It's almost word for word an alliteration. Kline isn't dumb, and he isn't just smart. He's brilliant."

She stood. Adjusted her white dress.

"Do you have any idea what that other song was? What it's about? Its history? Its meaning?"

White looked up at her. He didn't know. She gave off a frustrated sigh.

"Look it up. Layers on layers. He sent you … all of you … a gift-wrapped message that told you *exactly* who he was and *exactly* where he was headed. And you didn't read it."

White studied her, confused. This was not her arena, and she seemed to know something he didn't. Truth was, he hadn't questioned the song, nor done much more than check it for political and ethical reasons.

"I guess that's really more my arena." She seemed to read his mind. "But I'm telling you, that was important, and you treated it as a passing fancy. Which it was not. And he'll learn from that, and I'm not sure I want him to learn about the industry that easily." Her disappointment hurt White.

"You think he's the next Lloyd?"

"No," she said. "I think he might be more."

He blinked.

"No. He's not prepared. He's not polished. But there's more to him than you're willing to admit. You saw a placeholder. A stand-in. That's not what he is." She pushed a finger into the coffee table before rummaging in her purse.

She painted her lips, dropped the tube back in her purse. She wasn't sure she believed that. She just knew that's what she'd expected.

"You talked to Clara yet?"

"Briefly."

"She's not as simple as you think. She saw it, too. That's why I brought her in."

Aiesha stepped around the table, leaned down to White's level.

"This man? He's the kind that moves mountains. Changes how we think about music. And he doesn't even know it yet."

"Why did you bring Clara up? What did she say?" White asked.

"They had a conversation, before the show. She said that she saw something in him that he doesn't even see in himself, but she's seen it before. She said it's terrifying." Aiesha watched White for a response, but he didn't know how to take it.

"Clara also said you should understand, if you listened to her at USC. That this guy is starving."

She straightened up and started to walk away.

"And she said that if you didn't get the reference, you were just as lost as the rest of the industry.

"Anyway, not going to get there on his own. And I don't mean Aberdeen. You. He won't get there without you. Choose sides. You know what I mean, and I don't say that lightly."

A pause. Her eyes cut into him.

"That's your job."

She walked out, heels clicking like a metronome.

Excerpt from "The Voice Was Never Theirs"
BY CLARA COWLEY

"Greg Holden didn't care about ghosts. Not really.

So, when Paul White pitched Kline Thomas to sing—pitched him not just as a tribute voice, but as the headliner—I imagine Greg didn't hear the risk.

Did he even know? What did he know?

What we do know is that White masterfully boxed in the Lloyd Brannon Foundation—and their answer was emphatically no. And who could blame them? Blame Misses Brannon?

But Aiesha Holt had just pulled off a miracle with the streaming show, and Holden couldn't argue with the return on investment.

For him, it was about momentum. And they had it. The specifics likely didn't matter to him anyway.

Because we know now what his motivations were all along: Extract as much profit from Aberdeen as possible—then cut them loose.

In that moment, he didn't see Kline Thomas as a man. He saw him as a headliner. A walking ROI who could make the numbers bulletproof for at least one more show.

He said yes.

Because dead men can't headline.

But echoes can."

NDA

22

Pacific Coast Records, Los Angeles, CA

"Make it quick, White. I really don't appreciate missing my stand-ing tee time," Greg Holden said from behind the expensive desk. Only the hallway lights of the PCR building were on. Holden cut the end of the cigar that he'd just fished out.

"I wanted to discuss the results from last night, and I hope you might reconsider some things." White got straight to the point.

Holden lit up the cigar with a butane torch and sat back in the plush chair. He rested his hands on the top of his bulbous stomach. White braced himself for the possibility that Holden or the voice on the other end had picked up on what transpired an hour or so ago. Neither said anything. Aiesha had done her job, but he knew she would. It would come out, but if it happened later, rather than right now, that was a positive.

"I've seen the results. And I am impressed. It was a healthy return on our investment. You're welcome," Holden answered. White tried not to grimace. PCR had written the checks, but it was Aiesha who had brought in the money from sponsors. White took a step forward towards the desk, the conference speaker.

"And the Lloyd Brannon Foundation, Miss Brannon?"

She didn't answer at first.

"There was a noticeable uptick in ticket sales." That was all the voice would offer.

He couldn't say he was surprised, nor could he blame her for keeping it simple and to the point. They'd exchanged texts and agreed that they would be limited in what they said in front of Holden. White was not proud of what he was about to do, what he had already done. But he'd spent all last night and into the early morning deep in thought after he'd pored over the initial data Aiesha had sent him. But it wasn't the data that had convinced him. It was what he'd seen and heard with his own eyes and ears.

"I'm going to suggest we add Aberdeen to the benefit concert bill … with Kline and Eddie participating."

"No fucking way," the widow's voice came through. White had expected a visceral response from her, but not like that. She was so calm and professional. Holden seemed confused at her response, but only initially. Holden would guess why she didn't want this, but it was not the right reason. Being as confident in his own intelligence as he was, he didn't second-guess his assumption. He just didn't know the truth.

She just doesn't want to see her husband replaced.

"The band is meeting and discussing, right now. And you certainly have a vote." White crossed his arms and stared at the speaker.

"I vote no."

"Noted. And may I remind you that you are a silent partner, and you are under very specific requirements under the NDA and your own contract that you designed and signed to not interfere. You have your vote. You have cast it. Under no circumstance can you discuss it with anyone."

She said nothing. There was nothing she could say. White was glad he wasn't in this very room with her, but he knew a phone call would be coming soon.

"It's my show," she finally said.

"Our show," Holden corrected. "All of the other stuff, your auctions and your dinners, you can do whatever you want. But they are still my band, and I am financing the vast majority of this show. And if White says they can play and they want to play, then I am going to squeeze every fucking dollar out of this money pit I can." He spoke emphatically, which was exactly what White had expected and planned from the man. Holden looked up at White. White kept the mask in place.

"Assuming the vote is yes, which it better be if they want to cut this record and get out of my shithouse, then my requirement is that they play some smaller venues first. With real fans.

I don't need these two amateurs melting down in KC in front of sixty-thousand-plus."

White nodded. That was already handled. Had been. It just wasn't in Holden's arena. "Done."

"And, in the meantime, recall I did what you asked and rented Eveningview for you to record. You get a little bit of leash for last night's ROI. But not much. Sign them. Don't sign them. I don't care. Comes from your end, though. Get their ass in there and make some fucking music." White assumed he meant Kline and Eddie, and he also noticed Holden didn't say "good music." That said a lot. Perhaps everything that the head of PCR was thinking had been conveyed in just that one sentence. Holden dismissed him.

White already had his phone in his hand when it started ringing. He was barely out the door of the building. Paul could visualize her counting down how long it would take him to be out of earshot of anyone.

"You fucking set me up," she said simply and emphatically. White opened the door to his car and transferred it to hands-free.

"I did, Miss Brannon. And I am sorry about that. It's not my way. But I thought it for the best. For all of us." He meant it, even though he knew that she would not agree. White knew that he could be wrong, but he was desperate.

"I assume that you already knew how the vote would go?" She had calmed and was right back to being the businesswoman he knew she was.

"Honestly, I don't. Kilmore is a no, I assume. He's been pretty clear on his plotting and scheming. Ben set this all up, and I don't think he's seen anything that would change things. You know Jose is going to go with Ben. Markus? He's the wild card."

White heard her sigh.

"You know how this ends, Paul."

"If it ends, that means something began. We're all in this together. Me, you, your foundation, and the band. Your foundation may hang on for a while, but it's still tied to Lloyd's music and this contract, one way or another."

"You really believe in him, don't you?" she asked.

"I don't know if I'd go that far. The shows are one thing. Laying down a new album is something else, entirely. What I will say is, we'll know soon. But, to answer your question: do I believe in him? I'm not sold. Do I believe in his voice? I don't think there's anyone that could say no," White answered. He wanted to ask her so much more.

"What would Lloyd say?" she asked, and it caused him pause as he turned out of the parking lot and validated his parking ticket. She'd said it so fast that she couldn't have possibly thought it through. She may have known Lloyd better than everyone else, but her judgement was clouded. White couldn't blame her.

"I think, if Lloyd were here and knew everything, he'd say Kline deserves a chance for redemption, even with his own legacy at stake. That's the kind of thoughtful, forgiving, and kind man Lloyd Brannon was. He believed in art. In music. Does Kline deserve it? Time will tell."

"Indeed, it will. Best of luck with that." She hung up.

⋮

"No? Why?" Cantrell didn't hide his frustration. He expected pushback from Kilmore—just not this blunt, not this bold. Still, if Mike wanted to be that forward, fine. Let him defend it.

Kilmore leaned back; arms crossed. "Explaining my vote wasn't part of the deal."

"We're all in agreement—except you," Cantrell shot back, gesturing to Madera and Kenney. "You owe us an explanation."

Kilmore was surprised by Cantrell's bite. "I shouldn't have to explain myself beyond saying no. But if you're going to make a thing of it..." He exhaled. "Fine. Let's talk about it."

Madera gave a small nod as he crossed his dark, tattooed, and muscular arms with the Hispanic hue. "Please do."

Kilmore leaned forward. "Eddie? He's not built for this. He's got a family, a full life outside of this circus. Two weeks into a ten-show tour and he's homesick, then what?"

"Valid," Cantrell conceded. "But they're not a package deal. And Kline wants to be here. That counts for something."

Kilmore didn't blink. "You ever ask yourself *why* he wants this so badly?"

Cantrell's voice dripped sarcasm. "Gee, I don't know—fame? Money? Chicks? Groundbreaking stuff."

Kilmore smirked. "Get to the point," Madera snapped.

Instead, Kilmore rose and made his way to the bar. He mixed a drink methodically, the click of the stirrer loud in the quiet room. Took as much time as he could dare. The air thickened with smoke as he exhaled a long drag.

"I did some digging." His voice was calm. Controlled.

Cantrell scoffed. "You hired someone? A private investigator?"

"I asked questions. Pulled threads. This isn't just some bar gig. If we bring him in, he becomes the face of Aberdeen. That means something. Especially with our standing at the label."

They listened, despite themselves. The truth was, Kilmore wasn't wrong about *that*.

"Kline's got baggage," Kilmore said finally. "Recent. Messy. Tied to us in ways you don't want to unpack."

Cantrell pointed a finger. "Bullshit. Everyone in this business has dirt—including you. You've had more tabloid ink than the rest of us combined."

Kilmore shrugged. "Exactly. Look what it's done to me. We don't need more."

None of them knew exactly what that meant. It was common knowledge that he had some failed ventures, but over their lifetime earnings? Drops in the bucket. Kenney spoke up, voice even. "We're talking about a benefit show. One night. Guest set. No strings. If it works, we talk next steps. If it doesn't, no harm done."

Kilmore stared at him, then at the others. The vote was clear.

He took a long sip and gave a wry smile. "Suit yourselves. Just remember this moment."

He didn't push further. Not now. There would be other moments. Funny how small the world really was, sometimes. Cantrell noted that there was more there. Kilmore knew something, and he needed to know for himself. Ben stood.

"I'll make the call."

$$\vdots$$

"That was quick," Kline said, voice flat over the line.

"This wasn't a murder trial," Cantrell replied with a chuckle. Then he shifted. "The vote's yes. But we need to talk."

"We? Or do I need to grab Eddie?"

"Just you and me. Eddie can join later."

Kline hesitated. Odd. Why not just say it now? Still, he had a promise to keep. "I'm heading to a bar near the hotel. Someone owes me a drink. I'll send you the address."

"Someone?"

"Not like that," Kline muttered, already cracking open a fresh beer. "Just a promise."

⁚

Thirty minutes later, Cantrell ducked into the beachside bar. Classic spot. Familiar. He didn't see Kline, so he took a stool near the door and ordered a beer. The bartender gave him a look like she might've seen him before. He ignored it.

"Interesting spot for a summit," Kline said, materializing beside him.

Ben smirked. "Figured you'd want privacy. Being the new star and all."

Kline grunted, nodding toward the bar. "That's the woman I told you about. Haven't talked to her yet."

"You work fast." Kline frowned at this, considering what had just transpired between he and the want-to be-influencer.

"She offered a drink. I keep my promises."

They found a quiet table. Kline leaned back, arms crossed, eyes scanning the room.

Ben got to it. "If we're going to do this, I need to know more about you. Not just your voice."

Kline didn't move. "You voted yes."

"I voted on your commodity as a singer and performer. But that alone isn't enough."

"But Kilmore didn't," Kline said flatly.

Ben didn't answer.

"Because he wants the job."

Ben didn't deny it. "I came alone because four-on-two feels like an ambush."

Kline nodded. He already knew. Let him talk.

"We're a family, Kline. Dysfunctional as hell, sure—but family. And we've had our power struggles. Now we're trying to fill a void we never expected to have. Lloyd was the guy. Made the calls. Wrote the songs. Fronted the band. And now he's gone."

"So, who fills the void?" Kline asked.

Ben didn't answer.

Instead: "Can you write?"

"Plenty. No clue if it's good," Kline said, honestly.

He didn't elaborate—but the truth ran deeper.

His notebooks were full. Lyrics scribbled for years. Margins scrawled with edits. Riffs penciled in the corners. Most of the songs had been born in isolation—during lockdown, during hangovers, during nights too silent to bear. All of it shaped inside a small, self-built studio wedged into a cluttered guest room. A beat-up mic. A salvaged interface. Acoustic foam duct-taped to the walls.

No one knew about it.

Not even Eddie.

He'd wired it himself. Taught himself the DAW. Sang them. Sampled every instrument. Arranged the songs.

Performed them—for no one. No one except Destin.

Because it was his. And no one else's.

It was never meant to be heard. That would make it real. He didn't believe in a future—not really. And he didn't want the echoes of his soul reaching anyone else's ears.

In those notebooks—those pages—was everything he felt about himself.

It triggered a memory, mostly because not all of that was true. Someone had heard them.

A woman in his bed—emotionally battered, grateful. She'd reached for him, wanting to offer comfort. Needing it in return. Needing *him*.

Instead, she found a notebook pressed to his chest.

He gripped it in his sleep. Tight. Like it was sacred. Like it meant more than she ever could.

He'd never been able to explain why.

And now it was too late.

Ben finished his drink.

"So, I ask again. Can you take all that shit—the pain, the weight—everything on your chest and make something out of it?"

Kline didn't flinch. Just stared back.

"That's the only reason I'm still here."

Even as he said it, something twisted inside him.

He knew what came next. He'd have to use the lyrics. The real ones. The ones buried in that notebook. The ones he never meant to share.

Suddenly, there was another level of pressure—one he hadn't admitted until now.

He had a choice: Write more. Or hand it over.

He wasn't sure which was worse. Or what going back to that place might do to him.

Later, as the sun dipped low, Kline thanked the bartender and promised to return. Said the bracelet she'd given him had brought him luck. He tried to return it and she'd refused. Told him to keep it, for now.

Out back, the bartender pulled her vape and made a call.

"He's ignoring me, Ava. Came in, sat down with Cantrell, and barely looked at me. I brought the damn beer. That's it. Like I'm some common bar wench."

"But he came," Ava said. "That's something. Might have something to do with getting slut-shamed on Instagram his first night on the job. You think he's in?"

She thought about it. Answered the last.

"Yeah. Said my bracelet brought him good luck, on his way out the door. Tried to return it. Must have gotten good news." They'd watched the live stream together, last night, after their gig. Aberdeen would be fools not to let him join. They'd also be fools not to know he wanted to change direction. She wondered if they'd caught that, yet. No. Why would mighty Aberdeen ever think someone would change them?

"Then we've got time," Ava said. "He's in. Now try harder. Be more forward. He's obviously willing. Maybe not today, but men are quick to forget when it comes to sex. He'll get over that situation fast enough and be on the prowl and you will be there to box him in."

She hung up. Rayne exhaled smoke into the ocean air, already replaying everything she *should* have said. The things she wanted to say about using her body, even if it did produce a meaningful result. In the end, what was the difference?

⁝

Eddie was sitting in the living room of Eveningview, simply in awe that he was playing guitar inside the hallowed mansion. Playing

Aberdeen. In Eveningview. He strummed some more, trying to come up with more rhythm riffs for their classics. Wrote down chord progressions. Kilmore would have to okay them, surely. Or would it be Kline? Eddie wasn't sure, but he there was unease in his soul at what was obviously brewing between the two of them. It hadn't just started on their song selection. It had started the moment the limo door had opened.

Eddie found himself mindlessly strumming, now as his mind wandered. Some of the excitement began to ebb as realities set in. He set the guitar down, looked out of the floor to ceiling windows at the ocean. His phone began ringing.

"Hey, baby! Sorry I was so short with you last night. I was exhausted."

"I can imagine. The energy was palpable, even through the TV. I bet you were wore slap out," Chandra replied.

"Incredible experience. Just. Incredible."

"You sounded great. You and Kline change the sound so much."

"For the better, I hope." Eddie paced the room, waiting.

"You know it does. And you played great, especially with how little time you had to prepare."

Eddie hesitated. "So... I have some news."

"I'm all ears, sweetheart."

"They've asked us to stay. For now, at least. There's a benefit concert in Kansas City—for Lloyd Brannon."

She didn't answer immediately.

"When is it?"

"September twenty-fourth." He winced, bracing.

"That's like... another three weeks, baby." Her tone was calm, but it hit.

"I know. But we're getting paid. I just don't know how much yet."

"So, what? You're going to take leave without pay? Ed, you don't have that kind of cushion. They might just fire you. Then what?"

He didn't have an answer, not a real one. "Kline says he has work taken care of. I didn't ask questions. The KC show is going to be big. More than worth it. We're doing a few small shows, too. There's income coming. "

"Like the gigs you play here?" she asked dryly. She didn't ask how Kline was taking care of work. It sounded a lot like Kline was all-in, no matter what. He wasn't coming home. She knew her husband and whether Kline was telling the truth, he'd listen. What about insurance? Once again, she didn't want to be the pragmatist in such a big moment, as much as she wanted to. It just seemed so unrealistic.

"No, it's different. Bigger. They want us in the studio, Chandra. They want to make an album."

"And how's that going to work if you're not even officially in the band?"

"I don't know yet. I'll find out. We're meeting for paperwork. There are contingencies, I'm sure. I read over the boilerplate stuff for when we first got here. I'm sure we are covered. Nothing would tell me otherwise."

Silence. Then a sigh. He could picture her rubbing her forehead.

"I told you I would support you, and if you think this is the right move, then it's the right move. But don't let the excitement of last night skew your emotions and rule your logic. If you think that this is real and lucrative, go for it."

"I will. I believe the offer's going to be solid. Even if I come back afterward, it'll be worth it. Hell, it already is. With the job Aiesha—"

"Wait. Who? With a name like that? I don't need another queen prowling" she cut in.

Eddie grinned. "She's the publicist. Look her up when you get time—she's the reason we've got a real online presence now. We won't be playing for six-packs anymore, even if I came home today. She works for us. Not just Aberdeen." There were some semantics there, since she was on retainer, but Eddie didn't want to open the door of uncertainty.

"Speaking of which, have you even reached out to the rest of your band?"

That stopped him. Shit. He hadn't.

"Not yet. But I will. Soon."

He softened. "What about you and the baby? I'll try to come home for a few days. I'm sure White would understand."

"We'll be fine. But yes, you should come back—even for a short while. Put your affairs in order. And make sure Kline does, too. But I doubt he will. You need to see to it."

Eddie frowned. He knew exactly what she meant. He hadn't heard from Kline all day.

"I will. I promise. I love you. You're the best."

"I know. Now handle your business. And don't forget to call me tonight."

Excerpt from "The Voice Was Never Theirs"
BY CLARA COWLEY

"Paul White always said "Denied" wasn't just Lloyd's best song. It was the one that mattered most. Boy, is that an understatement.

I know he says it from a place of love-for Lloyd, for his legacy. And truthfully, it is one of the most beautifully, brutally written songs I've ever heard. But we've only heard it with Kline's voice. Not Lloyd's. What a shocking thing to consider, all things known.

Paul White struggled with turning that creativity over to Kline—a man he barely knew and somehow knew all too well. He knew what that song meant. To both.

He'd held on to "Denied" for Lloyd as long as he could. Lloyd had told him he'd know when the time was right.

But was that time right? I can't see how it was.

And yet—I understand why White leveraged it. From a professional standpoint, it made perfect strategic sense. Everything had gone exactly the way he and Aiesha had hoped. The numbers were up. The myth was working. There was reason to believe it could keep working.

But I don't write this as a strategist. I write it as an outsider. And, yes, some of this may be revisionist history.

Still—I'll say it clearly: That song should never have seen the light of day. My feelings on this are well known. As is the conversation I had with White, while Kline was baring his soul onstage to sing it.

I'll never forgive White for that. And neither should anyone else.

You can argue that every step leading to this point may have been unavoidable. But not this one. This one was a choice.

This was the step that everyone should look back on and say: That simply should never have happened.

And these people are assholes for what they did to Kline.

While Kline and Eddie were signing their contract? A dream realized for Eddie and escaping a past for Kline—Paul White handed them a sealed envelope.

And inside it was the song that would seal their fate."

business card

23

Pacific Coast Records, Los Angeles, CA

"It's a standard deal for you two, replacing a band member. This is what you get, if the show is a success. This"—he referenced the much smaller contract—"is a one-show deal worth ten thousand, each." It was less than they'd hoped for, by about a third. Eddie frowned, knowing he'd have to explain that shortcoming to Chandra. It wasn't the three months' salary he'd hoped for. It wasn't even one. But, it gave them insurance, at least temporarily. Eddie had given a sigh of relief. At least that would be good news to give to Chandra.

Kline and Eddie met with White and Holden alone, with the other band members in an adjoining room of Pacific Coast Records. White had wanted to use his own office, but Holden wanted to size the two up, though he remained mostly silent. The reality had set in that Eddie wasn't going back to work and that felt odd. This didn't feel like a job, and he'd always had one, one way or another. It was weird to just quit, but Kline said he'd taken care of it. No one had reached out to Eddie.

"Just to make sure I understand, each of the other members get roughly two to our one, in pretty much every circumstance." Kline never looked up from the set of contracts set before them.

"It's very generous, considering your lack of experience in the industry. They have decades of proven work and success. You two represent significant risk, and that is represented here." Holden's words were sharp and his eyes were hard, unflinching. White adjusted his spectacles, watching their response.

"Of course, you have the potential of song and album credits, which is extremely lucrative, if you pursue that. You already have a head start on that." White softened the moment. Kline assumed White referenced Kline's notebook of lyrics. Kline's eyes narrowed.

"The selection of those songs are not really up to us," Eddie pointed out. Eddie looked to White, then to Holden, who smiled the smile of someone who had been through this thousands of times.

"That's correct. I understand your hesitancy on that. If it's a good song, they aren't going to veto it. It's counterproductive." White shot a look towards the closed door of the label's main office. That was *mostly* true.

"The likelihood of them turning down songs is low." White looked at Eddie, then to Kline, who wore questions on his visage.

White leaned towards the two. He understood their cautiousness. Holden sat forward and ashed his cigar.

"If they coulda wrote, they woulda wrote. And you just let me know if they start turning down any good songs." Holden's voice cut like a knife, even through his chubby smile that munched on a cigar.

White could sense some hesitancy in the two men, who just stared at the two stacks of papers.

"People don't like managers and agents. It's natural, and I completely understand. You don't know me. You know I've represented their interests for decades, and you aren't sure to whom my priorities lie. What I want to be paramount in your minds is, if you sign this, I represent your interests just as much as theirs. Greg and I want you to be successful. We both have skin in the game." That lightened the look on Kline's face. White plowed on.

"Now, between now and the show, things get tricky. Because of the existing contract for the next album, you won't be nearly as compensated as any additional, future ones. The two of you are not obligated to do anything, other than rehearse and do the show. But, if you do and don't join the band, the label wouldn't be obligated to pay you for your work, other than as contractors at a reduced rate." White side-eyed Holden, who looked smug.

The label really has them over a barrel. Us, too. At least for now, Eddie realized.

White swept his hands across the contracts. He peered from over his glasses, gauging the two men.

White referenced the number: a quarter-million dollars. He wondered if they'd read the clause—understood the structure. The bonus wasn't free money. It was an advance against royalties, recoupable at source. Until the full amount was recovered, every dime the band earned from streams, sales, and syncs would go to the label. Only then would their royalty rate revert to the standard backend.

Holden didn't know what these guys made back in Alabama, but he knew this: most artists signed deals like this thinking they were getting paid. They weren't. They were getting leveraged. And if the record flopped? They'd owe the label and have nothing left to show for it—except maybe a few photos and an anecdote about how close they almost came.

"This show? What are we obligated to do?" They pretty much knew, but Kline wanted to hear them say it.

"Most of the show is other bands paying tribute. You perform a few songs"—White looked up to gauge them," and at the end, you unveil a new song. One that Lloyd wrote before his death."

This was news to Eddie and Kline. There was something in White's eyes and the look that Holden gave him that said White had been holding this song's secret and waiting until the perfect time. Or for when he had no other options. The fidgeting from the stalwart White told them that this song had a story.

"If things work out, you work on releasing an album that the band is already on the books to produce. All those details for the financials are in there." Eddie picked up the contract and pretended to read it.

"Does this mean that Lloyd will still get royalties? Even if we do the work?" Eddie asked.

"Well, his estate will, something he changed before his death and threw a kink into things." That caused some eyebrows to go up, but the two men decided not to ask about that, right now. There had been whispers.

"Now, hold on. That doesn't seem right…" Kline began. Holden looked to White, knowing the history on this one. White sighed and adjusted his glasses.

"It can't be helped," was all he was willing to say.

"Well, that's kinda bullshit," Eddie said flatly. Holden laughed. He agreed. Kline's thoughts were elsewhere.

"Assuming this song is any good. It's the first I've heard of it." Kline crossed his arms and pushed back from the shiny black table.

White slid something out from a notebook. An envelope. It was still sealed, and Lloyd's handwriting was on it. A chill filled the room. A dead man wanted to speak. It sat on the table, but White wouldn't lift his hand off it.

"Lloyd's last lyrics. It's good. Great, even. I hope someone can do it justice, somehow." A lie. A bluff. He'd never read it. Couldn't bring himself to do it, especially because the words that were written had been addressed solely to White. It read: *You'll know the time. But the time is not right now. -LB*

As Kline tried to take it, White instinctively snatched back Lloyd's last artistic expression. A secret that had been entrusted to only him, years before. White could remember the conversation as if it were yesterday and the pain in Lloyd's eyes knowing the greatest song he'd ever written was one he knew he could never perform. And now he found himself about to hand it to Kline Thomas, of all people, to express his final thoughts.

He wasn't letting anyone see it until Kline proved good on his word that he could write. First his song. Then?

"Not now. Not here," White said simply and stashed it. Kline didn't fight him on it. Holden, shockingly and almost respectfully, said nothing.

White still couldn't believe he'd revealed this. But somehow it felt right, even though he'd one day pay for this moment, if things worked out the way he hoped. It had also been a carrot on the stick that he needed for Holden, and the man was practically salivating at its potential. White looked to Holden, and the label man's eyes told him what White hoped they'd say. The thought of a last Lloyd Brannon song had tremendous financial opportunity that might buy some good will, if he played his cards right. White turned to Kline.

Filling the shoes of a giant. I don't envy you. White wouldn't want that pressure, yet he recalled what he'd seen just days before. Kline set it down carefully, reverently.

"Guess we have some work to do," Kline finally spoke.

As they signed, the rest of the band clapped and cheered. Eddie would spend an hour watching the social media posts from the band's official account announcing their performance with the band at the upcoming show. Aiesha was on the ball, as always. Eddie would beam with pride when he called his wife and told her that they were going to be at least ten thousand dollars richer for one night's worth of work.

Kline, however, would spend the rest of the night in his hotel drinking and fussing over a notebook page, suddenly overcome with pressure. Pressure that wasn't even upon him yet. His eyes went to the stack of notebooks on the corner table. They called to him. He pretended not to hear them. This new one that was already missing pages that lay wadded up on the floor. Eventually, he would take a sleeping pill, finish the sixth bottle of beer, and pass out on the couch of his hotel room.

Excerpt from "The Voice Was Never Theirs"
BY CLARA COWLEY

"When Kline invited Rayne Harlow to rehearsals, it didn't feel like a gesture. It felt like a test.

Not for her. For him.

And she'd been waiting on that moment.

See, for weeks, the trap had been carefully laid—but Kline never walked into it. Not because he was deft, but because his mind had been anywhere and everywhere else—especially not on women.

Not after what happened to him after the streaming show.

I always found it interesting that nothing ever came of that. Was Kline embarrassed? Shamed?

Maybe he just didn't want to let his guard down again. As far as I know, he never brought it up again.

No, Kline did what he always did: internalized it.

And I can't imagine what that must've felt like. His sense of self-worth was already eroding under the weight of the role he'd been forced to fill. From that perspective, it made sense why he avoided Rayne entirely.

I remember watching them in the rehearsal room—Rayne with her feet planted like defiance

and Kline pretending she wasn't there.
Not out of spite. Out of what he thought
was duty to the band.

There's a belief in music—especially
rock—that the best collaborations come
from chemistry. But this wasn't chemistry.
Not yet.

Rayne had watched the industry build
a golden staircase for men like Kline and
dig a grave for women like her. This wasn't
a meeting. It was a collision. And it was
nearly silent.

Two troubled souls, standing in a driveway,
talking for the first time. Really talking.

Rayne doesn't remember much of what was
said. Just that she issued a test. Who she was.
What she did. And Kline passed it.

That was her first mistake. Because it
turned him into a person—not a commodity.
Not a man she wanted to manipulate and hate."

24

Moonshadows, Malibu, CA

They ducked into a beach front bar on the Pacific Coast Highway each trip in the late afternoon. Eddie had taken the early flight from Huntsville International to LAX after spending the weekend with his family. Although White would complain that he could have sent a car or at least hired a rideshare to pick Eddie up, Kline had volunteered to pick up his best friend.

Truth was, Kline was lonely and missed his best friend. Between not having friends and feeling the pressure of producing music, Kline had spent the weekend shut in his new apartment that White had set up for him. Eddie had been perfectly happy just staying in his hotel room until he had a firmer grasp on things. At least, that's what he had said. Kline surmised that Eddie needed to see what Chandra wanted to do this weekend. Apparently, she had passed, at least for now, on coming to LA. Until that changed, Eddie wasn't ready to commit to anything.

Kline had inquired on how his family was, how Chandra was handling the change. Eddie had simply answered that she was dealing. Kline didn't ask him to explain. From the way Eddie had answered, he could tell that there might have been some second-guessing going on. The fact that she hadn't come counterpointed that firmly. He wanted to ask Eddie more, but Eddie had been short about it, as if he didn't want to discuss it in any more depth.

"What did you get into this weekend?" Eddie asked as they neared the bar they'd stopped at a few times. Eddie found himself grinning. He knew exactly why Kline kept coming here.

"Focused on the music, mostly. Did some writing. We did play with some songs but didn't get much done." Kline didn't have the heart to tell him that he'd drunk himself stupid, all alone, every single night. The rest was true, however.

"That's boring." Kline didn't refute that.

"You still coasting on leave?" Eddie asked.

"Yeah, but they're starting to ask questions. You?"

"Same," Eddie answered. Management knew something was up, but it was their leave to burn.

"How did the band take it?" Kline asked while Eddie surveyed the coast as cars whizzed by on the other side.

"Honestly, they were very happy and excited for us. I told them that if things didn't work out, the work Aiesha had done was really going to help us. I told them that we might start working on some originals." Kline turned to the passenger side and scowled.

"Of course, that's totally up to you," Eddie held his hands out, defensive. Kline turned back to the road, lifted a beer from the cupholder, and took a sip. Eddie followed suit.

It did bother the band that Kline hadn't said anything to them himself. But they understood the situation and had said as much. They knew that Kline had the talent to take it to the next level and were frankly surprised it had taken him this long. They also reminded him of how good a friend Kline had been to get him involved.

"Thanks for having some cold ones ready. Needed that, after the flight."

"Of course, man." Kline tilted the beer and set it back in the console. They drove in comfortable silence. Eventually, Kline spoke something that had been weighing on him.

"I know this must be stressful for you, having a family in the balance. I think about that more than you realize. I think about it all the time. One of the reasons I stayed in the apartment this weekend was because I have all this pressure on me to make good by you and Chandra." Kline turned to Eddie, and Eddie could see just how much his friend meant it.

"Some of it is for the music. Hell, maybe most of it. But I also don't want to do something stupid and fuck it all up. Can't do that from an apartment." It pained Eddie to see Kline's concern with himself and his knowledge of his own self-destructive tendences. It hurt even more that Kline wasn't thinking of himself. Kline was thinking of him and his family. But what did he really want? Why was he here?

"It's all gonna work out, man. Even if it doesn't work out like we hope, who can say that they've gotten to do the things we've done? The things we'll get to do? We only live once, man." Eddie's head bobbed as he took another sip of beer.

"I appreciate it more than you know. Thank you. But this is about us. That means you, too." Kline nodded. He hit the turn signal and pulled into the parking lot.

They ordered a set of craft beers, which the familiar female bartender brought back quickly. There were patrons sitting in various booths and tables of the upscale, open-air bar, but the dining room was empty and waiting for the rush. The air was thick with sea salt, but the sound of the waves was muffled by the traffic.

The two watched the ocean roll its timeless dance, the sun starting to dip close to the horizon.

"Well, hey, guys! Long time no see. What's new with you today?"

"Hey, Cherie. Just picked this fool up at the airport. Headed to work." Eddie was almost giggling that his friend refused to let on why Kline had brought him here.

Cherie smiled at him, waited for him to say more. She played the game. When he didn't, she started to walk away. Kline fumbled with words but eventually found them.

"You doing okay, Cherie? How's your day going?" Kline fumbled over his words, almost desperate to get her to turn around as she walked away. Cherie stopped, cocked her head to the side, like a dog hearing words she couldn't understand but knew they meant something. Aside from directly answering any questions she had, he never really asked her anything.

This is a change, she thought. He was finally engaging, which meant it was time for Cherie to go to work. Do her job.

"Oh, you know. Grinding away?"

"Know all about that," Kline answered, tiredness in his voice.

"Where ya headed for work?" She knew the answer, but she had to start somewhere.

God, this is going to take forever, but at least it's progress, she thought.

"Into Malibu," Eddie answered. Kline drummed his fingers on the bar, slightly rocking along with the rhythm of the ocean. She nodded and smiled. Inside, she was glad Kline didn't hear the exchange. He might recall her slip up in the airport when she, stupidly, admitted that she knew why they were there. Kline didn't catch it then. He didn't catch it now.

"No one works in Malibu, didn't you know?" She raised a thinly drawn eyebrow, which brought a smile to Kline's face, one that Eddie hadn't seen in a while.

"You work in Malibu," Kline offered as he smiled.

He had such nice teeth, she thought. And, truly a beautiful smile, when he gave it. Kline was thinking the same about her. Even with braces. But the colors weren't just cute. It gave her personality.

"Oh, this? This isn't work. It isn't too bad. Dealing with rowdy customers later at night, but not too bad. Assholes gonna be assholes, ya know? Nicer the suit, worse they are. So, you guys must be okay." She eyed the two of them, hands on her wide hips. Her waist was thin, and she looked like a bodybuilder of some sort.

If I had those thighs, I'd show them off too, Eddie thought to himself. The sight hadn't escaped Kline, he noticed.

Eddie watched Kline watching her.

Her screen-printed shirt was sleeveless, and it was only then that Eddie noticed the logo. It was colorful, but not nearly as colorful as her eyes. Her arms were chiseled, not overly muscled, but obvious. The shirt had been torn from the neck down below her cleavage, showing the sun-kissed skin of her small, freckled breasts. Hazel eyes with yellow flecks around the edges, a hoop nose ring. Multiple tattoos that peeked from the skirt, both out from the waistline and from the edges of where it ended above her muscle-knotted thighs. He couldn't look away.

"I'm gonna make a guess that you guys don't cut grass or swing a hammer." All of this she said as if she already knew, Eddie thought. Her hazel eyes darted from one to the other, but they held knowledge that betrayed her words.

"You cut me to the quick, lady. These hands have hammered many a nail," Eddie quipped, faking hurt. She laughed, ran a hand through her auburn hair, and surveyed the room.

As she turned away to retrieve something, Kline surveyed her. She was slightly taller than he was, but so were most women. Her short hair bobbed as she walked. Kline watched her go, intently. When she was out of earshot, Eddie leaned close.

"Did you see her shirt?" Eddie asked.

"No, was I supposed to?" Kline responded, almost joking. Truth being told, that was the last thing about her that he was looking at. She was striking.

Why hadn't I noticed?

"It's an Aberdeen shirt," Eddie said and jabbed a long finger at her back as she walked away.

"So?"

"*So?* We *are* Aberdeen. You are the lead singer for Aberdeen, remember?" Eddie chided him and guffawed.

"For now. And?"

"And? She's a smoke show and you're a single rockstar? Why am I having to explain this to you?" Kline started to explain how his run in had put sex on the backburner. Or maybe it was all the other things. Eddie knew about the situation, vaguely. He'd laughed about it. Seemed stupid to him. Yet, he hadn't lived it and Kline had.

"I doubt she knows that. Besides, we aren't *her* Aberdeen. She probably doesn't know who we are."

"That's the point, jackass. Tell her. When are you going to go for it? You aren't fooling anyone, man. She's the reason we even come here, and when you met her, she was all you talked about for the entire ride." Not necessarily true.

Cherie started to return, and Eddie hushed. She carried two beers and set them in front of the two men. Kline chewed his lip right until Eddie elbowed him in the ribs and mouthed "go for it."

"I told you I'd buy you a beer, but you've barely spoken to me. I was starting to think you didn't like me or something. But why you kept coming? I couldn't guess. The food ain't that good."

"Huh. Well, I don't know what to say," Kline defended himself by her directness.

"You can say thanks. And you can tell me why you've done little more than wave at me every time you've come by." Kline smiled back at her, a glimmer in his eye, which Eddie hadn't seen in so long. And there was a confidence in the air about him.

"I'm sorry about that, Cherie. From the bottom of my heart. Just been under a lot of pressure. If we haven't been talking about work, I've not really wanted to talk at all." There was truth in it, but not the truth she thought of, about that influencer. That woman likely fucked up her chances, at least for a while. Put him on his guard for women just like her. Yet here he was. He's willing and vulnerable, Cherie reminded herself. At the same time, Rayne felt for him. She pushed that away.

"Oh, good. I was starting to think I was ugly or something because typically when a woman offers to buy you a beer, it means she's interested in you. And you've shown no interest in anything except buying beer. Seemed to be a clear sign of disinterest." She winked, drummed her hands on the counter when another patron beckoned her, so she left them alone for a second.

"Well. Isn't this a new development? Speechless Kline. Nothin' to say?"

Eddie elbowed Kline and gave him a toothy grin.

She returned—leaning in close, invading just enough of Kline's space to rattle him. His discomfort poured off him like sweat. He leaned away. She smiled.

She was testing him.

Her long eyelashes batted deliberately in front of hazel eyes flecked with something curious, unreadable. Her scent lingered, soft and sweet.

Muted, almost quiet, an Incubus track played low in the background. It was "Echo." She waited for the verse that lingered on eyes and light. When it hit, Cherie tilted her head and met his gaze, lashes fluttering. He held it for a beat, then looked away.

"So, hey. Uh… like your shirt. An Aberdeen fan?" She glanced down—at the logo stretched tight across her chest, clinging to what little skin it could. Kline tried not to notice. Failed.

"Oh? This old scrap? Nah. Found it at the thrift shop. More of a thrash metal girl," Cherie said flatly. Kline turned red.

"Oh," Kline said, dejectedly. He couldn't hide it if he tried, and Rayne felt bad for him. She started laughing at him.

"I'm joking. It's a joke. Of course I am. Can't be my age, living here, and not be a fan of Aberdeen." She smiled and laughed, braces on her teeth showing. "I basically grew up here. They're legends.

Shame about Lloyd." She sighed, then wiped the condensation from the glasses she'd just set down in front of them. Without looking up, she kept talking.

"Greater shame was how they sold out. Their music was never the same after the Eveningview album. Good songs here and there, sure. But it lost something—after he got married to that model or whatever. Guess he lost the fire."

Eddie and Kline both lifted their beers at the same time, neither quite sure what to say.

She kept wiping.

"You'd think after the messy divorce, after Celeste got strung out, started disappearing into weird sex cults in Topanga or somewhere? Maybe that would've lit a fire under his ass."

"Huh. Never heard about that," Kline muttered.

"And you wouldn't have. Word is, the whole thing's sewn up behind some ironclad NDA. But the way it went down? Getting left like that?" She paused, then said it quieter—more pointed.

"Pretty powerful motivation. To write songs, at least."

Then she looked him straight in the eye. Waited for him to flinch in mentioning his predecessor. Crossed her arms over her chest—small frame, sharp posture—and held her gaze like she knew exactly who she was talking to.

Was she testing him? Poking the bear? He couldn't hold that gorgeous gaze so beautiful that he completely missed it.

Kline's eyes dropped to her tattoos—detailed and intricate pieces down both arms, stories inked into skin. Shoulder to elbow, a tapestry. He caught himself wanting to know each one.

She followed his eyes but didn't seem bothered by it. Though he blushed, Kline mistook her acknowledgment of his gaze as something else. He assumed she was simply used to it, a pretty woman with lots of body art designed to attract the very attention he was giving her. Just another man at her bar. When he locked eyes with her again, she let out a high-pitched laugh.

Kline, face full of confusion and surprise, searched those hazel eyes with the yellow flecks, studied her painted black lips that parted like a curtain to show those white teeth in braces. When his eyes saw the different colors of the glued-on metal, she hid them in her well-practiced way, as if she were ashamed to be her age and in braces. Perhaps she truly was.

"What's so funny?" Kline queried.

"You. You're funny."

"I didn't say anything." She laughed again, that high-pitched laugh that she offered so rarely, mostly because she hated it but also because she had a heightened sense of cynical humor.

"Exactly." She brought a finger to her lips, chewed it, her eyes became tight, and eventually she extended the finger towards Kline.

"I'm curious. Tell me. Truly. How long were you going to bait me before you admitted who you are? Or were you ever going to tell me?"

"I'm sorry?"

"Come now. Don't be coy. I know who you two are. You're the new guys in Aberdeen."

"You knew the whole time? You were just pushing my buttons?" Kline asked curiously. She nodded an affirmative, palms to cheeks, head titled, as if to say she's just an innocent little girl. She straightened.

"It's been all over social media for days! And, I have a secret. I watched your show. Why do you think I bought you these beers? Ain't 'cause I've got an abundance of spare change, I can tell ya that."

Kline started to ask her about the show but saved it. He deflected.

"Maybe because we are two handsome men that planned to pay for them, and you enjoy the conversation of a beautiful woman?" Kline asked, trying to get a deeper glimpse into her. She held those striking eyes on Kline.

"Hardly. I get all of that I can stand already. Malibu, remember? Everybody is conversational after a few beers, especially around beautiful women. Though not quite sure I agree with the beautiful part, in this particular case. But, to better answer your question, I wanted to see what kind of guys you were. Are you the kind of rockstars that make sure everyone knows who they are? Or are you the kind of rockstars who are just normal people?" She turned her face back to Kline, leaned in close, the tatters of her shirt open. Kline tried his best not to look, but he was only a man. She didn't mind. She knew what she was doing. He'd venture a guess that she wouldn't be leaning like that unless she had planned it.

"Oh, come on. Who's being coy, now? You're full of it if you don't think you're beautiful. And I am no rockstar," Kline said. Eddie was shocked to hear him be so forward.

She blushed and pushed her hair back again as she looked away. This was an honest emotion, and she felt butterflies that shouldn't be there. She changed the subject slightly.

"And you're a fool if you don't think you're a rockstar." She let the silence hang. It had come from somewhere and nowhere. Part flattery. Part jealousy. All truth. She self-corrected.

"I find that typically, handsome men rarely have anything interesting to say, at least about anything other than themselves. Not much of a conversation."

"What about rockstars?" Eddie asked, but her eyes never left Kline. She shrugged.

"About the same. Worse, really. Now, men who have a story to tell? A real story? Stories of pain and suffering? Amazing journeys of self-discovery? That's rare around here and far more compelling of a conversation." She winked at Kline. She lifted the beer she'd poured for Eddie, clanged it off the one in front of Kline, and drank from it. Eddie looked at his best friend. If there were ever a man that lived her definition? Kline was it. It was like she really knew him.

"Those are the men I buy beers for. Those are the men that need beers bought for them." She took a sip. Her hazel eyes remained locked on Kline from behind the glass. After a long sip, she set it back down and winked at Kline, yet again. Ran a black nailed finger around the rim and pushed her hair back. For the first time in a long time, Kline felt desired. There were only so many signs he could account to coincidence. She was thinking the same thing.

"Look, I've got to get to work. Fun time is over. It was nice to finally meet you. Eddie. Kline. Shame it took so long. But I guess I can appreciate the humbleness." She jerked a head towards the men, even as more were filing in. She offered each a handshake, her black-painted fingernails digging into Kline's hand as she squeezed. Kline started to pull his hand back but found resistance from the calloused hands of hers. Eddie noted the feel of the fingers, much like his. He knew what that said: guitarist.

"I'm sure normal women aren't your thing, rockstar that you are. But, if you'd like to hear some stories, have some real conversation, maybe you could ask for my number. Been waiting to give it to you for some time, ya know?" When the shock wore off, he opened his mouth to ask for that very thing, but she pressed a finger against his lips and pressed a card into his hand. Then she was gone, headed down the bar. Eddie finished his beer with one big gulp, then slapped his friend on the shoulder.

"That's our cue, good buddy. Time to go to work, anyway." Kline stood, a pep in his step that he'd not had in a very long time. But then, he remembered something. He turned back.

"Hey! You gave me this, back at the airport. It did bring me luck, just like you said." He dug it out of his pocket and extended it to her. She smiled.

"Keep it. For now. I won't say it's brought you luck. Because you've earned it. But I would say it has brought you fame and fortune, which is more than it's ever given me." She winked at him and turned to leave. As they traversed the parking lot towards the rental car, gravel underfoot, Eddie snatched the card from Kline's tight and sweaty grasp. He started to complain, but Eddie's laughter ended his plea in his throat.

As they stepped toward the door, Scott Weiland's voice rang out—low, aching, prophetic. STP's most popular song, but the lyrics cut her. Leavin' and Lyin'.

"Cherie Antoinette, Painted Queens Entertainment Group, LLC."

•

The band cackled with laughter, all of them. Even Kline had to admit that, in retrospect, it was comical.

"Welcome to rockstardom, Kline. Barely a few weeks in and already have the porn stars knocking down the doors for you and buying you beers." Kilmore gave him a salute with his whiskey tumbler.

"She could be an exotic dancer. Or just a model. Or an influencer. Maybe she owns the company. But one thing's for sure, that's definitely not her name." Kline hadn't considered that, and it caused him doubt. The room overlooking the ocean grew quiet, with each of the band members looking at one another until they all cackled wildly with laughter.

"Only one way to be sure." Cantrell used his long arms to snake the card away from Kline, who kept staring into it as if it would divine to him secrets he couldn't easily find on his own. Kline launched himself across the couch towards Cantrell, who passed the card to Kenney, who passed it to the farthest member from Kline. Kenney, reading the social media handles, fished his phone out and spoke into it. A few finger swipes later, he stopped suddenly, and his eyes grew wide. His finger swiped through a gallery. One woman looked oddly familiar, but he couldn't place her. Then, he stopped on whom he assumed was Cherie. The description Kline had gushed was spot-on.

"Whoa! What have we here!" He passed the phone around. Kline crossed his arms and sank into the couch as the different members ogled at the promo pictures.

"Didn't figure you for tatted up muscle mommas, Kline. You only continue to impress." Cantrell punched Kline lightly, jokingly.

"She's outta your league, pal." Kilmore looked up from the screen.

"That ain't saying much," Kline offered in a self-deprecating tone.

"Oh, come now, friend. Give it a few more months. A few songs. God willing a show or two, and much finer chicks will be lining up by the dozens," Kilmore added between laughs. Kilmore couldn't help but notice that Kline was in a mood he'd never seen before. Jovial. Almost. And certainly a bit embarrassed. And, he had to admit, he was happy for the man. This was a Kline he didn't mind being around and working with.

"I seriously doubt that." Kline's tone didn't change. It took him mere seconds to understand, and Ben knew how Kline felt about himself and the doubts he carried. He had those himself.

"Call her." All the heads in the room turned quickly to Eddie, who ignored all but one set of eyes. Yet the eyes he sought were not looking up from the glass-topped table.

He's really conflicted, Eddie realized. It didn't take a genius to understand why, and it wasn't just because of whatever her profession was. He didn't want to be hurt. To find out that she was only interested in him for his stardom. But she hadn't known that at the airport, right?

Kline was wondering the same thing in his moment of conflict:

She didn't know who I was in the airport. She couldn't. Which means that she doesn't care anything about me being in Aberdeen. Which means…

His thoughts went another way.

What if this was a mistake? What if she was just being polite? Kline hated the way his mind worked, always questioning, always pulling back from anything that felt good. Eddie jarred him.

"Dude. Call her. Ask her to hang out. She's clearly interested," Eddie emphatically pleaded again.

"Yeah?" he implored. If Eddie believed it, maybe it wasn't so crazy after all.

"Absolutely, man. She was into you. You were into her. She literally told you. What've you got to lose?" Kline raised an eyebrow.

Kline was shocked that they'd shown this interest in him seeing this woman. Tonight was a work night. Songs to write. Songs to rehearse. At some point, White was going to come by and tell them when and where their first real gig would be. Perhaps it wasn't the best time.

"Kline! Wait! Don't you need her card?" Ben waved the card, and the band laughed.

"I already have it saved." Out of sight, his voice echoed off the walls of the adjoining hallway. The massive front door opened and closed quickly. This elicited even more laughter from the band.

Everything is going to be okay. Kline convinced himself. Still, there was doubt.

It doesn't matter what they do. It matters who they are. He justified to himself.

But what does it say about me that this is what I attract, whatever it is?

Doubt.

Meeting Destiny was exactly what he had needed, at the time. Maybe Cherie was what he needed, now.

Born to wonder. Born to wander. Born to push away.

The man had understood. That was enough. And the man had stood, put his hands on his only possessions and pushed away.

✦
✦
✦

The pacific breeze cooled his scalp and ruffled his linen shirt. From the brick steps, he fished out a pill from the bottle, lifted the beer, took a gulp, and pressed the send button. Strange how fast these pills could make him feel better, he thought. It rang and rang. About the time he was going to give up, relieved, she answered. The background noise was chaos but lessened as she put distance between herself and the crowd inside.

"This is Rayne." He paused, looked at the number again. It was right. Unless this was a prank. His stomach dropped. But it was her voice.

"This is Kline. Thomas? I thought your name was Cherie." Silence.

"Oh, hey, Kline. Didn't think you'd call. Certainly not on the first night. Isn't that a violation of some sort of bro code?" Taken aback, he realized he was woefully unprepared for this conversation, especially with how it had begun. Sensing this, she spoke first.

"I'm kidding, Cherie is my professional name." She left it at that. The noise was still there, in the background. Kline tried to picture her taking his call, in the back alley of the bar. Yet, he knew that there was no back alley that he had seen. She'd gone somewhere else. A break room, perhaps?

"Ah. Right. Well, in that case, I guess I should give you my real name…" He tried to joke.

"You don't need a stage name, Kline. I do." Her voice was steady, but there was something underneath—a weariness he couldn't place. He wanted to ask why, but something told him not to. He already knew. She said it in such a way that conveyed many possibilities to him, namely the recklessness and danger that a woman like her had to face.

On a daily basis.

"So, what's up?" she asked, the voice muffled. He imagined her pinching the phone between her ear and her orchid tattooed shoulder.

"I just wanted to see, you know, if I could buy you a drink? Maybe have one of those interesting conversations?"

She laughed lightly, ending in a sigh.

"Is this a bad time?"

She snorted, and it led into that unique laugh.

"A bad time? Calling me on the rare occasion I get to lounge in the bath is a bad time. Calling me at six in the morning after I've worked my second job until two in the morning is a bad time.

Right now? In a rush when there's a line outside waiting for shitty, overpriced designer cocktails? No, that's not what I would define as a bad time. Inconvenient, maybe."

"I'm sorry. I can let you go…" Just a minute ago, he was happy if she didn't answer. Now he felt devastated that she deemed so dismissive. Yet, even hearing this, he wanted to keep hearing that voice. Didn't want her to hang up.

"No. It's fine. I needed a break, anyway. Sorry, honestly. I know I'm being short." He didn't know how to steer the conversation from here. She took the lead.

"Look, shift change is at eight. I'll be out around nine. Gotta roll silver and do my side work. We can hang after that, if you don't mind me smelling like BO and alcohol and looking like a drowned rat. Been sweating my balls off tonight, and I look like it, too. You don't want to see me looking like that. I don't want you to see me look like that." Her boldness took him by surprise, but the self-awareness, more so.

He wasn't sure how to answer. She took his silence for dismay.

"We can get together some other time, if that's better." The hurt in his voice was evident, even as he suggested it.

I really want this? Yes, he did. *Of course I do. I picked up the phone.* He went on.

"Really, I don't care what you look like or how you smell. I probably won't be much better, in the smell department. Tonight would be great. We're just rehearsing." He slapped his face when he realized how pompous that sounded. As if he were threatening her with "this is the only chance you're going to get to see Aberdeen in its natural environment."

"Really?" Her voice picked up in interest. "God knows when that will be, though. Monday through Wednesdays are my slow days.

Only one job. So, tonight will be the last night until the weekend is over, and I don't figure you rockstars do much during the days."

"No, not really."

"Didn't think so. Besides, my days do stay pretty booked up."

"Another job?"

"Something like that. Girl gotta grind, ya know?" She moved the conversation past it, but the words hung there; unfinished, waiting. "So, whaddya say, rockstar?" she asked. Deflected. Got the train back on track.

"Tonight is fine, I mean, if that's okay with you. We're at the Eveningview house. You know where that is?"

"*Do I know where Eveningview is?* What a dumb question. Of course I do!" She suddenly perked up, but it was forced. He just didn't know it. She respected the band, the mansion, and the lore. But it didn't do anything for her. Still, it was a cool experience.

"Come by when you get off, then? But call first. I'll have to get security to let you in the gate."

"They gonna charge me cover too?" she joked, and he, once again, was speechless in the face of her sarcasm. But it was infectious.

"I'm joking. Of course you'd have security, big shot. It's Eveningview, after all. See you then."

She was gone. Rayne leaned against the counter, her thumb hovering over the keyboard. She thought about Kline—his awkward smile, the way he'd watched her in a way that was different than what she was accustomed to. That wasn't what she'd expected, but maybe that was the point. Still, there was something else that bothered her about that. He saw her as a person. She couldn't explain it, other than it hurt a bit to know Cherie had a job to do that was going to hurt a guy she might appreciate. Hell, even like.

But she'd thought that many times and they were all the same, Cherie knew.

Rayne punched up the messenger app and sent a single text to the number listed as Ava Palatco.

I'm in. But I gotta listen to fuckin' Aberdeen rehearsals. Dot dot dot. Ava was typing. Rayne regretted saying that and realized she was overcompensating. Aberdeen might not be her style, but they were great artists.

Ooooffff. Did he even ask them if that was ok? Bet it ain't. Guess you'll find out. Good work, anyway. Stay focused. Eye on the prize.

She called to let him know she had arrived, so he popped another antidepressant, washed it down with the last of his whiskey in the tumbler, and bounded through the house while calling security to let her in. He met her on the steps of Eveningview as she exited her well-used car that was at least a decade old. It groaned as she leaned out of it, and she added her own grunt. Both were tired. It was in fine shape, and she had obviously taken care of it, but it was dated. She fished her small clutch purse out of the passenger side, black with cartoon characters on it. Kline stepped down into the gravel to meet her, offered her a handshake, which she took with a smile before pulling him into a hug. She did smell of must and alcohol, but he didn't mind.

"Wow. Okay." He pulled himself back from her.

"You don't look like a drowned rat," Kline broke the ice. When he looked her up and down, surveying her height again, taller than he was, she pulled the high heels off her feet and swapped into some black flats.

"God, that's almost orgasmic. Better than three shots of tequila and five minutes of silence." Rayne slung the purse over her shoulder. Her arms slapped down to her sides. The way she said it, with her eyes rolling into the back of her head, made it sound like it wasn't a metaphor. What was he supposed to say to that?

The gravel crunched underfoot. She was unlike anyone he'd ever met—forthright, confident, and completely unapologetic. A far cry from the always proper woman he'd been married to for so long.

"So, here I am."

"Here you are." He smiled at her, realizing that he hadn't thought beyond this moment. Truthfully, he didn't believe that she'd come. Yet, she'd texted him over the last few hours updating him, as if to make sure he hadn't forgotten. The ocean crashed in the distance, and the two simply looked at each other.

"If it makes you feel any better, I probably smell like BO too. We've been rehearsing. Kicking around some song ideas. Playing with them."

"How that going?" Cherie asked, as if she understood what it was like.

"Strikes and gutters, really. It's harder than you'd think. Especially with our…dynamic."

"I can't imagine." She said it almost sarcastically, and had he not seen her eyes, he could have imagined her rolling them. He laughed, but her tone had struck him as odd. Like she did know exactly what that was like.

"So? You gonna offer me a drink or are we going to stand out here all night? I've been serving all night. Time for someone to serve me." She tapped a foot. He smiled and motioned to the front door, but she stopped just short. Cherie disappeared into a shadow, just for a second, and Rayne turned back to him.

"Before we go in, I think it's fair if I level with you." Rayne waited for him to acknowledge him.

Don't. Cherie warned.

"First, I think it's fair to address the obvious. Yes, you are a rockstar…"

"Hardly," he said, trying to humanize himself to her but also be self-deprecating.

"You are, even if you don't think so. I'm not sure what I expected," she said, her voice softer now. "But you're… different. In a good way, I think." She poked him lightly in the chest, and for a second, he froze. It wasn't the touch that threw him off—it was everything she'd said. He hadn't expected her to be so honest. He didn't know what to do with that kind of transparency. People didn't usually say what they meant.

"And me. Yes, I'm an adult entertainer. No, I'm not easy or looking for a hookup. And no, I'm not sleeping with you tonight—I smell like a men's locker room at the gym, so count yourself lucky I put on perfume. Shit gives me headaches like you wouldn't believe." Kline gulped. She smiled at his nervousness.

"I, uh…" She waved him off.

"Sure, sure. Wasn't on your mind." She pursed her painted black lips. She cocked her head to the side, hands on her hips, then shook a finger at him with a braces-filled smile. Rayne eyed him deeply and went on.

"But, you know, in your case I think I actually believe you. And I like that.

"I just want to hang out with someone normal for once," she said, her voice softening. "That doesn't happen much in my line of work. Too many people either put me on a pedestal or tear me down before they even know me. That's it. Fair?" The steps of Eveningview glowed faintly under the porch light, the sound of waves crashing in the distance. Kline could sense that while she was confident and direct, some of this was a show. Defensive. This last was the most honest she'd been, and he could see it in her body language and eyes.

"Fair."

"I mean, I'm not gonna sit here and say that this isn't an awesome opportunity. I've heard a lot of pick-up lines, and 'you wanna listen to Aberdeen rehearse' is way up there. Just don't get it twisted. Also fair?"

"Also fair," he repeated.

"Great. Let's get that drink." She took a step in front of him and up the steps.

Waiting in the studio, Kenney turned to Eddie.

"I don't think this is what we had in mind." The way he said it caused Eddie pause, but he quickly deduced that they were uncomfortable with having a stranger here. Not knowing what he could say or do, he searched the faces of the other bandmates. Kilmore smiled.

"What could it hurt?" he asked. Jose looked to Ben, shock on his face at the response from the man who had always been the most adamant about playing in a vacuum. Ben shrugged. No, Kline hadn't asked. He probably didn't think he needed to. Yet, they had encouraged him and what they'd learned about Kline so far was, the man was direct and worked fast.

Kilmore sounded almost too willing. As if he knew this would become a bargaining chip. Maybe even Kline's liability to exploit. Surely White would take care of this.

•

They played.

Rayne watched.

Kilmore watched Rayne.

Jose watched Kilmore, still confused.

Whether Kline wanted to admit it or even realized it, she had become a distraction.

In his mind, he'd done the right thing by mostly abandoning the younger, uniquely beautiful woman curled on the couch in the sound room. During short breaks, he ducked in—asked what she thought, offered another drink—but otherwise acted like she wasn't there.

Because that's what they'd want, right? Kline had surmised.

He'd seen the looks. No one had said anything. But it was clear.

And if there were any doubt, White made it obvious when he found a quiet moment to pull Rayne aside and politely, firmly ask her not to take any pictures or videos. No posts. No content of any kind.

She'd nodded, expression calm, as if she expected that request. Then he pushed an NDA in front of her and she had to pretend that she hadn't expected it, nor was it a big thing. It was very evident that Kline had sprung this on them all, but White wasn't going to stop him from progress. Couldn't afford it.

But privately, she bit the inside of her lip until blood rose—copper-warm and bitter. Half from the reprimand, half from the ache to be involved, not just *there.* Her fingers twitched as she watched Eddie and Mike Kilmore play. She ached for one of the guitars on the rack. Ached to show them all how to play. Kilmore was exactly as she expected. But Eddie? Eddie was good, if for no other reason than his versatility.

Even if she'd wanted to argue and complain, she couldn't deny it: watching this unfold was intoxicating.

Rayne admired Kline in that moment more than she wanted to. Not just the voice, though it was worthy of envy.

Just weeks into working with this group of hardened, legacy-wrapped rockstars, and he wasn't backing down. He pushed them. Reshaped the sound. Challenged their muscle memory.

He didn't flinch when they resisted.

He led.

It was subtle but undeniable.

How? she found herself asking.

This was Aberdeen. Not some aimless garage band. This was *Aberdeen.*

And Kline Thomas? He controlled the room like a man led by a vision years in the making. Like he'd been waiting—plotting—for these moments.

Not improvising. Executing.

Four hours passed in what felt like twenty minutes. She blinked at the time and realized she had to get home to Lanna. She stood slowly, legs stiff, her mind still half in the music.

Kline finally looked up. His expression changed. Recognition. Regret.

He grabbed a towel, draped it around his neck, and jogged toward her, buttoning his shirt mid-stride.

"Guys, I've about had it for tonight," he called back to the room. No one objected.

Kline's work ethic had already spoken for itself. When he said he was done, he was done.

"You go ahead, man," Kilmore replied with a smile that didn't reach his eyes. "We'll finish up on the track. You've done enough."

Kline nodded, grateful.

Behind him, Kilmore watched the door. *Maybe I can wrangle*

this song back from whatever direction he's steering it. He glanced at the others. No one else seemed to notice.

Except White. The manager stood, arms crossed, reading everything.

Kline caught up to Rayne halfway down the hall. He suddenly felt self-conscious; sweat still streaking down his stomach, shirt sticking to him. He stopped, buttoned it fast, then jogged to meet her.

"Hey," he said, breathless. "Let me walk you out."

Rayne smiled, a little tight but sincere. Another chance. And something else. Butterflies?

"You don't have to. I've worked in worse neighborhoods, and way later."

He shook his head. "I want to."

She raised an eyebrow. She'd been ignored all night. And now this?

"Just give me five minutes to make up for tonight. The breeze'll feel good. I'm dying in here."

She crossed her arms, tapping her flat shoes against the tile. After a pause, she nodded.

"I've got a few minutes."

He smiled—real, unguarded. The first time he'd felt seen someone like this since… Destiny. A pang of guilt tightened his chest. He hoped she was doing okay. He needed to reach out.

They passed through the monstrous kitchen, where Kline grabbed two bottles from the fridge. She twisted one open with a nod, and they wandered around the mansion, following the carved stone path and wrought-iron rails toward the front drive.

Kline talked—music, mostly—and she let him. At the gate, under the glow of the security lights, he realized he hadn't asked her a single thing about herself.

"I'm sorry," he said, running a hand over his sweaty scalp. "I guess I haven't had anyone to just talk to in a while."

"Job hazard of being a bartender," she said, kicking off her flats to feel the cool stone. Her fingers worked the hem of her skirt, fidgeting.

Rayne didn't want to care what he thought—no, *Cherie* didn't. But Rayne did. Why?

"Why'd you invite me if you were just going to ignore me?" she asked, eyes forward. "I've got tough skin. You can give it to me straight."

He studied her profile in the moonlight. Sharp cheekbones catching the glow. Watchful, unreadable.

"I've been around," she said before he could answer. "I'm a tatted-up, muscled-up bartender-slash-entertainer in Malibu. You thought I was easy. When I wasn't, you lost interest. Happens all the time." She took a pull from her vape and didn't look at him.

He laughed, shaking his head.

"Are you serious? From the moment in the airport, I never thought I was in your league. You're gorgeous. And interesting. And frustratingly honest in a world that isn't."

That got a smile out of her. She reached out and ran a finger down his cheek.

"You don't owe me anything," she said. "You don't even know me. But I bet I understand more than you think."

Kline rubbed his short beard, his voice low. "I hate clichés, but I feel like I've been tossed off a boat into the ocean with no land in sight and no light to see. I don't know which way to swim—and if I stay still, I drown. If I swim the wrong way…"

He trailed off. The silence hung heavy.

"You're still swimming," she said.

Rayne looked away, then added, "You've got a great song, if you can get it to the finish line."

"One of life's great ironies," Kline said. "Put your soul. Your deepest fears, regrets and pain into a song so people can either celebrate it—or hate it. It's why I never shared mine before."

"All the great ones have."

"And most of them end up killing themselves for it."

It seemed an odd thing for someone to say. Perhaps terrifying. Yet, she understood what he meant and said nothing. Rayne slipped her hand into his. Then pulled away just as fast, adjusting the headband holding back her dark red hair—now black in the moonlight.

"Did you look me up?" she asked, watching for the truth.

"No."

It was true, though everyone else had.

"You'd be the first," she said softly.

Her tone shifted—distant now, almost disappointed. She stepped off the curb and slid into the driver's seat. The door creaked shut.

"If you still want to know me after that, maybe I'll believe you. Until then… like I said, you don't owe me a thing."

She started the engine. "But if you do, call me tomorrow. We'll get coffee. Or something."

She drove off. The taillights faded down the hill.

Rayne gripped the steering wheel and looked in the rear view.

She saw him. Then, she saw herself. And wasn't sure which one scared her more.

Kline didn't say goodbye to the band. He just grabbed the keys and left.

⁞

Rayne considered calling Ava to give an update. And there was progress. Kline had opened himself up, even if it was a little. Well, that one line he'd said about artists? Frankly, terrifying. She moved to the rest of the conversation. She'd seen it in his eyes, that flicker of regret. He *had* wanted to spend time with her. It hadn't been him who pulled away in the end. It was her.

And she couldn't blame him. She saw the conflict in him—the way he looked at her like he wanted something but wasn't sure he deserved it. Or couldn't let himself have it.

Still, she felt discarded. And Cherie—the mask she wore—couldn't understand why that stung so much. The mission had been a success. He'd interacted. He'd asked her to stay. He'd expressed interest.

Those were the goals. Those were wins. So why did it feel like a loss?

Maybe it was because it was another day with her daughter—wasted.

The regret settled in, heavy and familiar. Echoes of excuses long buried: *"I did it all for you." "You'll understand when you're older." "I had to work. I had to survive."*

Rayne had hated those words. Had sworn she'd never say them. Now here she was—another night gone, chasing something that wasn't hers, whispering promises she hadn't kept.

Rayne hated that, but that wasn't it.

She focused on the empty road ahead. Lanna would be asleep by now. Another night she'd missed for what? A performance? A ploy? A manipulation that was destined to fail?

Or worse—Time spent with a man she secretly admired?

If she dropped the pride, if she peeled back the sting of being ignored, the truth was harder to hold: *Kline Thomas was insanely fucking talented.* The Queens would kill for even a tenth of what Aberdeen was wasting in that studio.

Watching them flush it down the drain—while Kline stood there, delivering gold and getting dismissed—was a kick in the teeth. A front-row seat to creative malpractice. Whatever the game, the overwhelming feeling was simple and unwelcome: She wanted to be with him. And he hadn't chosen her.

Not really.

And that made her question everything.

Rayne entered the apartment, tossed her keys on the counter, and opened the fridge. She was starving.

Something was off.

The light hit the side door—and she saw it. Two handprints traced out in marker. Colored, messily. One small. Lanna's. The other? Massive. Ava's.

Scrawled beneath them: *We love you, Mom.*

Rayne blinked.

On the couch, the beautiful, overgrown Barbie doll stirred. Ava shifted; legs comically draped over the armrest. She sat up, yawned.

"How'd it go?"

Rayne didn't answer right away.

"I've got him hooked. Only a matter of time," she heard Cherie say. A lie. *Complete and utter bullshit.*

She'd had the whole ride home to think. Kline might be intrigued, sure—but he was guarded. Defensive. Especially with women. Whatever had happened to him, it had left damage. Damage she'd need *time* to work through.

Time they didn't have. Time *she* didn't have.

"Good thing your girl is organized," Ava said, stretching. "You forgot to tell me about that field trip meeting. But we made it."

Rayne flinched. She slapped her forehead. "Shit—I forgot."

Words she'd heard a thousand times growing up. Words she'd *sworn* never to say.

Ava waved it off. "No worries, Rayne Rain Go Away. Momma Ava saved the day. But we definitely got some looks."

"I bet."

"I don't know if they think we're lesbians or what, but one of the teachers thought I was her mom. Go figure."

"Half right."

Rayne pulled a frozen dinner from the back of the fridge—the only thing that wasn't mustard or beer.

"You know she's been getting in trouble at school?" Ava asked.

Rayne sighed but said nothing.

Ava grabbed her keys, pulled Rayne into a hug. Held her tight.

"Just don't fall in love with him," she teased. "I know that's gotta be hard."

Then, softer: "Lanna said she missed you. And to tell you she loves you, even though you forgot about the field trip meeting. I think she's just scared she's in trouble. Go easy on her, okay?"

The door clicked shut behind Ava.

Rayne stood for a beat, holding the microwave tray.

Then she sat down on the couch, placed her head in her hands, and breathed like it hurt.

$$\vdots$$

By the time Eddie called, Kline was already winding along the Pacific Coast Highway, the rental humming beneath him like it knew the way.

Eddie asked where he was.

Kline lied. Said he was just exhausted from performing.

Eddie didn't push, but Kline could hear it—the tension in his voice, the tight concern about him driving after drinking at a late hour. Kline told him he was fine.

And, at first, he was. The pills and beers he'd taken had flattened the edges of the night. The road ahead looked smooth.

For a while.

Then Eddie said it.

A show. Whiskey a Go Go. Friday night.

Eddie sounded giddy. Borderline euphoric. It should've felt like everything they'd worked for.

But to Kline, it felt like a weight. Another knot in his chest. He pretended to care. Gave Eddie the answers he wanted.

The truth? The music—the pressure of it—only added to the pain. So, he pushed it away.

He was alone, driving under the stars, contemplating what felt like failure. What had he said—or not said—that changed her mood? What did he miss?

For a moment, he'd felt something he hadn't in twenty years. Then it slipped away, leaving only the ache. The only way he knew to answer was a song.

He made it to his apartment and drank himself into sleep—but not before opening the notebook. He flipped past years of lyrics, aimless pages from other lives, until he found an empty one.

And wrote:

Toss me in the ocean's deep
Flip off all the lights.
Water's cold begins to seep—
No refuge left in sight.
Only way I know is down—
Start kicking or I'll drown.

Excerpt from "The Voice Was Never Theirs"
BY CLARA COWLEY

"I wonder what Aiesha and White really discussed that morning, in its entirety.

Obviously, I know I was part of that conversation—at least eventually. We spoke later that afternoon, and that's when I was formally brought into this project.

But what I didn't realize at the time was that I wasn't brought in to document the story. I was brought in as a hedge. A failsafe.

A witness.

There were too many wild cards already in motion, and they needed someone who could curate the fallout.

I think the real trigger was Lloyd's last song. That it would be the catalyst, just as soon as it was opened, and the lyrics were read.

White still claims the letter was sealed until he opened it. I was there. I watched him break it.

But I don't believe he didn't know what the song was about. I also believe there were other concerns. Things they could see coming but couldn't stop.

Rayne, maybe.

Knowing White and Aiesha, there's no way they brushed off her sudden appearance as coincidence. White had met them before. How could anyone forget those four? All the information they needed was a Google search away.

Just another question mark in a story full of them.

So why let her in? It wasn't because she and the Queens were talented musicians, I can promise you that.

I don't know. Maybe it wasn't about Rayne at all. Maybe it was Kilmore.

I understand the temptation to let the band's internal dynamics play out—to let them push and pull each other creatively. But Kilmore's financial troubles weren't a secret. And while White wasn't his advisor, he had to know Kilmore was sinking.

And when someone's drowning, they don't always care who they pull under with them.

Or maybe the wild card was Kline himself. He was wearing the mask well. Saying the right things, showing up sober. But the signs were there.

I saw them. The sleepless eyes. The missing hours. The way his hands shook just slightly before the first note.

I'd bet anything that Kline was saying he was clean while secretly binge drinking, using, numbing.

The version of Kline we eventually came to know? I think he was there the whole time.

So, what I still don't understand is—Did they not see it? Or did they just not know, and decide it didn't matter?"

clara

25

Cavatina at the Sunset Marquis,
West Hollywood, CA

Aiesha spotted White across the veranda, sitting at one of the small tables looking over the gardens. The sound of her heels clicked, barely audible over the sound of dishes clattering. She passed the two- and four-top tables where people were enjoying breakfast. Aiesha unbuttoned her suit jacket and sat. White looked up from one of his three phones and motioned to the carafe that sat on the table. The smell of the garden was wonderful, just muted by the smell of food being served. Aiesha poured herself a cup of coffee.

"You look like shit." Aiesha smiled, her perfect teeth contrasting against her skin.

"And you look wonderful as ever. Good morning to you, too." White set the phone in his hand down.

"What's on your mind, Paul?" She had worked with him long enough to know that he must be in some sort of mood to come here and stare at the garden over coffee. These were his peak get-shit-done hours.

"This band will be the death of me," he said, in defeat. She raised an eyebrow. He looked at her.

"I just need someone to talk to." White had his wife for emotional talks. He talked to no one about his professional issues because he always had an answer. This meant it was a combination of the two. She softened and leaned forward.

"I'm here for it." She cut the tough exterior.

"The LBF and Kline. I'm just trying to control when and how that happens." She knew exactly what he meant. She could control the band's brand. She couldn't control the band, itself.

"Kilmore?" She asked.

"If he doesn't know, he'll figure it out soon enough. The fact that certain tidbits of information haven't come out is shocking." She nodded in understanding.

"And, I did something so stupid. I don't know why I did it. I mean, I do. From a business standpoint." He stopped, and she knew he had more to say, so she gave him room by sipping the black, steaming coffee. Her expensive lipstick stuck to the cup.

"Before he died, Lloyd wrote a last song. He'd been dealing with severe writer's block. As bad as I've ever seen…"

"It's not like he hasn't written hundreds of songs. Eventually, you run out of ideas," she offered.

"Well, he wrote this one and he hid it. He hid it in the only place he thought he could. With me. He said I'd know the time."

"I'm tracking." She nodded.

"I don't know what Kline Thomas is capable of writing. He's got some ideas they're working on, but there's some pushback between him and the band on creative direction. But I needed something to get a head start and hold over Holden's head. I sold the idea of this last song, debuted at this benefit concert."

"A brilliant plan. I don't see why you're worried," she said warmly, encouragingly.

"That's the problem. I lied and said it was his best work. Truth is, I don't know what the song is about. But I know when it was written. More or less. And I know what he was going through."

"Oh. *Oh,*" she said, realization settling in with weight. The crash of plates from a dropped tray echoed across the veranda, but Aiesha didn't flinch. Her eyes locked on White's, reading him like a book. She saw the cracks beneath the practiced calm—the guilt, the exhaustion, the years of silence grinding away at him. He had protected Lloyd's final song like it was sacred scripture, shielding it from the world despite its commercial potential. And now, he was handing it over—not in tribute, but as a bargaining chip. To Kline Thomas, of all people.

It wasn't just about preserving Lloyd's legacy anymore. White was breaking a promise. And it was eating him from the inside out.

"It could be about anything, Paul," she offered. White nodded.

"That's true. And, even if it's about what I think it is, it could be vague. You know how he was."

"Yeah, a great songwriter. And great songwriters don't tell you what they think."

"There's more. So, just bear with me."

"I'm listening," she implored him.

"Kline has met this woman. Brought her over last night."

"That's a good thing, right? Considering."

"Could be. Normally, I would never have let anyone watch them rehearse, but I thought it was a good idea."

"Another solid idea. Soften the blow. I assume you did my job and made sure she was radio silent." White nodded that he had done what Aiesha would have done. She could see the logic. Kline moving past his ex-wife and that travesty of an influencer using him for clicks would be a step in the right direction. It didn't take a genius to see the pain his ex-wife caused him and the self-doubt that influencer bitch would also cause him.

"But then they left together. Kline didn't bother checking in. He just … checked out." Now he lifted his cup before going on, his expression changed as he peered into the tops of the garden's trees.

White rubbed at his temple. "And I know this woman from somewhere. I just can't place her."

Aiesha saw it bothered him more than he let on. His ability to stay three moves ahead was part of what made him invaluable.

She tapped her phone without thinking. "Want me to look into her?"

He shook his head. "No."

"You sure?" she said. "I just got all that shit locked down from the morning after the streaming show. She didn't put up much of a fight when she got served. Everyone wants to be famous—until you make them famous to the wrong people, for the wrong reasons."

She was proud of that. He didn't blame her.

White leaned back. "Does it bother you that Kline hasn't brought it up?"

"Would you?" she shot back. He guessed not.

He tried to let it go, but something still itched in the back of his brain.

"Whoever she is, however I know her? That's the least of my concerns right now."

He sat up straighter. "Kilmore is up to something. And I don't just mean dragging his heels on Kline's sound. That, I can understand. Totally not Aberdeen."

"That was fairly evident from the streaming show." Aiesha laughed. The songs had been, well, culture shock. Yet, the lyrics had lived rent free in her head and she's spent hours reading up on the origins of Temple of the Dog and the reasons Only Dying wasn't released.

"He's scheming. Plotting. He doesn't think I notice."

Aiesha snorted. "He was never subtle. Strippers, porn stars, dumb money in failing restaurants, vacation homes no one uses. The man bleeds cash." She narrowed her eyes. "But lately, he's still not quiet. He's evolving. Manipulating."

White nodded. "Clever, now. Smarter than he used to be. For what? To torpedo them?"

"Okay, but why torpedo it?" she asked. "What's his endgame? Just wants to be frontman?"

"He's had solo deals. Real ones. Before Lloyd blew them out of the water." White paused. Something occurred to him. "Maybe it's not about a solo career. Maybe it's about making this album fail."

Aiesha stiffened. "You think he's trying to kill the record?"

White nodded. "Feels like it."

She frowned. "But why?"

White exhaled. "Maybe... he's in worse financial shape than we thought."

"You're saying bankruptcy?"

"I'm saying it's crossed my mind. And I hate that it makes this much sense."

Aiesha let that sink in.

"Markus evolved," she said. "He grew. Got constructive. Maybe Kline pushing Kilmore creatively is a good thing. Maybe he will push Kline towards some sort of middle that works even better."

White looked at her. She meant it. And he respected her for saying it.

"Kilmore's just used to thinking he'd be the shark in the room," she went on. "He wasn't prepared for someone showing up with sharper teeth."

White looked thoughtful. "Can I just say something you just touched on?"

Aiesha raised an eyebrow.

"Kline pushing Kilmore? That doesn't seem odd to you?"

"Oh, it's weird as hell," she admitted. "We bought a story. We were fine with it—even knowing what we knew. But now?" She leaned forward. "I think we got more than we bargained for. Not sure that's a good thing."

White exhaled hard. "We wanted a shill. A stand-in."

"And Kline Thomas," Aiesha said, "is anything but that. And I don't mean from this current landmine we are dancing around."

They sat with that. Aiesha didn't follow that up in the direction White expected.

"He came in ready to write," she continued. "To create. Not just mimic. That's the part that keeps catching me off guard. It's like... he was waiting."

"Waiting for someone to take a chance on him," White finished.

He shook his head. "We never asked. We assumed. And I regret that. It's not like me."

Aiesha gave him a rare look of agreement. What struck her wasn't that White had failed to dig deep enough to see the genius—but that he hadn't looked for a way out from the start.

Or maybe he had. Maybe this was the way out. A calculated gamble based solely on Kline's ability—subconscious or not. Even with the past connections.

No. That wasn't Paul White.

Unless it was never really about Kline at all.

Maybe White had a quiet vendetta. Against the LBF.

That made more sense than she wanted to admit.

And Paul White? If that was the case—no one would ever know.

She hated to even think about it. Looked to her colleague's face, hoping not to see the look that told her he was caught. But, no. She didn't see that at all.

On some level, White had wanted Kline in this band. It never happens without him. She moved on.

"So, what do we do?" she asked.

White stared at the floor. "I don't know. Maybe nothing. If this record doesn't get cut, PCR drops them. Holden already has us halfway out the door. He's just waiting for an excuse."

"*In Utero* was produced in two weeks," Aiesha said. "You said it yourself—we underestimated Kline. Maybe now we support him. Give the proper nudges."

White had already thought it. Hearing her say it out loud made it feel real. He just didn't know how.

"And if they fail to make this record," she said, "Kline doesn't suffer. Not really. I'll see to that. He'll find something else."

White didn't flinch. He didn't take it as a threat. Just a fact.

"That's not it," he said quietly. "He doesn't want to fail *Eddie*."

That landed like a body blow.

Aiesha blinked. "Okay," she said. "That adds up."

"That," White said, "and the music—those are the only things keeping him together."

Aiesha looked down, then back up.

"He doesn't even know what door he's walking toward. Not yet." White nodded.

"But he's going through it. Whether he's ready or not." Silence followed the ending of their train of thought.

"Do you know Clara Cowley?" she asked, and he looked up with a look of confusion, not because he didn't know her but because he wasn't sure how she fit.

"Yes. Of course. She was on the USC panel with us. She was at the streaming show the other night. Wrote a terrific article for us. Why?"

"She's been looking for an opportunity for a very, very long time. If you ask her, she will tell you that rock is dead. Being someone that has been covering it for a very, very long time, it would be foolish not to believe her. And here we are, with an incredible story on our hands. Especially if it goes south. You're worried about legacy, and I totally get it. But it isn't just Lloyd's legacy. It's the legacy of them all. More importantly, it's compelling, regardless of the outcome." She shifted just slightly in the wicker chair, a thought occurring to her.

"But what if it becomes huge. Bigger than Kline. Bigger than Lloyd. Bigger than their common bonds?" She conveniently sidestepped the legal issues, and he appreciated that, even as he was treading close to the line, himself.

"What if there is a hidden story? A hidden gem hidden among all this, and we just can't see yet?"

He crossed his arms in thought.

"You want her to write a book about it?"

She snapped her fingers when he figured it out. White considered it, and it held water.

"There will be pushback. But right now, only one person we need to sign on knows everything—and she's no dummy."

White knew exactly who Aiesha meant. There had been tension in the beginning—territorial, maybe even personal—but the two had logged too many hours in the trenches for there not to be some level of mutual respect now. Aiesha was handling the public side of the benefit: the auctions, the dinners, the press. And from what White had seen, those pieces were shaping up to be the most profitable part of the entire affair.

But not just because of Aiesha. He despised the idea of selling Lloyd's legacy. White didn't betray his emotions.

"We make it so she can't say no. Give her whatever she wants. We don't have to break the story. Someone else will do that for us, which will let us avoid that landmine." He saw the truth in it. A bestseller in the face of complete destruction would give him peace, knowing he'd managed to profit the band and the LBF, regardless.

"Where would I be without you? You really are good, you know that?"

She flashed her predatory smile. "I am a boss bitch." She held her arms out and smiled. There was something else.

"There's the minor issue with Kline. When he figures it out, he'll realize what I've done to him. It will kill him. Or, at least any trust he has in me," White said, face full of concern. Aiesha considered it. There was no way around it.

"That, my friend, is just something you will have to live with. You must make a choice. Who means more to you? Whose legacy is more important?" He couldn't argue with it. One way or another, he would bear this burden for the rest of his life.

"You assume that Kline's legacy won't be bigger," White found himself saying, shockingly. She realized she'd made a huge assumption on that and laughed.

"I suppose you're right. He's a great singer. But, truly, what are the chances he becomes what Lloyd was? You can't hitch your wagon to 'what if.'" She tapped a manicured finger on the table, final punctuation to her point.

White didn't respond. Neither did Aiesha—for a long moment.

Instead, she picked up her phone, expression unreadable, and fired off a text. *Lunch?*

A beat passed.

Long as you're buying.

She locked eyes with White over the rim of her coffee. "Let's go sell a legacy."

As White walked to his car, he made a call. Kline picked up.

"There's something I've been meaning to ask," White said. "And I don't think anyone has."

"Shoot," Kline replied.

"I know you've been writing songs. I've seen the notebook. And I can appreciate how secretive and possessive you are with it. Truly, I do." He was thinking of Lloyd—how protective he'd been of his final track.

"How much do you have written?"

Kline laughed—but it wasn't warm. White didn't like the sound of it. He knew why. It should've been asked a long time ago. Maybe during the first call.

"A good bit."

"'Good bit' doesn't help me. I need you to help me here."

"Why?" Kline snapped. "So they can shoot down even more of my work? So I can serve up my soul and live with the rejection? No, thanks."

White exhaled. "Okay. Just between you and me. And I'll tell you... there could be other things in the works for you. But I have to know."

He heard Kline sigh.

"Thirty songs? I don't know. Somewhere in there."

"Thirty songs of lyrics?" White asked.

Kline chuckled again. This one more bitter than the last.

"No. Thirty fully arranged songs."

White sat in his car in stunned silence.

Before he could speak, Kline kept going.

"And I've written more since I got here. The ones you've heard—the ones that got passed on? Those were written just for Aberdeen. The rest?" He stopped himself. He'd said too much.

"How? Why..." White whispered.

Kline exhaled.

"Before the divorce, my therapist told me to write my feelings down. That sounded stupid. Instead, I made them into songs. I always loved to sing, but having songs without sound made me crazy. Eventually, I built a studio. Makeshift. Barely functional."

A pause.

"During COVID, after Chrys left." White winced at the name, "I started learning to record. It wasn't perfect, but it was close. Dozens of tracks."

"Have you told anyone this?" White asked.

"No. No one knows. Not even Eddie." The call ended shortly after pleasantries.

But that wasn't entirely true.

Someone *had* heard the songs. And had called a few days ago. Kline hadn't picked up. He wasn't ready to hear her voice—not after the post-live-stream disaster. Not after everything.

Destiny called today.

Kline looked at the notebook in his lap. He wrote the words down absently.

Destiny called today,
But I let it ring.
Didn't know what to say.
Didn't owe her a thing.

He set the pen down. Picked the phone up. Dialed her number—hoping she wouldn't answer.

"Hey, stranger," her voice came through. Warm. Familiar. Unshakable.

"Been a long time, Destin with a Y," he said.

"Because why not," she shot back, that crooked smile in her voice. Their inside joke.

"How are you?"

"You probably wouldn't believe me if I told you." He looked around the empty studio. Nowhere else to go.

"Oh, I know," she said. "That's why I called. It's been a long time. Lotta water under the bridge. But I wanted you to know… Destiny still believes in you."

"Thank you," he said softly. "It's not been as easy as I thought."

"Nothing worth it is," she replied. "You know that better than most."

He did. All too well.

He hadn't fought hard enough for Chrys. And Destiny… she'd fought *for* him, until he pushed her away. Now they were strangers again. Strangers on a phone line.

Born to push away.

"How are you?" he asked.

"Living that married life. Wife with kids."

Kline smiled.

"I guess I have you to thank for that," she offered.

It wasn't a dig. It was true. Kline was very proud of that, even though moving on from him had hurt deeply, for how easy it had seemed. Deep down, he knew it hadn't been.

She'd been there after Chrys. He'd helped her get her daughter back. She'd found someone since. Built a life. It all felt like a lifetime ago—when they danced around each other in his house, needing something neither of them could give.

She'd wanted love. He'd needed escape, seclusion, comfort and none of that needed love.

"I don't want to take up too much time," he said, rubbing his head. "I just wanted to say—"

"That you're sorry you missed my call," she finished, letting him off the hook. She knew how hard it was to show emotion.

He laughed, weak. "Yeah. That."

"I miss you too, Kline," she said. Calm. Direct. Like she'd always been. "And I am so proud of you."

Her words hit like a wave. He blinked hard. Tried to hold on.

"The world needs to hear your voice," she added. "To hear your words. I can't be the only one. I don't deserve that honor."

Tears came. Kline wiped at his face.

"You're the reason I'm still here," he said, quieter than he meant to. And it was true. He wouldn't have survived if she hadn't forced him to face himself back then. He never told her that before. Maybe he should have. Or, maybe, one day he would find the strength to say that to her face. Which, she deserved and he'd denied her of that.

"You deserve much more. So much more."

"I already have more than I deserve," she said gently. "And it's because of you. I want you to know that. I'm always here for you."

She paused.

"Your destiny is out there. Grab it—and don't let go."

And then she hung up. Because they both knew where it would go if they didn't.

Nowhere. From high enough, it only looked like a step. For him, standing there? A chasm.

Kline picked up the pen.

She looked like a prayer,
I never learned how to pray.
So I gave her a room
And drank myself away.

BY CLARA COWLEY

"We met at The Laurel Room—quiet, upscale, forgettable.

They arrived together. I'd assumed the text from Aiesha meant they'd been meeting about me. That's what I get for thinking too much of myself. At the time, I told myself they reached out because of the article I'd written on the streaming show. It was good—tasteful, restrained, almost glowing. I praised Kline and Eddie.

I left out the part where Kline's final
song felt like a warning shot.

I wish I hadn't.

They pitched me. I signed the NDA.

I listened.

I should've walked away.

But greed got the better of me. That,
and the belief I'd carried since the first
time I saw that man onstage.

I'm not above scrutiny for it. And I
own that.

We all do.

As hard as I am on the others, I gotta
admit: every one of us carries baggage into
this story.

But I was right about one thing. I did see
the return of rock and roll. And this moment—
this lunch, this NDA, this handshake with the
machine—was the start of me witnessing it.

Up close. In real time. And with no
excuses left."

paycheck

26

The Laurel Room Midtown,
Los Angeles, CA

Clara Cowley shoved a fork full of twenty-dollar salad into her mouth, speaking around the food.

"Legacy, eh?" She swallowed the bite of spinach, cranberries, nuts, and balsamic before washing it down with a glass of iced tea.

"Seems pretty flimsy to me." She set the fork down and rested her pale, bare, and thick arms on the white tablecloth. Cowley looked from White to Aiesha.

"I don't know, guys. I'm not seeing a lot there." She lifted a hand and counted, holding up a finger for each new point. "No shows, no songs, no real intrigue. I don't know what I'd be writing about."

"Oh, there's intrigue," Aiesha offered with a tone that was meant to create interest. Cowley started to open her mouth, but Aiesha cut her off.

"And we will tell you, if you sign an NDA. Then, you can decide."

Aiesha bent down from the table and fished out a piece of paper, handed it to Clara. Clara read it carefully, but it was standard. She didn't offer it back, a good sign. But she did lay it on the far side of her utensils before picking up the half club sandwich and crunching through the toasted bread. She chewed loudly, watching each of their reactions. She got none and scowled.

"They've got me so busy, you know. Covering these up-and-comers." It was sarcasm. Clara's disdain for her current position was well known, and she made sure everyone knew it.

"Saw this band the other night. You'll love this. All women, right? Swinging from the goddamn rafters at H and S. Craziest shit I've ever seen." She spoke around another bite of salad, motioning with her fork, and thought about poking at the fact that the women were nude. Yet, that wasn't what had first come to mind, as it had when she'd listened to them. Clara realized maybe there was something there.

"Hella performers. Great musicians. But the song titles and lyrics?" She set the fork down.

"'Fuck Your Dick, Man?' 'My Sentence Ends with a Period?'" She shook her big, round head. Her brown and grey mop of curly, unkempt hair swayed. "But my favorite? 'Come to my Kitty.'"

"I'm sure there's a point, here, Clara. We have places to go."

Clara smiled. "My point is, rock is dead, guys. As much as it pains me to say it. Born in the wrong generation, I guess. And it will come back, I'm sure. Every year I think it will get better, and every year disappoints. I've been saying that since oh-one." She referenced the death of nu-metal.

"An interesting point, since that's when Aberdeen hit stride," White pointed out. Clara considered it, looked for her next quip at the ornate ceiling.

"John's voice in the wilderness."

"And what came after John?" Aiesha asked knowingly. There was silence between the three, the restaurant nearly empty before the lunch rush. Clara burst into laughter.

"That's your pitch? You want me to cover the Jesus Christ of Rock and Roll? I admit, your new guy? What's his name? Kline? Good. Really good. Great voice. Better taste. But second coming?" Clara rolled her brown eyes.

"Never thanked you for inviting me." She chewed away.

"Many thanks for the article," Aiesha reminded her. Clara rolled her eyes again but said nothing. Aiesha leaned forward.

"So what if he is? What do you have to lose? You don't want to miss it." Aiesha cut right to the point. They all knew that Clara had the time. Truth was, she was the perfect person to cover this story. Respected. Hungry. Disenfranchised. There was a standoff, and Clara folded her arms across her massive chest, sitting back in the chair, waiting for more. Aiesha pushed on.

"You said rock was dead. Then maybe it needs a good obituary.

But what if it's resurrection?" Aiesha waited for a response, but the only one was a series of blinks from Clara and a subtle tilt of her head. Aiesha pushed her over the cliff.

"They'll write about this anyway, Clara. But no one will get it right unless it's you."

"You guys are serious? You really think there's something here? You're asking me to chronicle a powder keg—and you're sweating like someone already lit the fuse."

Finally, White spoke, his words even heavier from his previous silence.

"I made a promise to someone who's not here anymore. And to keep it, I may have to break another." Clara watched him carefully and realized how hard it must have been for him to say that. Aiesha scowled; closing was her job.

"We know there's a story here, but we need someone we can trust that we respect," White stated without moving an inch. She looked at Aiesha, who just smiled back at her with a look that said she didn't want to miss it.

"Give me a damn pen and let's hear it." Aiesha already had one in her hand.

She signed and listened to the prepared and manicured pitch. Clara's pompous smile was long gone, and she was on the literal edge of her seat, hanging on every word.

"This is a gold mine. Or field of land mines. Or both." She regretted not bringing her notebook, but she didn't think she'd need it. It wasn't like she would ever forget it.

"You know that no one will walk away without getting hurt, right? I'm not going to sugarcoat it." They nodded that they understood. It confused her.

They must be desperate.

"And you aren't worried about that?" She crossed her arms again. No response.

"When can I start?"

"Right now. They're rehearsing every day. Playing at the Whiskey Friday night. We do have some loose ends to tie up. Got to get everyone on board." Clara nodded in understanding, but a scowl appeared.

"If everyone knows everything, there's no way." She searched their eyes. "Unless no one knows everything." She found the answers.

"Just give us some time. We will make it work. Until then, we are trusting that you will trust us... and we can trust you." She assumed they meant that she would honor the NDA and trust that they would get legal logistics together.

"I'll start now. You know I don't care about the money." Neither argued because they knew it was true and one of the reasons Aiesha had called Clara. Clara cared more about the music than the money. She drained the drink and belched loudly. Then, she stood. She began stuffing rolls in her purse. Aiesha looked around, embarrassed.

"Is that why you made me buy? Because you don't care about money?" Aiesha asked sarcastically.

With the last rolls stuffed in her oversized burlap purse, she slung it over her neck.

"No, I made you buy because you do." She donned a faded ball cap, tilted her head in thought.

"Or is it because I'm poor and need the money?" She shrugged and turned, but before she did, she fished in her purse and laid a piece of paper on the table, tapped it. Then, she reached into the bag, pulled out a soft pack of American Spirit cigarettes, and tapped one out. Clara dug into the pockets of her high-waisted, acid washed jeans for a lighter, sparked it, and gave a parting gift from the corner of her mouth and around the smoke.

"Take care of that parking ticket, would ya?" Aiesha and White watched her leave, and Aiesha couldn't help but chuckle.

"That woman." It was all she could say, but White knew what she meant, only because he knew that Aiesha could never understand the woman, nor would Clara ever understand Aiesha. They were complete and total opposites, other than their obsessions with their work. For that reason, there was a mutual respect.

"She's something, alright. But you can't help but like her."

"Now comes the hard part." White changed the subject. Aiesha knew what he meant.

"I'll take care of it," she answered, intently and deliberately. He started to ask why, but she beat him to it.

"You're on her shit list, and we're already working so closely on the benefit weekend. She absolutely would not want you to sell this to her. It's a no before you walked in the door."

"And what exactly can you do that I cannot?" White asked suspiciously.

"First, this is my arena, and it will sound a lot more natural, coming from me." He already knew this, but that's not what he had asked.

"She thinks I'm just a suit. Always has. And I've let her, because it made things easier. But now? Now she's in my world. And she's going to see what I *really* do." White fidgeted with nervousness because he was about to let Aiesha handle something he believed he should take care of personally. But she had a point. He'd already outmaneuvered LBF once this month.

"First, she's already seeing the financial gains for this upcoming weekend. It's going to make her a bit greedy. Second, and more importantly, I'll make it seem like it's her idea."

"And how are you going to do that?" White asked.

"I convinced you, didn't I?" He started to rebut her but snapped his mouth shut. She laughed at him.

"I already said it. I will give her whatever she wants but make her fight for it. More importantly, make it clear that this is going to happen, one way or another. Which it will. We might as well profit from it. Clara doesn't have to write for us. Better if she does. We can have an official autobiography, of sorts, or we can have a very unofficial biography that can say whatever the writer wants. Her choice."

"But she signed the NDA—" White started.

"She doesn't know that. You think in white and black, no pun intended, Paul. Sometimes you gotta live in the grey."

His phone beeped and he picked it up. Email.

> From: Greg Holden
> To: Paul White
> Subject: *Re: Aberdeen Timeline + Contractual Deliverables*
>
> Paul,
> Appreciate the update on tracking progress. Unfortunately, our internal projections no longer support an open-ended timeline for this project.
>
> Per Section 4.3(c) of the revised agreement, Aberdeen must deliver final masters within 45 calendar days from the commencement of full-band recording. That clock started on September 1.
>
> If the deadline is not met, PCR will be forced to reclassify the album as a "developmental hold," which

may trigger reversion rights for the publishing catalog—including the Brannon estate's holdings, under
the Lloyd Brannon Foundation.

Please ensure your artists understand the implications.

—Holden

White started to throw the phone but held back.

"Shit." The pressure was really on now. PCR smelled blood.
White only had one card to play. An envelope with his name on it.

Excerpt from "The Voice Was Never Theirs"
BY CLARA COWLEY

"Kline picked up the sheet of lyrics like it
was something fragile. Maybe he'd sensed the
weight-judging by the way White had handled it.

He couldn't have known the true
significance.

Paul White stood off to the side, arms
crossed like he was holding something in.
Because he was.

And me? I sat in the back with my notepad
in my lap and my hands still.

This wasn't a performance. It was an
exorcism.

Because what do you say-when someone sings
a dead man's goodbye for the first time?

I think that's all I have to say about
that moment."

27

Eveningview Mansion, Malibu, CA

"It's missing something. I don't know. Something isn't mesh-ing," said Jose Madera, tapping his full lips three times with his index finger.

Kline was scribbling in a battered notebook, half listening. It looked like it had lived most of its life rolled up in a pocket. Eddie sat beside him, idly picking on a guitar while Markus Kenney fiddled with the mix.

On the soundboard sat an opened envelope—Lloyd Brannon's final lyrics. White had finally handed them over. He'd read them, said nothing, and left abruptly. The way he left… it was odd. But no one asked questions.

Only one person knew. And she sat in her usual spot—Clara Cowley—in the corner, away from the artists. Observing. Writing. Her heart breaking. But she couldn't show it. Not even a flicker.

In the studio, beautiful art was being made as Kline and Aberdeen reverently poured their souls into an icon's last song. And it was killing an artist. He just didn't know it yet.

She jotted that line down.

When art became real—when it lived—the artist died.

White had let Kilmore read the lyrics first. Clara had found that strange. The lyrics were clearly entrusted to White. Why pass them off?

"Either their voices don't match his mood," Jose said, "or the sound doesn't match theirs. Or maybe… we're all wrong."

"Hard to know what a dead man wanted a song to sound like," Kline muttered, eyes still on his notebook.

Eventually, he looked up and sighed—frustrated, but careful not to lecture. He wasn't trying to beat them into submission. He was trying to lead.

"It's about wanting your cake, eating it too, and realizing how you hurt everyone around you because of your greed and lust," Kline said, his voice low. "And at the same time? The pain of knowing what you've done. Not for your own loss. But for what you've cost the people around you."

He spoke as if Lloyd had written it down for him.

Clara looked up at that, unsettled. It caused a shiver to pass over her and she remembered the old saying about when that happened. Made sense.

Kline understood the lyrics perfectly. And it would destroy him when he realized why.

Outside the booth, the remaining two bandmates diddled idly. Kenney rapped on the glass and motioned for Kilmore, who sat on an amplifier tuning his guitar. Kilmore heaved a sigh, carefully placed the guitar on its stand, and crossed the room, opening the heavy black door. The soundproof insulation at its edges scraped across the carpet.

"It's still off. They're far too…not Lloyd?" Jose didn't know what to make of it. For days, Kline had moved further away from Lloyd's sound, and Kilmore couldn't seem to let that go. The more he brought it up, the more Kline went another direction. Jose had the inclination that perhaps it was their play that was the problem, but he didn't want to bring it up.

Eddie had grown uncomfortable over the last hours of playing with the song, and the weight of being able to appease his new-found idols/friends was starting to crush his confidence. Spending up to ten hours a day in this space, in close proximity, had cut away what little brevity of a friend-courtship there might have been.

It was far more infuriating to Kilmore, in particular, to learn that the balance of power had already seem to shift, at least a tad. The fact that the band even listened to Kline was frustrating.

The diminutive singer looked up from his notebook at his guitarist with a grim look, closed his notebook, and carefully laid it on the armrest of the couch he had sunk into an hour ago as Madera and Kenney had played with the arrangement and mix.

"We've been hammering away on this song for hours and we aren't making progress on it. Maybe we should just set it to the side for a while." At that, Madera and Kenney turned towards Kilmore, who propped himself on the doorframe, arms akimbo, the sleeves of his shirt rolled up over heavily tattooed arms. Madera looked out the window to the mic stand. Kline followed his eyes and scowled.

"Oh? Just *set it aside*." Kilmore mocked.

"That's … not how we do things," Kilmore stated as fact, as he messed with his curly hair, which was tied up. Jose looked from Kilmore to Kline. That had been true for three decades. In this case, he wanted to hammer on this song for a completely different reason. Make Kline ask questions. Open the door for the answer.

"So, you'd beat a dead horse?" Kline asked, both eyebrows raised, the lines of his forehead creased. Kilmore cocked his head back, glaring at Kline. Kline could feel Eddie slinking into the cushions of the couch, trying to make himself as small as possible. Kline sat straight and then leaned towards the guitarist. Kilmore's eyes never moved from Kline's.

"Let's hear Kline out." Kilmore shot laser beams at the speaker, Kenney, yet he remained silent.

"I've been thinking," Kline said, and Kilmore immediately started laughing and cut Kline off, speaking through guffaws. Kline was undeterred. His eyes became cold, and Kline sat forward.

"Let's get something straight, Mike." Kline pointed towards the mic stand as he spoke. "If you'd like a crack, please. Be my guest. I have no intention of betraying the artistic expression that you think Lloyd would have, which is why I haven't fought it or complained.

"I am pouring myself out to appease you guys' opinion of how a man I've never met would sing a song I've never heard. Do you want me to sound like him or do you want me to be him? If you can't appreciate that challenge, I don't know what to tell you. Secondly, yes. I have ideas." The shockwave of his words rocked every member of the band, each blown back inches. Eddie's jaw dropped and he looked at Kline, first, and then the rest of the members. Lloyd was the only man who would have spoken to them in such a manner, and the voice he heard could have come from Lloyd, if he wasn't looking at Kline.

Kline replaced the page back into the book, laid the book on his thighs, and looked back to Kilmore with slits for eyes.

"This is not a happy song. It's a sad song. That's what makes it so damn good and different. It's because it isn't anything like what Lloyd would have written, and you guys keep playing it like it is. Meanwhile, I'm trying to sing it like I think he would, but you think I am the problem."

Wow. He's right, Madera thought to himself. They'd all been reading the lyrics and hearing Lloyd's voice and their sound.

No, not voice. Spirit.

Kilmore's jaw twitched. His arms were still crossed. For a moment, it looked like he might tear into him. But instead, he nodded—barely. He had to admit there was logic to it, especially since he knew what the song was about.

"I think we should just set it down and work on something else. Something I *do* understand." Kline shook the notebook but guarded it like a secret.

Eddie had expected a blow-up—hell, he'd been *waiting* for it. Kline and Kilmore had been circling each other for days like two bulls in a too-small pen. But now, the silence was louder than any fight.

Kilmore didn't respond. He just stared, chewing on whatever pride he still had left.

And Kline? He wasn't gloating. He wasn't angry.

He was *in control.*

And for the first time, Eddie didn't see the new guy in the room. He saw a frontman. Not Lloyd's shadow. Something else entirely.

⋮

The band filed into the studio. Markus stayed behind, lingering at the soundboard.

Clara noticed him pause—eyes locked on something near the console. A shape. A spine. A notebook.

He took two steps forward, slowly. Almost reverently.

Clara started to speak—maybe to warn him. But something in the moment told her to shut up.

Markus carefully lifted the cover. Page by page. He read the words.

But more than that, he *felt* them.

Randomness became rhythm. Feelings became words became lines became *lyrics.*

It was entropy—*order from chaos.*

Markus didn't say anything for a long time.

Then, quietly: "Jesus Christ."

The shock of actual emotion in his voice made Clara shift in her seat. It startled him. He looked up, caught. Shame flickered across his face.

"I… wasn't prying," he said. "I was just curious."

Clara raised both hands. *I didn't see a thing.*

Markus flipped forward, lips moving silently. She watched him process—not as a musician and artist, but as a man.

Then, softly, he read aloud:

"I read your book. I sat in the pew.
I've done everything you said to do.
Your yoke ain't easy. Your burden ain't light.
These are the things that keep me up at night."

He looked to Clara.

Waiting.

Clara blinked, then smiled. The smile wasn't warm. It was sardonic. Perhaps even a touch angry, but Markus didn't know her well enough to guess. She stood, eased past him on the way out the door, but not before she reached into her purse and pulled out her phone. When she spoke, Markus knew what the smile meant. Her voice was cold, cutting. Markus was a very intuitive man, and her body language echoed her voice. What did she have to be upset about? She looked him dead in the eyes.

"If you ain't praying to the rock god he's talking to…

You better get on your knees and start."

$$\vdots$$

**4:30 PM PDT Tuesday September 12, 2022,
Somewhere on I-10 Malibu, CA**

White didn't leave. He just…drove. He had been dreading reading those lyrics for years and had prepared for that pain of that moment for a long time.

Now, the pain was entirely different. What was once a powder keg was now a nuclear weapon counting down. And it could not be stopped.

Why is life doing this to me? he thought, over and over. The phone rang and the display of his car showed the name. Aiesha Holt. He nearly didn't answer it, but he did.

"Did you open it?"

"Yes," he answered, but the tone of his voice couldn't be ignored.

"What's wrong? Was it not what you expected? Was it not any good?" White tried to find the words. He swallowed hard.

"It's a beautiful song. Lloyd was right. It's his best lyrics he's ever written."

"That's great! What's it about?"

He sighed heavily.

"It's about his wife leaving him when she finds out he had an illicit affair with a married woman." More silence.

"You didn't give it to them, did you?" she asked, and he didn't answer. "Did you?" she reinforced.

"They're rehearsing it now." The sound that came through the speakers sounded like someone throwing a phone. That's because it's exactly what Aiesha had done.

He should've waited. He should've opened it alone. His sense of duty and sentiment had forced this. But the game had already started—and he wasn't the one moving the pieces anymore.

Another call. Clara Cowley.

She didn't wait for him to speak.

"I have to say something I couldn't say back there. Wasn't going to say anything at all. This is fucked up, White. Fucked. And that's saying something, coming from me."

"You knew it was the moment you signed the NDA, Clara. Keep your voice down. Are you still at Eveningview?"

"I'm outside. Alone. But that's not what I want to talk about, you sadistic fuck."

She was shaking. He could hear it in her breath.

"I want to talk about the man in that room. The one just pushing and pushing. And Kilmore is pushing back like he knows what the song means. Like he just wants him to sing it over and over. That man is going to pour his soul into that song—and when it comes out? He's going to burn. Maybe literally. Maybe not. But he won't come back from it."

"Let's not be so melodramatic."

"I wish I was, White. I really fucking do."

He lit a cigarette. It tasted like failure.

"I didn't know what the song was about. No one did."

"Bullshit." Her voice cracked. "Lloyd Brannon sang about two things his entire career—drugs and women. You really think his 'greatest song' was about fucking mushrooms? Of course it was about her."

There was a long pause.

"Why am I the one saying this?" she asked, almost laughing at the absurdity. "That guy in there is going to light himself on fire for you. And for what? An album? A book? A fucking tour?"

White pulled off onto the gravel shoulder. Exhaled smoke. Watched it curl into the setting sun.

"This was always going to happen, Clara. We've discussed this. Get the album done. Move on. Pretend the fire was just heat."

"Yeah, well, that was before Kline became a person."

Her voice cracked again.

"No one deserves what's about to happen to him. I don't care if he's Satan in a flannel. He's an artist. And your job—your *only* job—is to protect artists. Or did you forget that when you traded a soul for a paycheck?"

He didn't respond. He couldn't. Because she was right.

"I didn't think it would happen like this."

"You can still stop it."

"No," he said softly. "The pieces are already moving. All we can do now is control the pace."

And then he realized what he'd said. He'd used *we*.

"Who else knows?"

"You. Aiesha. I think Kilmore does, but he hasn't said anything."

"Have you talked to him?"

"Why would I do that? If he knows and hasn't said anything, maybe he won't. And I'm not giving him the satisfaction of asking. Besides, he's been playing nice. At least, by his standards."

"Or maybe he's waiting for the perfect time to strike?" she said, like it was obvious.

"Why would he? What would be his motivation? He needs this album as much as any of us."

White's voice hardened, weary.

"Besides, you're part of this now. Your job is to keep the secret. Document it. Frame it. This could be a tragedy. Or it could be incredible."

"Are you candy-stripping the cancer ward?" she snapped.

Silence.

"I'll write this," she said, her voice steadying. "From my perspective."

"That's why we hired you."

"Then know this—if things play out the way I think they will, history won't be kind to you. And I won't pretend to be."

Click. She hung up. White swallowed hard. He knew that had always been the case and he'd accepted it. That was before being threatened with it.

Excerpt from "The Voice Was Never Theirs"
BY CLARA COWLEY

"People like to say that Kline Thomas
walked into Eveningview and started
changing Aberdeen's sound. That he took
the reins. Made demands. Drew a line in
the sand.

That's not how it happened.

He didn't come in to change anything.
Not consciously. And certainly not to
rewrite Lloyd Brannon's legacy.

It was simpler than that.

Kline tried to put himself in Lloyd's
mindset—or at least what he imagined it
would've been. He tried to understand where
Lloyd was headed.

And in doing that, he took Aberdeen's sound
in a direction it had never gone before.

Was Kline biased toward grunge? Toward
early-to-mid '90s alt rock? Absolutely.

But he didn't walk into that mansion and
tell Aberdeen it was his way or nothing.

Did he know the world wanted a return to
that sound? No.

Did he care if it was a departure? Also no.

He had no investment in the Aberdeen sound.
Only in the sound that came out of him when
no one was telling him what to be.

People say the pushback from the band—Mike

Kilmore in particular—was harsh. That
there were fights. Yelling. Chaos.

There weren't. There were words, sure.
Tension. Clarifications.

But no one flipped a table. No guitars
were thrown.

The real story isn't in the pushback.
It's in the gamble.

Because somehow, Kline got one of his own
songs into the Kansas City setlist.

He believed in it that much. Enough to risk
it all.

Considering what happened that night—the
fallout, the fallout behind the fallout—it
turned out to be the gamble of a lifetime.

And it worked."

detune

28

Eveningview Mansion, Malibu, CA

They played it, over and over. Listened. Questioned. Tweaked. Repeated.

"It's still not there." Kline had a vision, and while they might not be able to see it, they knew obsession. A man with obsession was something they knew well and a premise they were very comfortable with.

"It's not dark enough. Gritty enough. It needs to sound like dirt and pain."

"I don't think your voice could do that any more than it has. I think you've nailed it. I just don't know how we could match it," Kilmore answered, and though it hurt him to say, he meant it. Kline's voice had shone like a piece of polished metal. His words were dirt and rust, pitting, and degradation and had done so flawlessly.

"We could detune. Maybe a half step?" Cantrell offered with a shrug, almost embarrassed to suggest such.

"We aren't a grunge band, Ben. Detuning might make it gritty, but it's not Aberdeen."

"What is Aberdeen?" Ben shrugged innocently. The point was made, even if Ben didn't mean to make it.

⫶

Kenney hit the pause after the last notes of the song concluded and before the bonus sounds of exclamation from the band bled through the recording. White removed his glasses, pinched his nose.

"Um. Okay? I don't know what this is, but it *isn't* Aberdeen," White exclaimed.

"I think that's the *point*, Paul," Cantrell offered from just right of the manager and agent. Markus looked at the graphs.

Timing, different. Tuning, different. Delivery, way different.

Markus looked at the graphs.

"What do you think, Mike?" White turned to Kilmore, and Mike looked at the faces of his bandmates and friends and already knew what they thought. It was good. Unique. Great, even. But different and uncomfortable. More importantly, he knew he was already outvoted on this.

"It's something different. Some sort of hybrid sound." White was struggling to formulate his own thoughts. He turned, leaned against the soundboard. Eddie finally sat forward.

"If you were to listen to this with fresh ears—not Aberdeen's ears—you can't deny that this song absolutely slaps. Kilmore, your ideas on layering our guitars, chef's kiss. But it's Ben's bass that really shines. Like a whale's tail, beating in the depths."

"I guess my drumming is just meh, eh?" Jose feigned hurt. Eddie, thinking he'd offended, spun around, a face of concern.

"Dude, you're Jose Madera. Your drums are always on point." Jose placed a hand on Eddie's bony shoulder.

"I'm messing with you, dude."

"Ah. Well, in that case, Jose's drumming is great, too," Eddie joked, and the band laughed. Markus took no offense that no one mentioned him, but that's because there had been no place for keyboards or turntables in this song. He couldn't be upset; the song rocked. To Eddie's point, the use of fills Jose had employed? The combinations were used to lead the percussion, not fill in gaps in transitions. It reminded him of Matt Cameron on "Fell on Black Days."

"Eddie is right. Can't deny how good that song will sound, driving down the road. Or, in front of a stadium full of fans. It's difficult in the right way. It's fun to play," Markus found himself answering.

"Stage tech's gonna love detuning for it, though," Markus added on, and it elicited laughs. Detuning it had been the key to matching Kline's voice and song.

"I do have a concern. Commercially? I think change represents a huge risk that shouldn't be ignored." White answered with truth, ambivalent and not willing to wade into the creativity side of it. But this was a test to see what the band members really thought about change of creative direction, even if it was small. He had a feeling it wouldn't stay small forever.

"I agree. We have a long history of sounding how we sound. It's what our fans, and more importantly, the label expect." Kilmore pulled at the thread. White wasn't surprised at this answer. He watched the others as he waited for Kilmore to finish.

"Furthermore, the content of the lyrics? Lloyd never blamed women. Or made drugs a crutch. That's a line Lloyd wouldn't cross," Kilmore explained. The rest of the band couldn't disagree and neither could White. But he wasn't going to bring this up now. He felt it more professional to address with the artists themselves.

"Why not?" Kline interjected, pushing for understanding.

"Lloyd believed—"

"I'm not Lloyd. My words and feelings aren't his."

"Granted." A one-word response from the guitarist that said much more. Kline's eyes closed into slits.

"Y'all needed me to give you songs. I gave you songs." He shook the notebook.

"Wait. Songs? How many?" Kenney asked, cutting the silence and deflecting the awkwardness. Kline had told them he could but not that he already had.

"You never asked." Kline thumbed the pages absently. "Four or five good starts. Eddie's been helping a lot." Eyes shifted to Eddie, who brightened at this. White watched the conversation, caught Kline's eyes. That wasn't what Kline had told him. White said nothing. Kline's eyes were appreciative that he'd kept that secret.

Eddie suspected there was more, but he'd never out Kline like that. Kline had been very guarded about it, and, knowing his friend, he knew the reasons.

"Bullshit. Give me that." Kilmore tried to snatch the notebook off the arm of the couch, but Kline beat him to it. A stiff-arm shot out and stopped Kilmore in his tracks. Kline pulled the hand back as fast as he pulled the notebook back, and Kilmore had to regain his footing.

"I'm sorry, Mike," Kline told Kilmore, honestly, and patted him on his bicep. Kline's eyes went to the floor. "But these are my personal thoughts, and I'd rather keep them to myself until I'm ready," Kline offered with a bit of morose in his voice.

White coughed to bring the attention back to focus.

He's not just writing songs, man. He's putting his soul on the page, Ben thought. The band turned to him.

"His first attempt was pretty damn good, though. I'm excited to see what else he has. When he's ready to share it." Cantrell nodded to the book, thoughtfully, and smiled.

Kline appreciated the vote of confidence and confidentiality that the bassist gave.

White saw the pieces moving on the board. He had managed enough bands to know that discord could produce greatness or destruction or both. Considering how close they already were with their lackadaisical attitude to produce anything until now, he figured this a good bet and applied the slightest push.

"Regardless, it's been a very long time since a new Aberdeen song has been laid down that at least half of you liked. I share Mike's concerns, but that's definitely progress. Keep it up, guys." With that, his shoulders slumped in exhaustion. He shrugged into his suit coat, the sweat stains of his dress shirt showing as he did so.

In the corner, forgotten and silent, Clara Cowley wrote furiously. Every word. Every look. Every silence. She didn't miss a thing, even if the band did.

This really is a gold mine and a mine field. So much was being said without words, and it was her job to bring those words to life.

White had almost made it to the gravel parking lot when Kline caught him.

"Before you go, I wanted to run this by you." White eased the door of his car closed, then shuffled in the gravel to face the short man in blue jeans and graphic t-shirt from some 80s cult classic movie.

"Alright. I want to run something by you, too." That surprised Kline.

"Shoot. You first."

"I will reiterate that while the decision is up to the band, I strongly suggest giving a lot of thought in this…change of creative direction. Certainly, the risk involved in alienating a large and important group of our fans. The majority of merchandise, for example, is bought by our female fans, and I don't think those lyrics would look very good on the front of a shirt." White wanted to make sure Kline understood.

What he didn't say was, sticking to Lloyd's sound was why they became stale.

"I think that's fair, and I will keep that in mind," Kline agreed, almost too easily. White waited, calmly. Kline leaned against the car.

"What if instead of just Lloyd's song at the tribute concert, we unveil two? If you agree, I'll make sure I give everything I have for Lloyd's, even if I don't like it. I'll do it just like the band thinks Lloyd would."

"Days in and already making deals? Sporty." He thought for a second, a man always quick on his feet.

"But brilliant, if you play your cards right. I'll make that deal with some slight tweaking. You do yours at Whiskey a Go Go, but you will scrap it if I don't like the reaction." Kline held out a hand, having truly nothing to lose, and took the man's smaller hand into his.

Paul White contemplated this deal. If the song struck a chord, regardless of the performance and the band's personal feelings towards the two, it gave Kline leverage.

A brilliant move. Truth was, if the concert didn't work out, none of it mattered.

"You've got a deal." Suddenly Kline felt the pressure of getting this song in shape in far fewer days than he'd thought.

White saw him consider this and smiled.

Let's see what the guy's got.

Excerpt from "The Voice Was Never Theirs"
BY CLARA COWLEY

"If you ask anyone when the legend began, they'll say Kansas City. They'll say the Lloyd Brannon Benefit. The contract.

Kline's viral show. Hell, any of his shows in front of dozens to a hundred. I could say all those nights, alone, in his makeshift studio.

The sealed envelope.

But I know better.

The legend, as we know it, started at the Whiskey. It was supposed to be nothing. A one-off. A fluke.

And it almost didn't happen.

I like to think the only reason Kline Thomas stepped back on that stage—the only reason he flicked the lighter was because of something Rayne Harlow said.

It's easy to vilify the con Rayne and the Queens pulled to get their shot. Easy to say they used him because they did.

Would they have made it without Kline Thomas? History says no.

And I get it. I've earned the criticism that I didn't hold the Queens to the same standard as the rest of them. But I've said it before: their survival wasn't the same.

The rest of them were never going to starve. But that's not the only reason I give them a pass.

I give them a pass because I stood behind Rayne Harlow that night—as Aberdeen played, as Kline became a myth, and I watched her cheer for his moment. I saw her cheer as a fan of rock and roll who wanted to see rebirth and was in the delivery room.

That woman wasn't clapping and screaming and dancing for her own set. She was cheering because she saw something sacred catch fire again. Real, original rock with a sound that did more than echo off your chest. It echoed in your heart because you believed what he said.

Rayne witnessed a legend born. She had faith, even if the prophet was the devil. After all, prophets don't meet you at the crossroads to make deals."

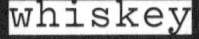

29

Whiskey a Go Go, Los Angeles, CA

"This is surreal," Eddie said, turning to Cantrell. "I mean, you guys started here. I'm getting to play this stage?"

"Hey, Clara? You want one?" Markus Kenney asked, grabbing a beer from the cooler Cantrell had raided.

Rarely acknowledged, she nodded, and Cantrell slid one all the way down the bar with practiced ease. The band had been around beat writers plenty and did what they were told: ignored her unless she spoke to them directly. Eddie and Kline hadn't that experience and had been far more social with her, treating her as a person. She hadn't taken it personally that the band ignored her. Truth was, they were far too shallow, outside of the story she was writing. She liked Eddie, very much. He was such a nice guy.

Perhaps too nice.

Same for Jose and Ben.

Markus? Unsung musical genius.

Kline was something else entirely, but he stayed guarded around her. She couldn't say she blamed him. She reminded him of some other brilliant artists from the distant past, but she hesitated in comparing him to those men and women.

"It's practically a requirement if you're a band from LA."

"I can't imagine," Eddie said, his voice tinged with awe. "Being a teenager and playing here—it's wild. I know a lot of bands did it, but still..."

"It was awful," Kenney said bluntly, lifting his beer.

"The experience? Or the playing?" Kline asked, sitting on the edge of a booth and twirling his beer bottle.

"All of it," Kenney said with a grin. "We were underage, couldn't drink, and they made our parents chaperone. Total buzzkill."

"They booed us," Kilmore added, chuckling. "Lloyd tried to sing louder to drown them out. Forgot half the lyrics."

"I snapped a guitar string trying to overplay the noise," Kilmore added, mimicking his younger self with an exaggerated air guitar. "Didn't have a backup guitar. Just had to power through with five strings."

Cantrell grinned. "By the time we were done, we'd swallowed half the beer the crowd threw at us. Great memories."

Eddie found himself grinning ear to ear, thrilled to finally see the band as regular guys sharing old war stories. He turned to Kline, expecting him to be just as awestruck, but his friend sat quietly in the booth, his expression unreadable.

Ben had a realization.

"You know, we were sitting right over there the night I called you. Called White about you guys. I was sitting at the barstool right there, where Clara is sitting."

Hearing her name, she looked up but realized they weren't talking to her. They were talking about her. She put her head down and wrote.

"Was that before or after fighting off that Amazonian?" Jose joked. All eyes went to Cantrell. This was obviously not a story he had told the rest of them.

"Pussy got your tongue, Benny Boy?" Kilmore joked. Cantrell looked sheepish and blushed.

"She was part of this band that was playing here at the same time you guys were playing in 'Bama. She was one of them."

"Well, who were they?" Eddie asked.

"I don't recall, honestly. Some half-naked women with painted faces doing acrobatics while playing horrorcore or shock-rock. Actually, it was like listening to The Cure mixed with Babes in Toyland. Quite the show, if you liked getting beat to death between the drums and bass and berated about toxic masculinity, pay equality, and periods. Never heard such foul language from a female group. Pegging? Who is into that?" With this, Clara looked up. Made a note. Said nothing.

"Sounds like at least one of them thought you were." Kilmore guffawed, his lips around a beer. Laughter erupted from them all. Cantrell didn't honor it with a response. Truth was, he had been amazed at what he had seen from them.

"The acrobatics were cool. Must not have been very good if we thought you guys were better," Cantrell chided. All laughed again. The sounds of the towering bassist's feet across the concrete floor echoed as he walked to the bar, leaned over the counter, lifted a stainless-steel cooler lid, and began setting beers on the bar top.

"Don't let Ben out of this. You should have seen the look on his face." At this, Cantrell blushed again and ran his hand through his hair.

"I've never been made to feel so small. That woman is intense."

"She was so hot, too. A hot, huge-ass woman," Jose explained.

Cantrell was flabbergasted that Jose even knew about her. He hadn't told Jose about her and certainly not that he had kept in touch for a few days before she ghosted him. Right about the time Kline and Eddie had shown up.

Small talk broke out among them, and Eddie considered that, if no one were the wiser, the six of them could be passed off as regular guys. Though, he considered Kline and himself still regular guys.

"Something on your mind, Kline?" Eddie asked gently. He'd started drinking a bit earlier than Eddie would like, but not enough to be truly concerned about.

Kline hesitated, rolling the bottle between his palms. "I've never sung a song I've written before," he said, his voice subdued. Worry. Pressure. They'd been rehearsing it religiously before settling on a master. Kline stood, walked behind the bar, and retrieved a bottle of clear liquor and six glasses. Silently, he poured for everyone, pushing the glasses across the bar. He held his own glass up, staring into the liquid as if searching for answers.

"I'm going to sing it tonight," Kline said finally. His voice was steady, but the tension in his shoulders betrayed the turmoil beneath. "We're going to play it." Yet, he seemed sure. Eddie could sense that he had been wrestling with this for God knew how long but knew it must be done.

"What? 'Drain'? Of course we are," Kilmore said, though his brow furrowed. The guitarist had a feeling he knew where this was headed. He let Kline continue.

"No," Kline said, locking eyes with him. "We're going to play *his* song."

The room went still.

"We aren't ready, Kline. It's too soon," Jose stated quickly. Eyes went from Jose to Kline. Now the eyes went to Kilmore. Kilmore thought about the song, itself and what it meant.

"I don't think it's the worst idea. We need to play it live before KC." While that was logic, it shocked the rest of the band to see Kilmore fold so quickly on a song over which, to this day, he and Kline continued to butt heads.

"We're ready," Kilmore stated, with finality that said he was with Kline and there would be no more discussion.

"You don't think White would protest?" Jose asked the guitarist.

"White doesn't control us once we're onstage. He just gets us there," Kilmore answered.

They'd mastered a dozen or more versions of that song. Clara Cowley looked up from the last stool on the end of the bar. The very one that Cantrell had pointed to. She raised an eyebrow.

"And we're going to play it first." Kline dug in. He made it clear that no wasn't an option, and the way he came out with it sounded like he hadn't just thought of it. He had been wrestling with when to make the declaration.

That's a power move. Or insanity. She wrote it all down. She'd learned so much about the band over the last few days, and while she was no musician, to say they weren't ready was a lie. They were just scared. Or perhaps not ready to move on.

"Whatever comes out, comes out. Maybe this is where we find that sound."

Now, wasn't that an interesting concept? She jotted down more notes. She could certainly understand Kline's perspective. He'd peered into every corner. Lifted every couch. Couldn't find the sound they wanted.

What would happen when he found the truth, hidden in the shadows?

⋮

The green room was dimly lit, the hum of anticipation from the crowd muffled through the walls and down the hall from the entrance of the stage. Kline sat alone on the couch, Eddie tuning his acoustic guitar on a stool. His fingers moved with precision. Kline felt the weight of the night pressing down on him—not just the performance but everything it symbolized.

A soft knock on the door jolted him out of his thoughts. Before he could respond, the door creaked open. Rayne stepped in. Her presence filled the room like a storm cloud—quiet, charged, impossible to ignore. She wore a black leather jacket over a simple grey dress, her auburn hair catching the light from the overhead bulb. Her sharp and beautifully unique eyes met his, and for a moment, neither spoke.

"Rayne?" He called her by her real name, and she realized that hearing him say it did something to her. Cherie disapproved of the feeling.

"Hey," she said, her voice softer than he remembered. She closed the door behind her, leaning against it. "Hope I'm not interrupting."

He shook his head, standing up. "No, not at all. I just..." He trailed off, unsure of how to finish. "What are you doing here?"

Eddie smiled at her, took his cue, and excused himself after smiling at Kline.

"Hey, good to see you again, Rayne." He tapped Kline on the back. "I'll see you out there, bud."

Kline realized that for all his talk about wanting to know the real her, he'd ignored her the last few days. Forgotten her. It had only been days, but still. He realized something.

She's been the one bright thing in my life. The thing I've been looking forward to. And I've ignored it. She asked me to call her the next day. I didn't.

She crossed her arms, a faint smile tugging at her lips. "I heard you guys were playing tonight." It was painful for him to realize that he hadn't invited her, much less reached out.

Kline nodded, rubbing the back of his neck. "Yeah. Feels... huge. Overwhelming, really." He paused, his eyes scanning her face. "I should have invited you."

"I almost didn't come," she admitted. "I thought about just sending a message and inviting myself, but that felt so impersonal. Plus, when you didn't call..." She shrugged and her voice trailed off, disappointed.

"I wanted to wish you luck. In person. Regardless. Not every day that you know a real rockstar and get to see them play. It's like having something personal at stake."

Her words hit him harder than he expected. Kline exhaled slowly, his hands resting on his hips. "I've been meaning to reach out. It's just—things have been insane. Getting ready for this. Adjusting to everything. Writing. Rehearsing. Recording." She held up a hand to stop him and smiled. There was genuine concern in both his voice and his face that gave weight to his words.

Rayne's expression softened. "I get it. Life moves fast, and you've had a lot on your plate. I'm not here to give you a hard time, Kline. I'm here for some kick-ass music." Kline wondered how she'd walked past what they called security around here.

He nodded, but the regret in his chest tightened. "Still. I should've called. I really meant to. I want to see you again."

"It's okay," she said, stepping closer. Her voice dropped, gentle but firm. "Really. I just wanted to say I'm proud of you. You are a man being asked to resurrect a ghost. I wanted you to hear this: you don't have to." He started to ask what she meant. She pointed to the bracelet.

"And you still have that." She pointed to his wrist. "So, now I know you're gonna fuckin' slay. I hope it brings you the luck you say it has."

That last sentence carried weight. He fingered the tree on it. It was no longer in his pocket; it was on his wrist. She'd put so much stake on it, he wanted to know what she meant. Another time. At some point, without thinking, he'd slipped it on. It felt like armor now.

"Your roots run deep, Kline. Deep and strong. Resilient. Tap into that, whatever it is. You can do this." She stuck a finger in his chest, and he felt like he could run through these walls.

Kline's throat tightened, and he forced a smile. "Thanks. That means more than you know." If he was nervous about pleasing people he didn't know, he really felt the pressure of having someone's opinion in the crowd that seemed to genuinely care about him. Had expectations. Other than Eddie, this was a first for him as a performer. Strangely, it meant just as much for her as it had for his best friend.

She reached out and touched his arm briefly, her fingers warm against his skin. "You're going to kill it tonight. I know it." And then she did something before she realized it. She pulled him close. Laid a head on his shoulder. He breathed deep, and they both felt something leave his body. He wrapped his arms around her.

"I'll do my best," he said, his voice quieter. "It's just... it feels like a lot to live up to. Lloyd's shoes are impossible to fill." He absentmindedly referred to his predecessor when he had meant the song. His chest quivered. He swallowed it down and forced himself to enjoy this woman's touch.

"You're not here to follow his footsteps," Rayne said firmly as she pushed him away to arm's length, but her hand stayed on his muscled biceps as she looked fiercely into his eyes. "You're here to *leave your own tracks*. Something only you can do. Don't forget that."

She said this with such conviction that it felt like she was an authority on the subject. Kline guessed that whatever it was that she did for a living, she had to understand what that was like to say it with such authority. He tried not to linger on this thought. If she could do whatever it was that she did to survive, he could do this. It almost felt simple, putting it in those terms.

Her words settled over him, grounding him. For the first time in days, he felt a flicker of calm. "I'll try to keep that in mind."

She kissed him quickly on the cheek, stepped back toward the door, her hand on the handle. "Good. Now, I'll let you get back to it. Just don't let the assholes in the crowd get you down. They can be relentless. You are on the stage, not them. It's your voice. Not theirs. They are an echo of you, not the other way around."

Kline laughed softly, though he wasn't sure what she meant. Once again, she said it with such authority and knowledge.

"Thanks, Rayne."

"I'll see you after the show and you can buy me a drink."

"You got it. I owe you one." She winked those eyes at him.

"Baby, you don't owe me a thing." She started to walk away but stopped. Smiled, hopeful. "But I'll take that drink."

And then she was gone. He heard her heels clack down the hall and disappear into the cacophony. The room felt emptier without her, but Kline's chest felt lighter. Her visit had stirred something in him—a mix of gratitude, regret, and determination. The last was the overwhelming feeling.

"Alright," he muttered to himself. "Let's do this."

He looked into the mirror, hated what he saw. Not himself, but an imposter of what all those people out there expected to see. Lloyd Brannon. Kline shook his head and walked toward the door. The noise of the crowd outside grew louder with every step. Claps. Chants.

"Ab-er-DEEN! Ab-er-DEEN!" He wasn't sure if he was ready, but he knew he had to try. For the band, for himself—and maybe, in ways he couldn't quite admit, for her. More for her. He found that odd, but it worked.

He didn't know who she was. She'd made sure of that. But he still felt like he owed her everything.

"There's no ghosts," he told himself. He wasn't sure if he believed it, but there was only one way to find out.

:

From the pit came a cacophony of noise—laughter, conversations, and shouted drink orders melding into a singular roar. When the house lights dimmed, the voices unified into a raucous cheer.

Mike Kilmore, holding a glass on each of his outstretched fingers, set them down on the nearest piece of equipment backstage. He uncorked a bottle of expensive bourbon with his teeth, spitting the cork to the side, and filled each glass to the brim. Taking a deep pull straight from the bottle, he swirled the liquor in his mouth, his long, curly hair flying as he exhaled.

The rest of the band reached forward to take their glasses, including Eddie and Kline, who hesitated slightly before following suit. Kilmore slung his guitar over his back and raised his glass.

"Guys," he began, his voice steady but strained, "I know the last few weeks have been tough. But, God, it feels good to be here. Real stage. Real fans. With you guys. Wow." His eyes flicked to the shorter man, holding his glass with both hands.

Eddie, glass raised high, added, "To the music. Let's burn this stage up."

"Light this fucker up," Kline echoed, his voice low but resolute.

The six glasses clinked together, spilling liquor onto the floor, and each man downed his shot in one motion.

Taking their cues from the veterans, Kline and Eddie watched as Jose Madera slipped behind the wall of equipment to take his seat at the drum kit. Ben Cantrell traversed the stage, his footsteps muffled by the rugs covering the cables, slinging his bass over his shoulder before stepping back into the shadows. Eddie followed, his guitar swinging at his hips, taking his place slightly off-center stage.

The crowd's noise dulled when the lights dimmed further, and the energy swelled to a fever pitch. The house went black for the briefest moment—an eternity to the electrified crowd.

The house announcer came on.

"Ladies and gentlemen, the Whiskey a Go Go is proud to present…ABERDEEN!" The crowd erupted, but it was clearly a mixed bag of emotions.

Eddie came in with his acoustic guitar, strumming an eerie set of chords, setting an ethereal mood. Three times through the progression and then it stopped.

Then a thunderous boom erupted as Madera slammed his bass drum.

Boom! Kick!

Boom-kick!

Boom! Kick!

Boom-kick!

The lights pulsed with every beat, illuminating a sea of faces. Each snare and floor tom strike sent blinding flashes through the room, a staccato assault on the senses. The rhythm built to a dizzying crescendo, culminating in a frenetic crash of cymbals before everything fell silent.

The crowd erupted in screams. In the darkness, Kline passed behind Kilmore, patting his shoulder as he took his place at center stage. Gripping the microphone, Kline's breath slowed as he stared into the void before him.

The crowd leaned forward, hanging on the silence, when Kilmore's guitar screamed to life. A piercing, crystal-clear solo filled the air and vanished just as suddenly as it began, leaving the room in stunned silence.

The crowd leaned farther.

Just as Kline opened his mouth to sing, a voice cut through the air and stopped his voice dead in his throat.

"GET THIS FAT-ASS TROLL OFF THE STAGE!"

Laughter rippled through the audience.

"FUCKIN' HACK!" another voice yelled.

"WE WANT LLOYD, NOT THIS POSEUR!"

More taunts about being a social media construction. A stand-in. A publicity stunt. A shill.

Kline's jaw snapped shut, his teeth grinding. His hands fell to his sides, his body rigid. Eddie, standing to his left, craned his neck toward him, concern etched across his face. Kline was supposed to come in after the four-count pause, but his voice was stone silent.

An empty beer can whizzed past Kline's shoulder, smashing against the drum riser. The crowd jeered, emboldened. Eddie turned to Kilmore, who just shrugged, jaw clenched.

This was Kline's moment. No rescue was coming.

Kilmore struck the intro again—louder this time. A wall of sound, chaotic and unanchored. Like an orchestra tuning before the conductor steps in.

"JUST SING!" he shouted.

Kline's head snapped up. He locked eyes with Kilmore, who mouthed, *you've got this.*

Kline scanned the front row. A wall of women—fierce and still. One, a broad-shouldered blonde with a stare that could kill. Beside her, a redhead. For a second, she was Chrys. But it wasn't Chrys. It was Rayne.

Another heckler.

"SOMEONE GET THE HOOK FOR THIS LOSER PIECE OF SHIT!"

The fire lit in his chest.

Don't tell me what I can't do.

He raised the mic. Rayne met his eyes. Her smile was calm. Her hands said *breathe. Push.*

And then—he let it out.

"A river of lava cascades down her body..."

Barely a whisper. Medium register. Crystal-clear. Heavy vibrato.

The lights went black.

The world held its breath.

Then came the hammer. Kline's voice exploded. Pure force. Madera adjusted on instinct, cymbals crashing to match the surge. Kilmore's guitar snarled in. Eddie followed.

In thirty seconds, the crowd forgot every insult.

From chaos came clarity.

Clara had heard this song a dozen times. But never like this. Everything messy and broken, suddenly converging. Crushingly precise. Perfectly Kline.

Red-hot as the blood in my veins.
For her I burn.
For her I yearn!

Each line soared higher, Kline's voice pushing against the limits of control. Madera's cymbals crashed in waves, Cantrell's bass thundered, and Eddie's harmonies underpinned Kline's raw delivery with haunting precision.

Kline fed off the energy, ignoring the ache in his chest and the sweat dripping down his face. He sang like a man possessed, pouring every ounce of anger, regret, and defiance into the lyrics. Occasionally, he looked down at the front of the stage. Rayne danced, twisting from side to side, one hand in the air.

She turned to the woman who towered over her during one of the guitar solos.

"I told him he'd kill it!" Rayne yelled as she pointed the raised hand, finger pointing at him.

Ava, shaking her blonde hair viciously from side to side, didn't have to say anything to let her know that she agreed.

On the last solo rift, Kilmore strutted over to Kline, purposefully, as he shredded. The spotlight was on him, and he entertained as he had for decades. Kline bent down to the guitar, held a hand to his ear. He turned his face to the crowd, nodded in appreciation. Waved them on. They responded as Kilmore's fingers danced on the neck, the pick in his hand flew.

This does feel different, Kilmore found himself thinking. Kline motioned for him as he smiled, pointing to him, giving him the spotlight, willingly.

"Give it to 'em, Mike!" Kline yelled into the mic.

It was all smiles from Eddie, who watched the growth before his eyes. Kline embraced the man that had fought him for this sound. Cantrell eased over to Eddie and the two faced off, strings to strings, and jammed.

Mike turned with his back to Kline and leaned into the singer. Kline leaned back into him, and they formed a dynamic pillar of power. Guitar and voice. He entered the last chorus, and he walked forward, menaced at the edge of the stage, bent forward, pointing at her as he sang and beat his chest.

Red-hot as the blood in my veins.
For her I burn.
For her I yearn!

The final note lingered in the air, ringing out over a now-silent crowd. Then the applause erupted—a roar that shook the venue.

The loudest scream came from the two mismatched women up front. Kline pointed at her, firmly, and smiled. Something coursed through the look to one another.

She'd done that. They both realized the connection, and Rayne beamed.

"LET'S FUCKIN' GO!" Rayne screamed at the top of her lungs as she bounded up and down. Ava turned to her, a look of confusion. Rayne looked up at the woman.

"You cannot say that didn't kick so much ass!" Ava nodded viciously. It had, but that wasn't the question she had for Rayne. One thing was certain: the man onstage had fallen for her. She wasn't so sure that Rayne was objective in this venture anymore. It pained her to think it, but so what if it wasn't, as long as they got what they wanted.

As Kline stepped back, grabbing a towel, Kilmore seized the mic.

"Ladies and gentlemen, thank you for coming tonight. We are Aberdeen." The crowd roared again. "That song was written by Lloyd Brannon. It's the last song he ever wrote, and this is the first time we've played it for anyone. We hope you liked it."

The heckler's voice pierced through the applause.

"BE A LOT BETTER IF LLOYD SANG IT! NOT THAT SHORT, BALD FUCKER!"

"IT AIN'T ABERDEEN WITHOUT LOYD! GET THAT SCAB OFF THE STAGE!

"SELLOUTS!"

"NOTHING MORE THAN A COVERBAND SINGER IN AN ABDERDEEN COVER BAND!"

Ben's head snapped toward the voice. His eyes blazing in anger, which happened so rarely. He stepped towards the voice, which came from Kilmore's side of the stage. They'd expected a rowdy crowd. Warned Kline and Eddie about this place. This was vitriol.

"Hey, fuck you, man!" he shouted. "You wanna get up here and sing it yourself?"

The man launched a beer can, but the errant throw struck Kilmore square in the face. Kilmore brought a hand to his face and found blood. With a look of shock, he looked back to the crowd and then turned to Kline and Eddie. More flew by his cheek, and he wondered why they were aiming at him when their ire was obviously towards Kline. But even as he stared at Kline, he could see Kline absorbing blows of his own. Kline stood strong because he had nowhere else to go.

These guys ain't worth all this.

"Fuck this shit." Kilmore walked offstage, and his gait said he wasn't coming back. One by one, each of the band members left, leaving Kline and Eddie alone. From the edge of the stage, Ben called to them.

"Get off the stage, guys. This shit ain't worth it." Kline looked to Eddie, then the crowd. Then he found Rayne, and there was something in her eyes. A look of concern for him, but something else he couldn't know. Ava leaned close to Rayne.

"What a bunch of pussies," Ava said. Rayne shrugged.

"If we had a dollar for every can and bottle thrown at us, well, we wouldn't have to play shitholes like this anymore." The crowd was restless and expecting them to come back.

"They ain't coming back," Rayne heard herself say. She leaned back into the tall woman.

"They aren't used to this anymore." Rayne tried to give them agency, but she knew Ava wouldn't agree. She felt obligated to, anyway.

"Then they've forgotten what it's like down here in the trenches with the rest of us," Ava returned.

"Ain't a safety net of security guards down in these trenches."

Two rows back, Clara Cowley watched it all unfold. Same conclusion, different takeaway.

Kline Thomas had power. That much was obvious. But he wasn't ready. Not for *this*. Not yet.

And the redhead that had been skulking around? The one Clara could now place?

There was no mistaking the dynamic. That kind of eye contact wasn't casual. It wasn't lust. It was need. Vulnerability onstage wasn't rare—but direction like that was. Too bad she couldn't see how she looked at him. That would have been far more telling.

Lastly, she caught the look on Kilmore's face as he wiped blood from his cheek.

That said it all.

He wasn't sold. And he sure as hell wasn't taking another can to the face for Kline Thomas. Clara didn't believe in violence. But silence? That was worse. Kilmore said nothing, did nothing, and when the blood came, he ran. So much for loyalty. Kline stood there alone—because when it got ugly, everyone else vanished.

⁝

Aiesha and White speed walked towards the green room. White opened the door, let Aiesha through, then closed it behind him.

"I'm not going back out there, White. Don't even try to convince me," Kilmore exclaimed before the door even shut.

"They weren't even trying to hit you, Mike," Ben pointed out. Kilmore wheeled on him.

"That's right. They were trying to hit him." Kilmore pointed a finger at Kline. He turned to White. "I've kept my mouth shut enough. This publicity stunt has gone too far. I am too old to be dealing with this shit, and we are too good to be doing bullshit shows like this. It's obvious that they don't want him here. Why do we?" Kilmore's fingers shot out in the general direction of the fans.

"It's just a couple of rowdy assholes, Mike," Aiesha offered up.

"Yeah? Well, let's see you go out there, then." She clamped her mouth shut. "That's what I thought."

Finally, Kilmore turned to Kline and Eddie.

"Look, guys. This was never going to work, okay? No offense. It's better to call it now than keep pushing."

White coughed, and Kilmore turned to see White's face harden. *Go no further, or else,* White's face said. Kilmore obeyed. White tried not to judge Kilmore's reaction too hard. Getting smoked in the face was enough for anyone to lash out. KC was a done deal. Kline was going to perform and he knew that. What happened after that, they would wait and see.

There was silence. White didn't know what to do. Neither did Aiesha.

The eyes went to Kline, who sat in a chair, hands folded between his knees, head slumped. He took a deep breath, and something caught his eyes. The bracelet on his wrist. Kline fingered it and thought. His back, the only thing visible besides the top of his head, rose mightily. He stood up.

"Come on, Eddie. Let's go."

Eddie hesitated at first, his back just inches from one of the walls, his arms down at his sides, shoulders slumped.

"Eddie, follow me. Now," Kline ordered, and Eddie looked around sheepishly as Kline opened the door and brushed past White and Aiesha.

Eddie followed his friend out, but Kline didn't turn towards the exit. He turned towards the stage. Eddie used his long strides to catch up with Kline.

"Wait. Where are we going?"

Kline never turned.

"If they don't want to play, that's fine. But we are. We have to. We've come too far and been through too much not to do this."

Kline bounded up the two steps of the stage. The house lights were on, and a mixture of jeers and cheers met him. Kline grabbed the mic from the stand, shook the cord, and investigated the crowd, whose noise muted before he went to the edge of the drum riser. Eddie had stopped short of the stage and watched, nervously.

Kline returned with two glass beer bottles. The crowd was silent. Kline stepped to the edge of the stage, twisted off one cap and then the other.

Rayne looked to Ava, who stood silent—stone-faced.

Behind them, Clara Cowley didn't move. She'd spent years chasing legends. Now one was unfolding in front of her lens.

"You want to throw bottles? Here—have two." He doused himself with them. Then, he smashed both bottles on the stage, the pieces of glass reflecting light in all directions. Every member of the crowd jumped a step back in unison.

He bowed his head and smiled. Nothing else flew.

Kline stepped to the side stage, grabbed an acoustic from the rack, and pressed it into Eddie's hands.

Without a word, he dragged two chairs into the spotlight—scraping metal on wood, slow and deliberate.

He sat, lowered the mic, and let out a breath.

The weight of it all had landed—but he wasn't backing down.

"Before this show, a friend said something to me. She said that I can't walk in footsteps. I have to make my own tracks."

Eddie nervously walked forward and sat down. The vitriol died and Eddie took a cautious breath. The crowd had been silenced from the two glass bombs Kline had dropped.

White started to mount the steps to the stage. He looked to Aiesha, who grabbed him by the arm.

"Wait. Just wait." He turned to her, surprised.

"So, if this is it…well…I have a track for you. If it's all I leave here with, then I can live with that." He cleared his throat, turned to Eddie, and gave him a smile that said, 'just do your best.'

Eddie shrugged and smiled. He didn't know why he'd followed Kline—until the chords hit. Then he understood everything. *Fuck it. Let's be us. Together.*

"This is called 'Drain.'"

Eddie needed a moment to think about how to play it, but he found himself strumming. After a few bars, Kline closed his eyes and began humming. Eddie and Kline felt each other out over what seemed like minutes. Finally, Kline's voice emerged, softly, painfully, but beautifully. He slapped a soft rhythm on his thighs. The venue was dead silent. Kline sang in a middle octave, and

Eddie noted this was not how it had been originally designed. Kline's voice shook and broke, searching for notes. It was haunting, but real and authentic.

> Walls of lies and pride,
> Form this cage I've built.
> Just a broken man in borrowed light,
> Someone's shadow twice my size.
> Cracks where shame can slip inside.
> No ceiling stops rain of guilt.
> Pouring down.
> Filling up.
> Do I drain it?
> Or does it drain me?

Eddie's voice echoed eerily in harmony on the last two lines as he ad-libbed a solo as Kline hummed again, sorrowful. Kline shifted up an octave, and Eddie harmonized in the octave Kline had just left. With Eddie's voice grounding him, Kline's notes were perfect. Clara couldn't help but hear tortured souls from three specific MTV Unplugged albums coming through the voice of one man. The hair on her neck and arms stood at attention, her skin prickled.

> You built these walls in silence.
> Brick by brick with spite and shame.
> Locked in here and further from home.
> Every song strikes a hollow tone.
> I wear a mask they paid to see.
> Is this stage freedom or a parody?

Pouring down.
Filling up.
Do I drain it? (Drain it)
Or does it drain me? (Drain me)

Kline let Eddie shine, leading up to the chorus. Eddie was a fantastic player, but Kline had never heard him play with such precision and grace. Eddie's foot danced to the rhythm; his cheek nearly pressed against the top of the guitar.

Left me to drown, went mad.
Now pour out the curse you had.
Do I drain it?
Or does it drain me?
Can't be happy wearing chains.
Can't be dry when it always rains.
I can't be myself
If I can't be free.
Do I drain it?
Or does it drain me?

They finished the song. The room was silent. Not empty. Not a vacuum. Just holding its breath.

Kline leaned forward. "Thank you, for that moment."

Ava exhaled like she'd been underwater. "Jesus Christ, Rayne…"

Rayne didn't speak. Didn't blink. Her eyes were fixed on Kline.

"This is legend shit," Ava whispered. "Like… real legend."

"I don't know what beer costs here, but I bet I can sing longer than you can afford to buy them. I can take bottles. I can take your hatred. Let me tell you something else I can take. Singing all

night. If you want *that*, then let's hear it." He didn't have to wait.
The crowd roared. Kline smiled—barely—and turned toward
the wings. The pack was ready.

Kline glanced toward Aberdeen and gave the smallest nod—
wait. You'll know when.

"Alright. That's what I was looking for. This one is called 'Last
Night.' You may know it."

The crowd cheered. Kline turned to Eddie, covered the mic,
and whispered. Eddie nodded that he understood and adjusted
the capo once, thought about it, and changed it. He hit the strings
hard and played Kline in.

"Heeeeyyy, hey, Momma! Momma, heeeyyy!" It was subdued,
but right in his wheelhouse.

Eddie stepped in, slow, steady, and grounding:

How could I ever deserve your love?

That way you look from above.

Let's go down to the shore without a care.

Who cares if we go in our underwear.

It was understated and bluesy but purposeful by choice. Kline
broke here and began humming. He turned slightly, giving a nod
to the band side stage, who understood and stayed in the shadows
as they took their places. Only Kilmore hung back. Behind him,
White and Aiesha watched, carefully.

"Fuck," Kilmore muttered as he strapped on his guitar. The
light stayed on Kline, who continued to hum softly with the play
of Eddie.

"You bastard." He dejectedly joined the stage.

Kline shot to his feet—kicking the chair behind him.

Jose's drums followed, slow and steady at first—then pounding
like blood in a vein.

Kline hit the edge of the stage, bent over the mic, screaming.

"HEY!" he roared, holding it until his lungs gave out.

Jose's drums cut.

The crowd erupted—his scream swallowed by hundreds of others.

Fingers poised. Sticks raised.

Lights—detonated.

He cupped a hand to his ear—daring them. They gave him their fury.

"WALK THE BEACH OF SAND SO WHITE!"

"YEAH, LET'S MAKE LOVE LIKE WE DID LAST NIGHT! UUUUHHHH!" He gave it right back.

He leapt into the drop—and the band exploded.

Kline landed hard on his knees, leaned back, and *roared*—a sound forged somewhere between fire and grief, with a finesse that didn't seem earthly.

Clara Cowley watched; breath caught halfway to her ribs.

She'd covered legends. Documented implosions. Written obits too early, she started keeping templates.

But this? This was different.

She should've written something down. Instead, she just stared.

If she'd pulled her eyes from the stage, she would've seen the same look on every face in the room. Even on the two women in front of her—women who shouldn't care. Should hate.

Women just like him, she realized. Pieces clicked.

They were all saying the same thing—Begging. Screaming. *Praying.*

I just want to be heard.

It wasn't a lyric. It wasn't a pitch. It was a truth. Raw. Ugly. Familiar.

She'd heard it in every scream he didn't let loose. She'd read it between every line he hadn't written yet.

Because something was happening. Something *real*.

Kline Thomas wasn't being born a rockstar tonight. He always had been. Tonight was just when the world caught up.

And Aberdeen? They'd played those songs thousands of times. They'd always sounded the same. That wasn't a knock. Unlike the streaming show, Kline didn't echo Lloyd Brannon. He sang the songs how he wanted to sing them. Aberdeen, professionals, had shifted time cadence and tone to match. Then, there was Eddie's guitar.

What would Aberdeen sound like if Kline seized creative control. Surely not that jazzy funk quasi-metal band. Certainly not songs about beaches and psychedelics or pondering the universe. No. It would be about struggle and pain. Something real people needed to hear because they could relate.

If they could hold it together.

The set ended. The lights fell. The stage exhaled.

Clara didn't move. She couldn't.

How? She found herself shaking her mane of greying curls. *How the hell did that just happen?*

Her feet ached. Her head pounded. Her ears rang like church bells.

I'm too old for this shit, she thought.

But deep down, she knew that wasn't true. Because something cracked open inside her—something she hadn't felt in decades.

That kid. The one who waited outside venues with a fake badge and a real notebook. That kid was screaming.

That kid wanted to run after him. To say *thank you*. To say *finally*.

That kid still believed in resurrection.

And then—the crash. The ache behind the awe.

Because Clara knew the pattern. She'd seen it. Lived it. Written it.

One miraculous set. Then the world takes its cut. Fame. Pressure. Subtraction. She'd buried too many like him. Voices that burned too hot. Bodies that gave too much. Legacies that never made it to *legacy*.

She didn't want to watch it again. Not with *him*.

Kline Thomas was too good. Too raw. Too fucking alive—when he became himself and put all the other bullshit to the side.

And now? She was afraid.

Afraid the world would never get the chance to love him. Afraid he wouldn't survive long enough to be hated properly. Afraid she'd be the one to write the final draft of something that deserved a hundred more chapters.

So, she stood there. No notes. No recordings. Just one quiet, silent prayer.

Let them feel him before he's gone. Please, God, if you're up there... Let them feel him.

Clara wondered what gods Aberdeen were thanking backstage right now. This could have been an apocalypse if it had gone sideways before KC. She could only imagine the chaos, the relief, the bruised egos swallowing their pride. Something more. Elation from salvaging this moment. This, she had to see for herself.

She made her way toward the green room, still humming with aftershock. She wasn't ready to speak to anyone—but she needed to see it. *Feel it.*

As she opened the door, she froze.

Kline Thomas was nose to nose with Mike Kilmore, finger pointed hard.

"What kind of bush-league bullshit was that? Walking offstage like some kind of fucking hack? Don't you ever walk out on me again."

He leaned in. "Get in line. Or get the fuck out of the way."

11 PM PDT, Friday, September 15, 2022
Apartments on Fountain Ave. and Vine St.
Hollywood, CA

Rayne eased the apartment door shut. Two sets of eyes flicked up from the worn couch. Ava plodded past the kitchen and dropped into the recliner across from Jen and Connie. In one motion, she snapped the footrest up. The metal clank made Rayne grimace.

"Sorry," Ava said. "But since you're already up and mad, grab me a beer, honey?"

Without turning, Jen held an empty can aloft and shook it. Rayne bit back a retort and pulled four cold ones from the fridge.

The four sat in silence for a beat.

"Least you could do is stock liquor if we're your free babysitters," Jen said.

"Wouldn't be very responsible of me to leave my kid with a couple drunks," Rayne shot back.

"Hey, I resent that. I'm responsible," Connie quipped.

"Yeah," Jen leaned toward her, "and it's her kid. Aren't you supposed to be the responsible mother?"

"That's why I don't have any of them little crotch goblins. I ain't ever growing up." Jen stage-whispered it like a confession.

"Miracles never cease," Ava muttered. "Considering you've been run through more than a school hallway." She popped her can. "But you're right about one thing. You ain't ever growing up."

"What's wrong with that? So I can be like her?" Jen jabbed a finger at Rayne.

Rayne said nothing. Ava knew why. She'd left Lanna again. But there was a reason, and she needed reminding.

"Rayne's got this dude hook, line, and sinker. Should've seen how he lit up when she walked in. Smitten. Even on stage. Couldn't take his eyes off her. Smitten by the red-headed goddess she is."

It unsettled Rayne that her hair had chosen her for this job. Not her voice. Not her rage. Not what she'd lived through. Just the genes she was born with. And none of them seemed to care. If the con worked, they were fine letting her be the bait. Which made them no different than the men they swore to despise.

"Yeah?" Connie asked. "I'm starting to have doubts about this little honey-potting-for-studio-time plan."

"No, you were rehearsing your 'I told you so' speech," Ava shot back.

Connie didn't flinch as she wiped the can with her shirt. "It's not about me being right. The whole scheme is outlandish. And it hasn't worked yet. I've seen no proof. Has she even asked him for studio time? Brought her around anyone who matters?"

Rayne stayed quiet. Because Connie was right. None of that had happened. Truth was, she'd barely been around him at all. Was it because he wasn't interested? Or because the mask cracked the second she tried to wear it — and she couldn't bring herself to use a man she might actually respect? Maybe even like. Which went against everything: her scars, the Queens' mantra that men weren't to be trusted, let alone admired. And that betrayal of the mask cut deeper than any plan. Guilt, sharp and familiar, filled the silence.

"Quit using big words around the child," Ava said.

"Ava's been asleep for—oh. You bitch!" Jen hurled an unopened can at her. Ava caught it, cracked it, and double-fisted both.

Connie's eyes narrowed. "Stars don't usually align like this."

"First of all, thanks to my planning, a well-placed cup of pop, and Rayne's red hair? Here we are." Ava tipped her beer toward Rayne. "Now tell them about tonight."

Rayne crossed to the couch, sat at their feet. "He didn't flame out," she said quietly. "He slayed."

Ava barked a laugh. "Slayed is an understatement. He's an absolute rockstar. Aberdeen flamed out. Kline lit himself up. Flame on!" She mimed the Human Torch.

"That's high praise," Connie said. Ava shrugged.

"Deserved."

Then Connie shifted. When she finally spoke, the room went still.

"If you'd quit jerking him off for a second, I'd like to know how this helps us." Her voice was small but sharp. "If Rayne's closing in on him? Fine. But remember this: the story is ours. Not his. We are the rockstars. We earned it — even if it's underhanded. Time's running out, and I'm out of patience."

Rayne stayed silent, heat burning in her chest. They didn't see it — how being chosen for her hair, for her body, made her no different than the women men had always used. And now her own sisters were fine with it, as long as the con worked. No different than the men they swore to despise.

"Step one, conveniently run into him. Done. Step two, see him socially. Also, done. Step three, get him interested in you, however you define that, but it has to be a real connection, at least for him." As Connie explained, Ava watched Rayne's face. She'd seen Rayne tonight. Not Cherie. Music was music.

"Sounds like you're almost there. Step four, get him invested enough in you that he gets us a break."

As Connie talked, Rayne picked up Lanna's baby Taylor from the stand, fished the pick from the capo. She strummed and tuned, seemingly lost, not paying attention.

Connie's eyes swept the room, landed on Rayne, hard and certain. "So let me make this clear: even if we don't show up in every chapter... this book is about us. It was always about us."

Rayne strummed a D minor chord, considered it. Moved the capo, hit it again. Strummed an A. Eyes closed, she swayed slightly, relieved as the conversation shifted away.

"Told myself I'd never be you,
Sellin' myself out and bein' untrue.
Got this plan called the honey pot,
Got these steps that feel like a lot.
Wearin' a mask to hide the truth,
Startin' to slip."

Her rasp was low, threadbare, carrying just enough breath to make the strings quiver beneath her voice.

"Slip, slippy, slip. Slippin' away."

The words seemed to fall out of her mouth more than she sang them, hushed, vulnerable. Almost dream-like. Ava froze mid-drink, the can tilted but untouched. Connie's brow furrowed; Jen pressed her lips tight, the joke gone from her face.

The room was silent except for the faint buzz of the fridge. Rayne's hands stopped on the frets, and the air hung heavy with what she'd admitted — to herself, and worse, to them. She kept her eyes lowered. Reset. Strummed again, as if starting over could erase the slip.

"Sometimes I wonder 'bout bein' a mom.
Sometimes I wonder if it's just a job.
Startin' to think I'm not enough.

Startin' to think it's just too tough."

Her voice cracked on *tough,* more breath than note, but she pushed through. The sound was raw — not polished, not pretty. It was jagged, scarred, alive.

"Pulled my mask back tight today, resolve to keep the world at bay."

She sighed, reached into the drawer, pulled out her hidden notebook. Flipped to a page, fingers lingering like the lyrics themselves might burn. She had written them years ago, still just a hopeful girl escaping poverty. Men had confused her terror for consent, her silence for acceptance. Sometimes she wasn't sure herself. But she was sure of this: coming here was supposed to be the answer. Somehow, some way, she'd become the Rockstar.

Life hadn't gotten much better, and that was the irony.

"Left that one-stoplight town in the rearview,

Sunset chasing me down the 10.

Told myself I'd never be you,

Never let a man break me again.

Packed up a voice and a pocket of dreams,

Traded dirt roads for neon scenes.

Standing under this Hollywood sign,

I call you up just to say the line—"

The chords softened, tender but uneven. Her voice floated — thin at the top, growling low in the breaks — every note feeling like it might collapse but refusing to. Connie shifted on the couch, uncomfortable, like she was hearing too much.

Rayne's eyes flicked to Lanna's door. Then her hand slammed down on the strings, loud, final.

"Momma, I made it.

Made it out, made it here,

Made it past all the years
That tried to cage me in.
Momma, I made it. Can't you see?
I'm everything you said I'd never be."

Her rasp tore into the chorus, the words ragged but full. Ava's jaw worked like she wanted to speak but couldn't.

Jen rose from the couch, slid down beside her, leaned into Rayne's shoulder. Their voices tangled — Jen's clean country twang clashing imperfectly with Rayne's cracked rasp. They sang together, though Jen faltered half a bar when Rayne's voice cracked again and came back harder, defiant.

"Momma, I made it.
Made it out, made it here,
Made it past all the years
That tried to cage me in.
Momma, I made it."

Jen rested her platinum head on Rayne's tattooed shoulder, her harmony softening as if to steady Rayne's rawness. Rayne kept shifting chords, refusing to let the moment close. Her eyes stayed shut, voice trembling but unrelenting.

"Can't you see?
This story is about us — it always was.
They don't know yet, but that's because
We're everything they swore we couldn't be.
And this story's *still* me."

Her final note shredded into silence. The strings buzzed under her palm.

No one breathed. Even Connie. The room wasn't quiet—it was stunned."

EPILOGUE

CHRYS THOMAS BRANNON
was curled on her couch, lavishness of this lifestyle still new. Reaching behind her to the couch-side table, she lifted the glass of wine. It was getting late, and this would be just enough to let her wind down just so. For once it was quiet, and she reveled in its peace after another long day of tirelessly working on the LBF benefit weekend.

The phone on the table began to vibrate, and her eyes shot to the closed door down the long hallway of her downtown LA apartment. Her head laid back on the arm of the sofa, carefully setting the glass on the coffee table in front of her, she peered at the name. Her hazel eyes grew wide. The only light in the dark living room. Curiously, she answered it.

"Chrys. Long time."

She sat up, flowing pajamas wrapping around her tightly. She hadn't heard this man's voice in some time.

"You're about the last person I expected to hear from, considering I'm never supposed to hear from you," she said politely. Guarded.

"Yeah. I can see that. Look, this isn't about the money or Lloyd. At least, not directly." That was a welcome relief, she thought. She shifted the phone to the other ear as she picked the glass up and took a loud sip. By God, she was going to enjoy this wine, even if the conversation turned unpleasant.

"I'm not entirely sure what we have to talk about." There was a sigh on the other end, the feeling that the man on the other side of...wherever he was...didn't want to have this conversation.

"It's about Kline," the man said simply, but with conviction. She said nothing; she still couldn't fathom it.

"I know you were planning on coming to the benefit show, right?" he asked.

"Well, yeah. Of course. As strange as it is."

He dug in with a chuckle.

"Life. It's a motherfucker, isn't it?"

"You could certainly say that," she answered with a firm, yet accepting, tone. There was silence.

"Were you planning on seeing him?" the voice asked. Her eyebrows furrowed.

"Of course not," she said.

But the way she held the silence after made it sound like a lie. "I think you should." Where was he headed? She was immediately on the defensive, knowing the man as a manipulator, even if he was a poor one.

"Why in God's green earth would I do that?" He didn't answer, so she pushed on. "I know you well enough to know that you wouldn't ask this of me, much less ever call me unless you somehow benefited. So why don't you get to it?" She took another sip, the glass clinking on the coffee table. He sighed on the other side.

"I'm just asking you to be human. That's all." Now it was her turn to laugh, but she quickly stifled it.

"I'm sorry. Go ahead. Please tell me how to be human," she chastised him.

"Do you want him finding out your dirty little secret second-hand?" Kilmore's voice was calm but carried a sharp edge.

"By who? By you?" Chrys shot back, incredulous.

"No, of course not. By the internet. Social media. I don't know. Certainly, this Cowley chick when her book hits the shelf. She's been prowling around and asking questions. I think she already knows. But it's going to come out. And when it does, it won't just hurt Kline—it'll hurt all of us."

He paused for a second. "I'm still surprised you let that happen."

"You're right. It will come out. But it will come out on my terms," she said confidently. "I've known one other rockstar in my life, and I see a pattern. They are all self-destructive. And Kline was self-destructive long before you guys came along."

It was a strange change of direction, but she understood where he was going, especially since she'd known both the men to whom he referred.

"Fair. You asked how I would benefit, so I'll get right to it. Because you're right. I do have something at stake. But so do you."

"I'm listening," she said.

"There's the new direction he's taking the band. He has support from enough members to see it through. We both have much to lose if his direction doesn't pan out."

"You don't think it's the right direction?" Chrys asked, a genuine question. She had no idea how it worked in the industry, and neither did Kline, so this was fair. While the dynamics between band members didn't concern her anymore, she saw how he was appealing to her financial senses.

"I know it's not the right direction, financially. It's a total change. And it's at the wrong time. I don't think I have to explain to you why that matters. To you. Financially," he said.

No, he did not.

"And what direction do you think the band should be going? Fucked up or not that my ex-husband is now leading my deceased husband's band, I have to ask. Because, from what I've seen, that seemed to be nowhere, fast."

Her words sliced through him. She pontificated even more:

"I have to admit that I am shocked that Kline Thomas, with no experience in this industry, could come in and change the direction of a powerful band like Aberdeen in what amounts to a couple of weeks."

She inflicted her own barbs, but he was in no position to challenge it, so he gave up on that path and switched directions.

"I know what I am asking. I wouldn't ask it if I didn't think this was the right thing to do. I realize how painful it will be, that you'd rather go the rest of your life without dealing with it. Like I said, life is a motherfucker like that." This sounded authentic.

"What are you asking? You've brought up risks. You've brought up veiled threats. Now, tell me what it is you want me to do."

"What do you think he'll do when he finds out, if it's not you that tells him?" Kilmore asked.

"You want me to tell him? In person? What do you think he'd do if I told him? I can promise you; it won't be much better."

"But it would be better," he said. "You just admitted it. Be human. I think you owe that to him. He's already out of control. Drinks too much. I think he's on drugs. He'll crash and he will take us with him."

He didn't know that, but he knew enough about their shared past that it would make sense. In as few words as they'd shared on Kline's involvement, it was evident that he was driven and under a lot of pressure, because of her.

She couldn't change that, but he was right. She could help shape it in a way that benefitted them all. She realized that she did owe Kline answers, as painful as it may be. She was hesitant to believe this man that she could help Kline, but if he needed help, it was against her morals not to try.

But perhaps he knew that, she surmised. Still. It would be a weight off her shoulders, and that did have merit. She'd never unburden herself, otherwise. Perhaps this was a gift in disguise.

"Hmm." It was all she could muster. She wiped away a tear but didn't sniff and give herself away. He sensed her agreement but knew her well enough to know that she wouldn't give him the satisfaction of agreeing with words. Her silence said enough for both of them.

"It's the right thing to do. By all of us. Especially by Kline. I'm afraid of what might happen if it doesn't come from you, and that affects us all. I'll be in touch."

He knew when to let it lie and hung up.

She downed the cup of wine in a gulp, stood, and walked to the window of what used to be Lloyd's downtown LA apartment. She ignored the lights below and saw only her own visage in the window. She wasn't looking at appearance but her own morality and choices in the reflection. She knew what she needed to do. But did she have the strength to do it? What if he was wrong and Kline spiraled even worse? There was shame in the admissions she'd have to make, but it was the pain that she'd inflict that caused her pause.

Some doors never truly close...

Follow me for updates on
Rockstar: Mirrors – the next book
in the Rockstar Series:
Facebook: zachtaylorbooks
Instagram: @zachtaylorbooks